We Have a Plan

Gregory Ulseth

Published by Gregory Ulseth, 2021.

First edition
ISBN: 9781393840664

For all whoever believed in me.

'Without family you have nothing'

-Georgiana "Gram" Ulseth 1929-2021

Foreword

'We Have a Plan' was a labor of love and the passion it took to get the words out was something that thrilled me. I know that this may not be the best story ever written and although it's not written by George R. R. Martin, J.K. Rowling, J. R. R. Tolkien, or any other initial crazed writer (C.S. Lewis, I'm looking at you), it's still a pretty good one. I believe that all stories should be told whether they are good or not—write yours!

The world put together here is inspired by so many different friends, rough drafts, false starts and, overall, the inner workings of my mind that finally exploded onto paper into coherence. The fictitious historical background was laid out so plainly to allow readers to have a mutual understanding on the situation the world is in geo-politically speaking and allows a more personal understanding of the story within that world.

The main character, Charlie Prescott, is not based on anyone specifically, but rather singular attributes from many of my role models. There are several cringey scenes that should make the reader uncomfortable with the main character but also help put into perspective his aspect on life.

I also need to recognize a sort of divine inspiration to write this as well. At first, this was going to be mostly religious with injections a lot more frequent but I decided that as Charlie's world view expanded the religious emphasis would intentionally fall to the wayside albeit highlighting religious persecution and the importance of Sacraments. I look forward to sharing this journey with you. Please enjoy 'We Have a Plan.'

Acknowledgement

There are so many people I need to thank and I don't really even know where to start—but I guess I will start with the reader, for real, you rock. I wouldn't be here without you. Otherwise, I couldn't have done this without all the support I had from my friends, family and strangers. I would like to thank both my editor Hannah who did a tremendous job fixing my '-isms,' my beta readers including my brother Joe and classmate Hannah (different Hannah).

As much as my wife, Sierra, kids, Baelynn, Zachary, Owen, Caleb, Eloise, Abigail, Madeleine, and Loretta (+ future kids) and parents, Greg and Laurie supported me through this process, I also need to recognize a calling to write this as well. This is definitely not a religious text nor a primarily religious book in any sense, but keeps a religious tone throughout, and for that I thank God.

Dearest Sierra, I'm sorry for complaining to you about this book, thank you for tolerating me and my shenanigans. I would also like to thank my parents specifically for their continued support of my lifestyle and dreams by never giving up on me—it means the world to me. I'd be at a loss if I failed to thank my fairy godmothers, Aunt Pat and Aunt Boo, for everything they have done for my family, you have blessed us more than you could ever know and I wanted to have it in print that it really does matter to me—thank you. One last honorable mention are my friends who supported my dreams of becoming an author. Thank you Hupka, Wilgus, Smith, Hansen, Stanton, Tan, Kwamin, Pearson, Chabak, and Gilliam for your help—I couldn't have done this without you. Dragon Soldiers!

Prologue

"Hurry or we'll be seen!" Claire said to her husband, Robert, as she opened the cellar door. "There are police at the front of the alley right now." She quickly shuffled down into the cramped space and looked up at him with nervous brown eyes.

Robert coolly removed his black and green baseball cap and handed the infant to his wife before climbing in after her. "Claire darling, don't worry about them. God is watching over us." He winked, ran his fingers through his crisp black hair, and leaned in to give Claire a kiss. Seconds later, he closed the door behind him, leaving the three of them in damp darkness. Robert whistled a short psalm and waited for a response. In the distance, Claire heard the rest of the psalm and thanked God as she clutched her baby and quickly made the sign of the cross.

The three of them headed slowly toward the whistled psalm and felt around for any point of reference in the darkness. They groped the air like children playing a game of hide-and-seek with their eyes closed until Robert felt the wall on the far side of the cellar and led his wife down the roughly hewn underground tunnel. They were in the underground now—a Catholic ministry in New Boston, Alabama developed specifically to allow worship to continue even though it had been outlawed. Although the church persisted, the clumsy craftsmanship of the underground was disheartening.

Since society was separated into different classes, and world politics had become such a threat to the American way of life, the Constitution was ironically gutted to safeguard the American people, but it actually compounded the problems. So many faithful followers had become martyrs as they were persecuted throughout the United States when laws were passed banning nearly all religious services—the official party became the national religion. After the first few years of wanton government-sanctioned murder, many went into hiding or outright complied in order to spare their lives. A small minority were devoted enough to continue practicing their faith in secret. The Prescott family, who had just entered a cellar in a back alley, were one such family.

The Prescotts were from "old party money," which Robert's grandfather had invested wisely, and it continued to build wealth through several generations. Robert was the sole heir to that fortune. He covertly donated large sums of money to local shelters and businesses that aided the poor. He had so much money that it was outrageous how much he could give without it affecting his lifestyle. To Robert, faith was his measure of success, and in this life, he planned to spread his faith as widely as he could. He was capable of doing so because his money was his personal business. That had not yet been restricted or tracked despite the fact that his religion had been outlawed. Robert shared God's glory through his treasure as best as he could.

As they made their way in the dark, Robert felt doorway after doorway until a dim light shone down one adjacent hallway where the whistling had come from. Once they reached a little oil lantern, they saw a priest kneeling with a ragged rosary in front of a small burnt, crumbling crucifix and a makeshift monstrance. Father Brian must have been in the middle of adoration when they came into the basement entrance of the underground network of pathways. Claire and Robert knelt and dipped their fingers into a small bowl at the entrance of the room and crossed themselves. They prayed for hope.

After a short while, Fr. Brian got up and said a few prayers before removing the Eucharist and placing it in a small and clearly salvaged tabernacle beside the altar. After quietly singing a song of praise together, Fr. Brian smiled and hugged Robert.

"I'm so glad to see you again," the priest said excitedly. "After last Mass I was sure you would be followed. How did you make it out tonight?"

Claire shot a nervous glance down at their baby and then over to Robert, who was grinning like someone who had just been asked a ridiculous question by a child.

"Father, there is never any reason to be afraid. God is with us," Robert started then paused for a beat and let out a short laugh before continuing, "Also, my pocketbook is deep. Deep enough for a few hours of time at least. You have to remember that the State is not the people who enforce the law. Policemen respect payment more than the law right now."

He winked again and chuckled before another whistler started a psalm in the distance. Fr. Brian whistled back in the same manner as he had with the Prescotts until the whistler and his company came into sight. It was Greyson White and his wife, Claudia.

Perfect, Robert thought, *they made it here safely too.*

The Whites exchanged long embraces with the Prescotts before sharing brief stories about raising their children outside the city in a farming cooperative where their children were homeschooled and largely got to experience freedom with the other members of their intentional community. The entire acreage was filled with religious minorities, such as themselves, and all of the families helped out one another. Claire, on the other hand, talked about dealing with a newborn again while also having a ten-year-old in the house and all the chaos that was causing. Claudia and Claire could have talked for hours, but they knew their time was short. So, after a few minutes, they paused and smiled weakly as Claudia's chin started to quiver and a single tear ran down her pale cheek.

Claire took a napkin and wiped away her closest friend's tear. "I know, but soon we will all be together." Claudia's resolve returned, and she kissed the baby, who made a small coo.

"Shall we begin?" Fr. Brian asked. The Prescotts and the Whites nodded as Fr. Brian pulled out a tattered leather-bound Missal—one of the few remaining Missals in North America after the raids. It had survived two fires and saved another priest from a stabbing about ten years earlier. Fr. Brian made the sign of the cross and said Mass. Afterward, they baptized baby Charlemagne.

Part I—Childhood

Chapter 1—Summertime

Truth was, this was a dark and hopeless time in America. Nothing meaningfully good was happening in nearly everyone's life. Innovation had slowed to a crawl due to both a collective fear of attack from foreign countries such as Persia or Russia, and the threat from the corrupt politicians who ran the government stateside. Criminals, all of them. Corruption was rampant.

Ever since the French loyalists had fled France in the middle of the War of Islamic and Soviet Aggression in the mid-21st century, nothing was worthwhile, yet many of the persecuted Christians in France and other occupied territories attempted to continue practicing nonetheless until they were all but hunted down or fled for America. Even in America, though, the French refugees found that nearly all religious practices were outlawed and religious symbols were found to violate new limitations of the First Amendment, but it was better than active persecution. The different classes of citizens established in the mid-21st century found that they were both taught and treated differently in society. Politicians no longer pretended that equality existed in post-war America.

Ceremonial weddings were permitted in private family residences, but if the couple wanted to wed in a public venue, they had to strictly adhere to the law and have an appointed judge read the required vows. Afterward, both parties would sign their marriage documents—end of story. Other religious ceremonies, from bar mitzvahs and confirmations to death rites, were nonexistent and therefore illegal in the country. In effect, all burials were illegal because human remains were now being treated through mandatory cremation and seeding to regrow forests in the state where the deceased had primarily lived in what was now called a planting ceremony.

Typically, families decided to commit several religious passages to memory that meant something to them, and because of this, many of the more popular stories from the Old Testament, such as the Exodus or Noah's Ark, were well known among those who still practiced. The New Testament was nearly all lost aside from the Gospels.

The Prescotts and the Whites were two of the very few families audacious enough to actually meet with a priest on a regular basis. It had been nearly fifty years since religion had been outlawed and freedom of speech was severely limited. Both Claire Prescott and Claudia White witnessed many of their friends being taken away for outwardly expressing their faith in public—either by wearing a cross, or reciting a verse on the magnetic-drive trams, or simply failing to surrender their religious items to police during the amnesty raids.

This was one of the reasons the Whites had moved out of the city and joined an intentional community. Undoubtedly, their friends were either imprisoned or martyred. Claudia often slipped into depression for weeks just because of the memories of her friends since gone. Claire kept her company and often hosted the Whites just to keep Claudia busy with something. Claire did so until her friend Claudia's suicide after the arrest of her husband about four years after that night in the cellar.

Claire was never the same after Claudia died. She struggled to find joy in most things and her relationship with her children began to suffer. Although it was clear that she still loved them, it was a distant love—the sort of love that was difficult to detect from outside the family but obvious from within. She grew stronger as time went by and the tragedies of her life—her mother being shot by police when her arms were linked in protest surrounding a church, her childhood home being burnt down by federal sympathizers, and her friend dying—solidified her resolve to fix the problem.

About eight years had gone by since Charlemagne's baptism in that dark cellar and not much had changed in regard to the Prescotts' livelihood. They lived in their gorgeous 21st-century estate just outside the city limits of New Boston, Alabama, and their kids loved playing out in their woods by a small stream all year long. Charlemagne's older brother, Alexander, had just turned eighteen and loved swimming at the small pool where the stream flooded during the early spring. He was starting to teach Charlie how to catch fish with a makeshift spear. Alex was definitely more outgoing than Charlie and had a knack for fieldcraft. He desperately wanted to teach his younger brother—if not to better him, to at least spend time with him.

Alex went out of his way to make sure Charlie knew everything that he himself knew. He was ahead of his age in both wisdom and maturity. Most would've called him a natural-born leader; for instance, when he was thirteen, he organized a group of older teenagers to develop a locally sustainable fresh produce market that now had over fifty small vendors and met once a month. Frequently, he was bored with kids his own age and was found reading whatever books he could get his hands on if he wasn't out in the woods doing something by himself.

He and Charlie now sat under swaying pines with cool earth underneath them. The smell of the water and the nettles was calming as Charlie whittled with a blunted pocketknife.

"Watch out for that knot there and be careful not to cut yourself. Duller knives are more dangerous than sharp ones," Alex critiqued as the spear slowly took shape. Alex continued to give him advice as his brother experimented with holding the knife differently. He showed Charlie several of the spears he had already made and motioned how to rotate the stick while he sharpened it. Eventually, it did come into shape.

"Now what?" Charlie said, adjusting his bright red baseball cap to position it just like how his dad wore it.

"Now we stand in the water and wait," Alex shrugged. Then he reached over and twisted Charlie's hat around, thoroughly messing up his little brother's hair.

It had been a long time since Charlie had gotten mad when Alex did this, and rather than pushing him away, he grabbed Alex's hat and messed it up even more than his own. They laughed at each other and made their way down the little trail through the woods. After a short and quiet walk, they got to the shoreline, took off their boots, and rolled up their jeans so as to not get them wet. Every time they did this, though, their jeans would get wet anyway.

"Now follow me, Charlie," Alex said as he made his way in the shallow water to where it went up to his knees. "This will probably go up to the middle of your thighs, but I'll be right here just in case."

Charlie looked at the slowly flowing stream and his heart began to pound. He knew it would be cold and the rocks would be slippery, but his big brother was waiting for him.

"Okay," he said. Charlie was hesitant about doing a lot of the things Alex made him try. He suffered from high anxiety and would typically shy away from doing anything outgoing. With Alex it was different, though. He trusted his brother. He loved him so much and admired him. Over time, Charlie wanted to emulate everything Alex did, but because he was ten years younger, he usually came up short.

"Make sure you go exactly where I stepped, too! There are some sharp rocks, remember?" Alex's last attempt at getting Charlie to spearfish about a week ago had ended with three stitches on the boy's ankle. Luckily, the stitches were treated with quikstitch, a medical advancement from the mid-2070s that used nanobot technology to reconnect and regenerate skin tissue—the wound was all but gone in about two days.

There was one thing great about living under government oppression—the State had a deep interest in healthcare. Mandated clinic visits were great for those who were sick, but missing an appointment would result in a fine many people couldn't afford. The idea of these mandatory appointments was to catch any early signs of serious disease and apply preventive care. During the 2020s, a global pandemic had killed over five million people over the course of the decade. Eventually, it had been brought under control, but the healthcare system had started to develop the initiative to prevent future pandemics.

Charlie looked up and swallowed nervously. He looked back down and made his way carefully out to his brother. Of course, his jeans were rolled up, but that didn't matter because the water was nearing Charlie's hips. It was colder than he expected it to be for the middle of summer in Alabama, but he didn't mind after his first few steps and started to move more quickly to meet Alex.

"Great! Now comes the fun." Alex began scanning the rocks in front of them and stopped for a moment as he looked in one direction slightly upstream. "Look at that, Charlie! A big one! This will be perfect for you, an easy target."

"What do I do?" Charlie let his spear hang in both hands, and his head was craned not looking at the fish but rather up at Alex. Charlie had forgotten what the entire adventure today was about, even though they left the back door of their house that morning talking about fishing and cooking over an open fire. He was just happy to be outside with Alex, because during the previous few weeks, Alex had gone camping all by himself in the woods and he hadn't let Charlie join in.

"You put your spear way back here and sort of jump forward onto the fish when you're ready." Alex was sure that Charlie didn't understand what he was talking about, but instead of showing him he figured that he would just correct whatever he saw.

Keep the spear back and then jump to the fish, Charlie thought to himself over and over again. "Where was the fish, Alex?"

Alex hadn't taken his eyes off of it the entire time and just pointed to its little pool slightly off course of the main current.

"Ah, I see him!" Charlie was getting nervous again and started repeating the same set of instructions over and over again as he rolled the spear eagerly in his hands. He slowly leaned back and put the spear into the position Alex had just described to him. Charlie slowed his breathing and closed his eyes. After a moment, he opened them and pounced.

LATER THAT AFTERNOON, the boys started a small fire out in the woods, which Alex took control of when Charlie started to smother it with greenery. Charlie stopped playing with the fire and sat nearby watching his brother fix the mess. He was just so happy with the day. Usually, his mother wouldn't let him out with Alex because he was so little, but luckily for him, she wasn't home today. His father was far less concerned with Charlie going out and exploring like he himself had done in his youth.

As they watched the fire die down into coals, they prepared the fish Charlie had caught earlier for a small feast. It wasn't much since Charlie had completely missed the big fish and accidentally speared a smaller one Alex hadn't even noticed. Alex laughed so hard when he saw Charlie pull himself up out of the water and hoist the spear up in the air in triumph. Charlie's clothes were so wet that they had to run back to the house for him to change. It wasn't really all that important to Alex, though, because he just wanted to spend time with his little brother before school started back up.

"That was a pretty good day, eh Charlie?" Alex said while lying in the grass and nonchalantly pulling at taller blades. "I wish this could be forever."

"Why can't it be?" Charlie was sitting across the fire and leaning against a small dogwood tree with a pile of unsharpened spears on one side and a much smaller pile of sharpened spears on the other side. "We could do this every day and I would love it!"

"Ha!" Alex smiled. "Everything is going to change. It's going to change soon, too." His expression was still happy as he sat up, crawled over to Charlie, and gave him a hug. "I love you, Charlie. I want you to remember that, no matter what. Okay?"

"Of course, you love me. You're my brother; you have to!"

Alex didn't have the words to correct his brother but rather decided to hum a song that Charlie recognized and kept hugging him. Charlie didn't know the words to this song but loved the way it sounded. It was both sad and happy at the same time. Charlie had learned that a lot of current music was very sad sounding but nearly everything gave the message of optimism. A lot of music in the technological age was centered on salvation and deliverance despite the circumstance of world affairs. All music that was happy Charlie associated with his family and the late-night trips they would take to various locations to celebrate Mass. There were times when his father was practically calling out to the night what they were doing, much like the night when Charlie was baptized, and other nights when Robert actually looked scared about what they were doing. Maybe there were shadows or whispers in the night, but nonetheless, they went to church.

From what Charlie remembered, most of the time there would only be one or two other families in the underground and it was always a very quick service. The homily was nearly nonexistent because the longer they were gone, the more suspicious it became. The Prescotts typically made it out to Mass once a month but sometimes it would be six months without bringing the kids because of an increased risk that their mother was not willing to make. Claire had times of increased paranoia for one reason or another and told stories of a friend's child who was taken away during a raid. The raids were increasing in frequency during Charlie's childhood, with the State Police taking religious images, texts, and people themselves from their homes, places of work, at random checkpoints in cities, and traffic stops throughout the road networks. Charlie even remembered getting tucked into a small suitcase one night when he was about four years old while they were driving up to a random traffic stop. He actually thought that this event was the start of his anxiety and so much of that night became a terrified blur to him. He was sure that something else must have happened, but he had no vivid memories of it.

Claire took no risks with her children after that incident, but there were plenty of reasons for her to feel that way too. Although she sometimes came off as overbearing and tough, she loved her children as fiercely as a mother bear does when it comes to her cubs.

"The sun's going down now, Alex. Shouldn't we get back?" Charlie asked.

"Yeah, we probably should before Mom gets home and gets mad at us!" Alex sat up and started putting his boots back on.

"Race ya!" shouted Charlie as he started running up toward their house.

"Hey, cheater!" Alex didn't even bother tying his other boot before jumping up to race Charlie to the back door.

CHARLIE WAS WORKING on his fire building skills one late afternoon that same summer when Alex came up with a small black and tan dog in his arms. This little pup was a purebred Australian shepherd no more than a month old. Alex fought with the dog to keep her in his arms as he approached Charlie. Eventually, he lost that battle and let her down to clumsily run circles around him and let out little chirp-sounding barks. Charlie didn't hear Alex until the puppy started barking.

"Whatcha got there?" Charlie said, dropping to his knees and trying to get the puppy to come over to him.

"This is President Barkley," Alex said, not expecting Charlie to catch the reference. "She's done nothing but bark and whine about everything."

To the average historian this would've been hilarious, but it flew right over Charlie's head. President Barkley was a president in the mid-21st century who had instituted a progressive agenda that paved the way for the eventual prohibition of religion and the limitation of free speech. This had been a pivotal moment in United States history, which led to its degradation as a world power. Sure, the United States Army was powerful and cutting edge, but even that could not stop America's decline in world power. What was the use in fighting if the home front was left in tatters?

"She's so soft!" Charlie couldn't care less about what the name meant or how it related to the dog; he just cared about playing with it.

"Well, she'll be here even after I leave," Alex said. "I'm not allowed to bring a dog into my school room, or else she would come with me!" At this point President Barkley started peeing on his boots almost defiantly. Shortly afterward, Alex pushed her away and she rolled a couple times, recovered, and scratched her ear before resuming her panting. She got up and continued her exploration of the surrounding area. Charlie was laughing at the entire exposition.

"Does she know any tricks yet?"

"I taught you tricks, didn't I?" Alex stuck out his tongue, then whistled for President Barkley to come over to him. She perked up and came bounding back to him from the wood line. "See, look at that. Already better than you."

Charlie was impressed at how responsive the dog was with only a small amount of training. It was obvious, though, that the breeder started training her before Alex even brought her home. Charlie was jealous of his brother. Alex was allowed to go camping for weeks during the summer away from home. Even during some other holidays, he didn't go with the rest of the family. Charlie felt like he was kept in a bubble, hidden away from the world for some reason. Alex was free to do so much; he drove around the city, he went over to the houses of his friends who weren't in the neighborhood, and—to Charlie's irritation—Alex simply spent time out in the wilderness by himself. Charlie had started noticing this about a year ago, and ever since then, he felt like their relationship was growing more and more distant. Charlie felt like the dog was some sort of bribe or peace offering. Even though she was adorable, he couldn't hold in his frustration anymore.

"Why can't I do anything like you do?"

"What do you mean?" Alex said after a short pause.

"You get to go on trips and stay with other people. You go away all the time, and I barely get to play with you or even see you anymore." President Barkley stopped prancing between them and cocked her head to one side as she watched a robin perch on a nearby branch. "I miss you and I don't know what's going on and I hate it."

President Barkley looked back at Alex before bouncing over to the robin. The bird quickly fluttered off. Charlie, who was now sitting by his small smoldering fire, pulled his knees to his chest and hugged them.

Alex crouched down and reached out to Charlie. "I know it's confusing. School doesn't tell you a lot of things that Mom and Dad know, but they can't tell you. I can't tell you either. If we tell you anything, we could all be killed. They know when we say things." Alex wanted to tell Charlie about the war and the underground struggle, but he wanted Charlie to be safe, and at eight years old, ignorance was best. Being safe meant being uninformed. Being uninformed meant being left out. After all, being left out had always been devastating to an eight-year-old.

"Well, you know how we can't talk about God outside of the house?" asked Alex.

Charlie nodded and Alex continued, "It's just like that, except that with what I want to tell you it doesn't even matter if we are in the house. They put stuff everywhere and they know when I say something I'm not supposed to say. If I say it, then they will come after all of us, all our friends, and everyone with a memory of us."

Charlie scrunched up his face and reached down to pet President Barkley, who promptly started licking his hand furiously.

"I wish it wasn't that way," Charlie said while he smiled at the dog. "I wish we could just talk about what we want to talk about."

"You and me both." Alex shrugged, then sat down next to Charlie and his dog while the fire slowly burned out and the sun began to set. They smothered the embers with a bucket of dirt and headed inside for dinner. President Barkley followed behind them with short and high-pitched barks.

Alex's words were comforting even though Charlie didn't really get the answers he wanted. The simple affirmations were enough to make him feel better.

The rest of the summer was filled with many days like this one—relaxing, calm, and playful.

Chapter 2—Back to School

Founding Fathers was a K-8 private school for citizens first class and opened to a limited number of citizens second class students based on a combination of scholastic merit, parents' heritage, and—probably most influential—the size of the donation sent in with the application. Therefore, students at private institutes had the newest technology and the finest teachers that the public schools couldn't afford even with overtaxing the lower classes. Meanwhile, citizens second class paid an increased tuition rate on top of higher taxes in order to have the school name on their child's records when they applied to high schools, trade schools, and colleges. Some things never change.

The single greatest benefit that private schools like Founding Fathers had over traditional schools was that they allowed citizens first class and citizens second class students to share mealtimes and recess times. This was not ideal for private schools that intended to segregate their students, however; it was simply that the classes themselves were so small that it made no sense logistically to split these times up among so few students.

Charlie was in a class of fifteen, which was the entire third grade of citizens first class students at Founding Fathers. Much to the chagrin of wealthy citizenry in the area, the third-grade class of citizens second class played with the third-grade class of citizens first class. Racism wasn't the issue anymore—it was classism.

This school policy, regardless of public opinion, afforded the children time to associate with one another, which was largely prohibited outside of official business and governmental activities. By extension, it was impossible for school friends of different class status to meet outside of the school environment. School, fortunately, was by its own nature deemed as official business, and their lunch and recess times were part of the overall transaction, according to the Department of Education and Scholastic Screening, or DoESS. It was in this way that Charlie made friends with François, a French businessman's only son.

François, who was half French and half African American, had seven sisters who were not very interested in academics and therefore would never have been accepted into Founding Fathers, so his father didn't even try to get them into the prestigious school. François was a truly gifted student and a fierce friend who stuck his neck out for all of his classmates whenever they were treated unfairly. About a year ago, François tried to stop the State police from dragging his friend Jameson out of his classroom after his parents had been arrested for crimes against the State—they were found in possession of a Torah. François had already been reprimanded publicly at school several times for all students and teachers to see prior to that moment. Despite this, he was not expelled because his father continued to pay the fines and penalties his son unfairly received. This is what caught Charlie's attention specifically—François spoke up against injustice and needed a good friend.

The start of the school year was boring for the boys, and although they couldn't speak freely all the time, they managed to catch up with one another during their mealtimes. After the first few hours of their first day back to school, the boys met in the cafeteria for the first of many shared lunchtimes.

"Hey François, how was your summer? I didn't do too much this year. My brother went somewhere out west for a couple weeks though. My mom and me visited a couple of my aunts outside of the city. I got to ride some horses!" Charlie rambled on for a couple of minutes and François nodded along and laughed at funny moments, such as when Charlie described how his brother accidentally caught his own pants on fire.

This was how most of their conversations went. It was almost natural for both of them because of their citizen status. They already knew each other's place and Charlie was essentially expected to dominate the conversation or it would have seemed suspicious to the teachers. François didn't mind because he now had someone to talk with, even if it was typically a one-sided conversation. This style of communication was typical in interclass friendships. There wasn't anything inherently wrong with being friends in the learning environment. After all, kids are kids, and have always enjoyed time with their friends regardless of citizenship class. François and Charlie had been friends for about a year and a half when they met back up in the cafeteria, and it was nearly four months since they had last spoken. Getting back to normal was a great feeling for both of them. François's little inputs in the conversation were heartwarming and they cherished every moment they had together.

"Wow, it sounds like you did a lot. I just helped my dad out with his carwash by the lake," François said in a fairly flat tone. It was clear to Charlie, even at eight years old, that François did not want to talk about his summer. It was better left not talked about, so he did what any eight-year-old would do and tried to change the topic of conversation, albeit unsuccessfully.

"Well, what about a different vacation?" Charlie queried.

"It's always the same."

Clearly, Charlie was unsuccessful in changing the conversation and the excitement he had about his summer quickly faded. Neither one of them wanted to talk about how unfair it was—after all, they were only kids. The two boys sat across from each other in the lunch hall, quickly eating their food in silence. For Charlie it was the school-served lunch of some sort of processed chicken patty and canned mixed vegetables, whereas François had a beautifully packed assortment of fruit, sandwiches, and even a couple desserts.

"Thank you ... for this food," Charlie whispered, mouthing "Lord" after saying thank you. He was looking down at some pudding with his hands folded in his lap before reaching in to take a spoonful of pudding. François's eyes widened and his jaw dropped for a second or two.

"You have to be careful about what you say, Charlie. I could have you expelled for just that!"

"All things are possible for one who believes," Charlie said defiantly.

François not only recognized what Charlie was doing, but that he was also referring to the story of Jesus driving out a mute demon—one of his favorite passages. François's father actually had a Bible tucked away at his home, where his family often read it. This well-worn copy of the Bible that his father had smuggled out of France was how they stayed optimistic throughout all of their hardships. This didn't take away his fear of losing his only friend and possibly even causing trouble for his friend's family. Because Charlie was his closest citizen first class friend, François knew that he wouldn't actually tattle; nonetheless, he thought that Charlie deserved an honest warning.

"You won't tell. I've known you for a year already and I know that you need a best friend." Charlie grinned a boyish grin, stuck a fork into his chicken patty, and took a bite out of it, practically daring him to say something.

François was seething and stared at Charlie with a furrowed brow while his new self-declared best friend finished chewing. "Fine, but I'm not going to like it." The two boys laughed and then were shortly dismissed from lunch back to their respective classrooms.

François understood what it meant to be in a lower class, and despite how he hated the injustice in the school system, Charlie was his best friend and he knew that it would be okay.

THROUGHOUT THE SEMESTER, they would meet up at lunch where they would talk about whatever happened at home the previous couple of days, and then at recess, they would play games just like every other school-aged kid. What made them unique was the secret messages they would send back and forth via Scripture quotes. Robert helped Charlie develop a simple code over the course of several weeks after Charlie had told him about how François was his best friend. The boys' code intensified over time as it got more and more sophisticated as well as more detailed. Their code grew to use little things such as referencing parables and different hand gestures found in the now outdated American Sign Language. Some things, though, were still too difficult in nature to convey with a biblical message, so other forms of covert communication began to take shape.

One day, Charlie felt like inviting François over to play but knew that the State would never allow it. So, he had to think of a way to play with François outside of school. He decided that talking to his father about it would be the best option, because so far nothing bad happened when following his dad's plans. Robert was daring, cunning, and he knew how to get things done safely.

This should be no problem for Dad, thought Charlie.

That afternoon, Charlie started looking for his father in all the usual places around the estate. His father loved the garden on the west lawn, where he planted many types of roses and hedges in a variety of colors. To the trained eye, the garden as seen from above was obviously a replica of Eugene Kazimierowski's painting called

Divine Mercy. Looking at it through the upstairs hallway windows, any visitor with a keen eye could recognize the deep red tulips in the rough shape of a human heart with taller and lighter red knockout roses through its center. Jutting out from one side, soft pink begonias drifted out in a small fan while blue periwinkles mirrored it on the opposite side. It was beautiful and complex with different levels of garden beds in complementing colors, which flowered almost all year with the assistance of their gardener, Jacques. Jacques was a very nice man who cultivated different plants and genetically altered them himself to ensure maximum beauty. He was also responsible for the greenhouse on the south-facing side of the house proper. Jacques was tending the garden when Charlie went out looking for his father.

"Have you seen Dad?" asked Charlie.

"Eh, no. But why doo 'ew asque, monsieur Presscaught?" Jacques questioned with a thick French accent. "Iz eet ourgent?"

"I just have a question for him, is all," Charlie pressed on and peered around the flowers nearest him.

"Oh, well, he deed go zat way," Jacques indicated the pathway leading to the front lawn.

"Thank you!" Charlie said. He skipped along the brick path around the side of the house to the front, where a row of strong and sturdy oak trees lined the driveway and street. He saw Robert sitting on a white bench by one of the oak trees where an old tire swing once hung. The rope was fraying pretty miserably at the end where the tire had torn off a couple of weeks ago. Robert had a book in his hand, but it wasn't fooling anyone—he was clearly staring at the rope gently blowing in the breeze.

"Hi Dad!" Charlie said to his father, who was startled and quickly wiped away a tear before standing up. Charlie hadn't noticed it and continued by asking his question in hushed tones so he wouldn't be overheard.

"Well now. I think that we should invite them to the next program!" Robert was visibly excited and began to bounce on the balls of his feet a little—he lived for this. "Here, this is what you need to find out. What priest does his family see? There are only a few in the city, but sometimes we go to the suburbs, and there are bound to be many scattered around out there. As soon as we know who to contact, we can get them to join us for an evening."

"You really think so?" Charlie said skeptically. He knew that his father was influential, but he was also starting to see that he was a little overly optimistic at times.

"I am so sure of this; I would risk it all." Robert winked and gave Charlie a big hug. He then swiftly ran his fingers through his own hair as he often did and went back to pretending to read the book on the bench where he had been before Charlie surprised him. His bookmark was actually an archaic printed photograph—not many people had printed photos anymore. It was a family portrait from a few years ago with Claire holding a toddler Charlie on her lap and Robert standing to her left with his arm around her shoulders. In the foreground was preteen Alex and a girl about the age Charlie was now. A tear dropped from Robert's face and splashed on the picture.

Charlie was too excited to stand around and watch what his dad was doing. On his way back inside, he accidentally tripped on the path and shouted, "I'm okay!" before running to the front door and careening up the stairs to his bedroom. He had some planning to do.

The next few days at school, Charlie was visibly moving slower due to exhaustion. Each day after school that week, he had been thinking of what to say to François to let him know his plan without actually saying it. It was a difficult process because he didn't take notes in fear that a random raid would discover it. Of course, it had been years since the last raid, but that's what made him even more nervous. The State could raid any house at any time. The fact that it had not happened for such a long time made everyone nervous.

Several vaguely religious oil paintings were confiscated from their house during the last raid, and that was even after an early warning from their friends in the underground.

François noticed that Charlie was tired the past few days but still acting normal. Today, however, something felt off. He would talk with him about it during recess. When the classes were released to play outside, François found his sleep-deprived best friend and escorted him to the playground. The boys were much too sophisticated to play on the playground, but it was a more private place for sending messages back and forth, away from the prying ears of their peer group. Only the kindergarteners and first graders really played on it anyway, and they didn't listen to the bigger kids. The two of them used this spot frequently when their codes were unable to convey the message they needed to share, and today François would use it for a couple of direct questions about his friend's bizarre behavior. They reached the top of the playground, passing several younger kids on their own way down. At the top, the two saw the open field between them and the school, where a game of kickball was taking place. Aside from the chatter of five-year-olds at the lowest level, they were alone.

"Are you feeling all right?" François asked Charlie as they got to the top level of the tower structure. "You look sick, maybe you should go to the nurse."

"No, I'm not sick. At least I don't think I am. I'm just tired, I've been thinking of how to ask you to meet me after school one day."

The two boys immediately stopped moving and stared at each other in horror for a moment before scanning the area to see who could have overheard. There were a couple of teachers sitting under the canopy by the building talking with each other—too far away to hear the conversation. There were some older kids on the field behind them—they were caught up in a soccer game. The other kids out during this hour were only the first graders, who didn't seem to notice. The two boys let out an exaggerated exhale.

"I can't believe it, but you accidentally found the perfect time and place to slip up." François let out a chuckle, which turned into another long sigh.

"Perfect time and place to say what?" Jo-Ann, a first grader, asked accusatively.

François knew that he would have to come up with something because it was clear that Charlie was in no place to be clever. Charlie apparently knew this too and just looked at François desperately for help.

"He just asked me to be his friend. He was too embarrassed to ask a citizen second class in public so he took me all the way up here to do it."

"Why would you be embarrassed?" Jo-Ann said with a puzzled face. She had bought François's answer, but wasn't completely satisfied.

"My parents don't let me play with any citizens second class, and I wasn't embarrassed, I was scared. I don't want anyone to tell my dad," Charlie said matter-of-factly.

"Don't worry, Charlemagne, I won't tell!" Jo-Ann scurried off the tower and down to a slide. François wanted to bolt after her but Charlie held his arm back. She got off the slide and looped around to the swing set. Charlie let go of François's arm and laughed.

"I'm not worried about her," Charlie said. "She was part of the plan."

François stood there; his mouth open in confusion. He started swinging his arms around wildly trying to grasp words to say, but he couldn't come up with anything. He felt surprise, happiness, confusion, anger, and irritation. After a minute of stammering, he managed to say, "So, this was what you came up with?"

Charlie chuckled and took a minute to form his response. "She was part of our alibi. She's my cousin and she comes over to our house with my Aunt Perpetua all the time. Yesterday she was over for a couple of hours and it hit me while we were playing."

"Why couldn't you just ask me without her coming up here?"

"I also knew that when you saw how tired I was today, you would take me up here during recess. You always take me up here when you have something to tell me, so I figured that you would probably do the same to ask me something. Besides, isn't it more convincing to have a witness?"

"You're crazy!" The two boys laughed for a minute, then climbed down from the tower and raced over to the other third graders and joined their game.

Chapter 3—Winter Break

"**N**ow's the time, Robert," a voice called from the entryway of their house. "Who knows when the next chance will happen. Go get the boy!" Charlie was sitting by the top of the stairs in a high-backed chair reading a Department of Education and Scholastic Screening-authorized leisure book when the front door swung open, but he had since put the book down and started eavesdropping on the stranger. He put his page marker in the book and haphazardly put it on the small round table next to his chair in the upstairs hallway before he crept on his hands and knees toward the top of the stairs to get a good view through the banister.

"I have to find him; he could be anywhere back there. I'll send for Alexander now—he loves the woods," Robert said to the man wearing a completely black jumpsuit and a small pin on his lapel. The pin looked like a gold half-circle, but a trained eye could tell that it wasn't quite round and it wasn't quite a half-circle, more of an arc shape.

The man's face was visibly anxious in the sunlight that shone through the open door and the spectacular faux windows around it. Normally, the Prescotts passed on the really fancy upgrades, but the difference in lighting that the faux windows provided was phenomenal. The windows themselves stored solar power and became usable light sources during the night. During the day, the user could dim them to zero percent light, or turn them up all the way to enhanced sunlight, which was in the realm of 125 percent in regard to natural brightness. Robert had seen them at a client's house and he had to have them. With this technology, window shades and curtains became a thing of the past. Parts of this world were not so bad after all, and innovation kept driving up the standard of living worldwide.

"Send for him, now! We only have a couple of hours until it'll be too late," the man replied, getting a little frantic. His sense of urgency was apparent even from the top of the stairs.

The stranger paced nervously in the entryway while Robert went toward the living room to get the butler and ask him to find Alex as fast as possible. The butler ran out the back door and toward the woods, where Alex had created a sort of lean-to along the side of a small cliff. Robert returned to the entryway and finally closed the front door behind the man.

"You look good for ten years in the underground, Valentine," said Charlie's father, embracing the stranger. "Hopefully you continue to look this good in the next ten."

"You know how it goes. Some days we lose and the government makes changes, other days we win and the government doesn't know or act like it matters at all." Valentine looked down at his wrist, where years before he had a watch implant placed. Charlie didn't know the man, but everyone with a watch implant checked their wrist as if they wore a watch only they could see. This technology was a little older, and nowadays people preferred to wear malleable screens on their forearm. "Bob, we have to go or we will miss it."

"I know, I know." Robert dropped his head and let out an audible sigh and sniffed. "I just didn't want this day to come. I knew it would eventually, I just-," He couldn't finish.

Valentine, who was standing at about arm's length, took a step toward Robert and grabbed his shoulders. He leaned his head over and whispered something into his ear. In response, Robert started nodding his head and reached up with one hand and grabbed

Valentine's wrist. They gave each other a tight hug, the kind of hug that only happens between lifelong friends when they have to say goodbye. It was somber, and Charlie started to feel sad but couldn't process what made him feel that way. Charlie decided that he shouldn't be listening anymore and crawled his way back to his book before retreating to his room.

He sat patiently in his room, struggling to respect their guest's privacy, but eventually he put his ear to his closed door. Charlie was just a kid and wanted to hear what was going on downstairs, but he still felt like a criminal trying to crack open a safe and felt bad about it. Unfortunately, even when he held his breath, the voices were too soft to make anything out. The only distinction he could make was when different people were speaking. Dad had a clarity about him. Valentine was a lower muffled sound. The butler was definitely a higher, precise tone and spoke very shortly and only a few times. Charlie could have sworn that the fourth voice belonged to his brother.

What is Alex going to do? Charlie was all sorts of confused and couldn't figure out what was happening. *When will he be back? What were they about to miss?* Charlie felt his heart rate increase and his pulse start beating in his ears as he began to sympathize with how Valentine and his father felt. Charlie didn't even know what was happening, but he knew it was not good. He couldn't explain it, but Charlie felt that his dad had expected this to happen. *What was going on?* Charlie heard the door shut, and Robert started crying loud enough that he could hear each individual sob. He wanted to comfort his father, but he didn't know what to do. *Should I go down there and hug him? Should I ask him what happened? Maybe I'm not supposed to know. Maybe I'll just stay here.* Charlie felt helpless. After a couple minutes of indecision, he heard the crying stop and then a blow into a tissue.

Whatever Charlie was going to do was now too late. The time had passed. Charlie made a promise to himself at that exact moment that he would never leave anyone crying like that again. No matter what the situation was, he vowed to be there for all of his friends and especially his family. Robert's cry wasn't from anxiety or depression—it was a sound of horror, the cries that stemmed from years of nightmares. It sounded like his father had just watched his oldest son die in front of his own eyes, even though he clearly just walked out the front door. The sobs were something that Charlie had never heard from his father before and never wanted to hear again.

LATER THAT EVENING, Alex wasn't at the dinner table and Charlie instinctively knew that under no circumstance was he to mention that he knew where his brother went. Both because he had heard his father struggle in private and because he did not know if his mother was aware yet.

His mother, Claire, had just gotten back from a visit to a friend's house who lived in the same community as the Whites. She told Charlie in the past that she left the city so frequently for her own mental health, and she always came back refreshed in a couple of hours. To Charlie it felt like she was simply visiting old friends and reminiscing about times since past—a better and kinder world. For Claire, it was hard to believe how fast things had changed because it had really only been a quarter of a century. The brief reprieve from the real world was a ruse however. The State owned and regulated everything. Freedom and liberty were considered a luxury now. Little did Charlie know, but his mother was part of the same movement as Valentine.

Claire was humming merrily with a spring in her step as she sat down. She looked around the table and noticed that Alex was not in his usual seat. Whether or not she knew why, she acted as if this were completely normal—after all, Alex was frequently absent from meals. This winter break was no different. In the first week he had only been back twice and only slept in the house once. She saw Robert sitting and staring at a painting of a long, empty table in lieu of the Last Supper. This version of the empty table was commissioned by the Prescotts around Charlie's birth and it was the only copy he had ever known. Claire looked over to Charlie and saw him staring down the table in the middle distance, not really focused on anything. He was trying to be distant and not call attention to himself, but this was unnatural for him and his mother noticed it immediately.

"What's the matter, honey, is dinner no good?" Claire asked Charlie.

"It's delicious, Mom, I'm just not very hungry." Charlie was trying to come up with an excuse as quickly as he could. "I just don't feel like eating, I guess."

"What's wrong?" Claire asked lovingly with a soft smile and concerned face. She had set down her fork just as a call came in on the kitchen screen and the chef answered.

"Mr. Prescott, it's for you. The caller's name is private and he isn't showing any video but is insistent that you answer right now." Robert got up unnaturally quickly, put his napkin down on the sturdy mahogany table, and rushed to the kitchen. A blocked number typically meant one thing—the government.

"That's odd. No one calls at this time. What could they want at this hour?" Claire feigned ignorance as even Charlie recognized this was a call from the official government. He didn't know much about what was going on, but both he and his mother anxiously waited for his dad to come back and fill in the gaps. Claire picked her fork back up and focused hard on her plate, trying to keep her composure for what was about to come. They both knew that it was only a matter of minutes until Robert would come back to the table with news. Charlie thought it would be about Alex going away, but Claire already knew it to be something else entirely.

The two sat silently at the table and slowly pecked at their food. The dinner table was usually full of conversation, but with Alex gone and Robert on the phone they didn't have much to talk about. Neither one wanted to start a conversation, so they simply flashed fake smiles at one another in a little game that they had played since Charlie was a three-year-old. Claire loved moments like this with her kids, but the seriousness of what was happening made feigning ignorance difficult. She was about to deceive Charlie and felt awkward about it. She knew that Alex had left earlier that day, but she wanted Charlie to think that it came as a shock to her too.

Robert called for her and she quickly flashed one last smile at Charlie before she stood up and walked into the kitchen. A moment later, horrified crying burst out. It stopped relatively quickly as she ran across the house and upstairs to her bedroom above the garage. Robert stood in the kitchen crying softly before walking back to the dining room. Charlie looked up and used his eyes to ask what was wrong. Robert knelt in front of Charlie, and hugging him tightly, said, "Alex is dead."

Charlie didn't know what to do. He hadn't expected this at all. He was prepared to be told that his brother had been taken away for a long time, but dead? He wanted to cry but couldn't, so he faked it. It's true that he was sad his brother had died, but it didn't feel real. He was struggling to process what he was being told.

"What happened?" Charlie asked, removing his dripping nose from his dad's chest. He needed to have his curiosity sated.

"Alex was on his way to a program and he got into a car accident on the bridge over Lake Adams. The coroner said he survived the actual accident, but he—" Robert was struggling to say the words out loud and swallowed hard. The program that Robert was referring to was the Prescotts' code word for church service. Charlie didn't understand but he sat quietly and waited for his father to continue speaking. "The car didn't release him from his seat and he couldn't get out." Robert's eyes were watering and his voice wavered as he concluded, "Your brother drowned."

This time Charlie buried his face into his dad's chest in genuine sorrow. He felt his brother leaving his life as he started to digest the reality. He really felt that his brother was no longer there. The pain wasn't because he wouldn't come back, but that Alex left without saying goodbye. Alex would have said goodbye. He was Charlie's best friend. This was impossible. Alex wouldn't do this to him.

"He didn't say goodbye to me," Charlie said with his head still buried in his father's chest. "Why didn't he say goodbye?" Charlie's high-pitched voice cracked as genuine emotion exploded out of him. His brother could easily have run upstairs to say goodbye. It would have taken only a minute. Robert could have called for Charlie to come downstairs when he was waiting with Valentine. Even during a period of time with rampant suicides and government raids, this was too much for an eight-year-old to handle.

After father and son cried in each other's arms, Claire walked into the dining room with her lip quivering and gently knelt next to Robert and reached into the hug. She didn't say anything for a while but just let the tears roll down her gentle and pale cheeks. Their new family of three comforted each other in their darkest hour until Charlie fell asleep in their arms. Robert carried his eight-year-old up to bed and sat with him for a while, gently stroking his hair while he slept. The stale tear trails on Charlie's face glistened with the glare from the soft light coming through the doorway. Robert sat there in silence until Claire came to get him in the middle of the night and bring him to bed.

A FEW DAYS LATER, THE Prescott family hosted a wake for their son. The casket was closed and the religious ceremonial parts of the funeral were permitted under the law, so long as no religious text was read aloud or religious official presided. Many people in government agreed that last rites weren't really offensive and all cultures had their own way of sending off their dead. In other words, they didn't care what people said after the death of a loved one so long as it was blatantly religious. They chalked it up to acceptable culture.

Essentially, the funeral service was Robert quoting parables long forgotten by the general population, yet he spoke directly to those who still practiced. He mentioned God and the angels and Jesus saving the world from death. This was against the law, but he did not have to bribe any police officers to turn a blind eye because many of the officers present were actually friends with the Prescotts and were upset about Alex's death—they would never turn him in. Others who didn't know the Prescotts well still completely understood the situation and felt their grief. The police weren't coldhearted; they had families of their own and wanted the same opportunity if their child died.

All the friends of the family and neighbors were present and offered their sincerest condolences. Many of them talked about how kind Alexander was and how he had helped them so often. Mrs. Quinan, who lived across the street in a massive five-story mansion, said that he once chopped enough firewood for an entire winter for her without accepting payment.

Charlie knew each one of these stories to be true. When it came time for him to say something, he had narrowed it down between this past summer when Alex had taught him spearfishing and something he remembered from when he was very little. The room was waiting for him to start speaking, and after a couple seconds of silence, Claire reached over to take the microphone and spare him from reliving a traumatic experience.

Charlie resisted. He gripped the microphone tightly and said, "No, Mom, I want to say something."

Claire leaned in lovingly, her face filled with sorrow, and gave him a kiss on the forehead. She smiled, grabbed his face, and mouthed the words, "I love you."

"A few years ago, Alex spent every moment he could with me. I would be playing in my room and he would come home from school excited to see me. It was so urgent to play with me that he wouldn't do his homework and Mom got really mad at him. She got mad at him a lot actually," Charlie recounted.

Everyone smiled and Claire started to tear up.

"But that's not what I wanted to say. I wanted to say that every time he had to leave me, he would say goodbye. Every time I was awake when he left, he would give me a hug and say goodbye." Charlie paused for a moment and swallowed. "But this time he didn't," Charlie's high-pitched voice squeaked a little. "This time he knew I was home and left anyway. He knew it would only have taken a minute, but he left. He left me."

Claire took the microphone as Charlie started crying. She was tearing up too, and nearly half the mourners were sniffling or wiping away tears. To see this young boy, brave enough to talk about his brother who had died mere days ago, made them even more disheartened. All of them felt so sorry for Charlie, but there was nothing they could do to make it any better. Robert pulled Charlie into a fierce hug and started rubbing his hair back as the boy violently cried. Robert whispered loud enough for only Charlie to hear, "Alex wanted to say goodbye. He wanted to. I need you to know that he wanted to."

As the day drew to an end and all the hors d'oeuvres were eaten, only a few people remained. Charlie recognized all of these people from the programs he had attended. The Fredericskes, the Kennedys, and the Durands were all there when Robert had some tea brought out. Charlie felt most at home when he was at church, but this was a close second, and being in the presence of his three friends, Gregory Fredericks, Juan Kennedy, and François Durand, helped a lot. He felt that those who were still present cared deeply for them. It was times like this that he felt a presence holding him.

It wasn't the feeling that most people mean when they say that. It was the physical sensation of his shoulders being held—actual physical pressure and presence. Charlie didn't know that there was a difference because that's what he had always felt. He hadn't mentioned what he felt to anyone because he thought it was absolutely normal. An invisible comforter was physically holding him in his time of need, and of course Charlie believed that this comforter was doing the same for others. The sensation was similar to the famous poem, "Footprints in the Sand."

"And call on Me in the day of trouble; I will deliver you, and you will honor Me." Mr. Kennedy spoke this out loud, and despite much personal risk, repeated it several times. Claire sat in Robert's lap on an armchair, laying her head on his shoulder while the Frederick's sang several hymns silently to honor Alex. There were classic Latin hymns of praise, as well as modern songs about persecution. Charlie would later recall hearing them mention St. Francis and tried to learn more about him because the song was so peaceful. The tune got caught in his head, and it would end up being what he used to honor his brother when he was praying. For now, he sat on the floor with his legs crossed, holding a cup of warm tea and listening to the adults talk about the plans for the next few days—Alexander's planting ceremony arrangements. After some time, Charlie grew too sad to sit and listen in on the plans, so he took a final sip of his tea, set it down on the table, and then went to bed.

IT WAS A BEAUTIFUL and mild mid-December day in New Boston. The cemetery was littered with several families making their way through the deliberate forestry to find where their loved ones' trees stood and to place mementos in their memory. The groundskeepers were treating the grass with some sort of herbicide and pesticide mixture that was an alarming shade of pink. This allowed the grass to grow to a uniform height, stopped all weed growth, and no insects could survive contact with it. The grass was always perfect because of this formula and never needed to be cut. Of course, government and public places were treated in this manner, while private citizens themselves were forced to make do with older ways.

As several plots were being prepared and some were being manicured by grieving family members, the Prescotts and several others attended the planting ceremony in the gorgeous sunlight. The Prescotts' family plot was one of the older ones in the section, and they were able to keep their ancestors' remains in their graves next to some trees that grew out from more recent relatives' remains. Alex's actual gravesite was directly at the foot of a small birch, which came from their grandmother Lydia Prescott. Alex would have loved the spot.

There was no formality and there were no spoken words. The family was simply allowed to gather while the cemetery employees placed the small box of ash, fertilizer, and seeds into the ground. Claire had collected herself over the past couple days and kept her composure throughout. To any passersby she would not look like a grieving mother, but rather a distant relative who was largely unmoved. Underneath all of this, though, she was torn apart and deeply missed her son already. Robert, who normally was quite cheerful, was not himself, but he too kept his composure to the best of his ability. Charlie looked on in utter disbelief. He wasn't quite crying, but he felt the teardrops sliding down his freckled cheeks. Soon the ground in front of him was littered with tears. They looked like dew on the grass.

Chapter 4—Confession

There was a draft in the small, cramped underground room where everyone was gathered on that late spring afternoon. Just over a year had passed since Alex's planting ceremony, and Charlie was starting to really come to grips with losing his brother. The first few months were tough, then the next couple of months were filled with psychologist appointments, and by the time he turned nine in September, Charlie was starting to feel anxious about the first anniversary of his brother's death.

A couple of candles illuminated the altar in the center of the room, and two chairs were set on either side, with Father Brian sitting on one side and Charlie sitting on the other. Charlie bowed his head in thought as he went through what he could remember from his examen. He thought about how difficult it was to clear his mind and let God's wisdom guide him during that reflection period in front of the priest. He knew what he was supposed to say and do, but he felt so ashamed. Father Brian had been the Catholic community's priest for nearly ten years now and had grown to be a resilient and caring pastor. Charlie was embarrassed to be telling a man he knew so well about all of the sins he had committed. Any eight-year-old knew that cheating was illegal, but he knew it was also wrong according to God's law. He wanted to qualify it; he wanted to explain why he did what he did, although he still knew it to be wrong and sinful. As he sat there in silence for a moment, he got anxious about what Fr. Brian was thinking. *He is reading my mind*, Charlie thought, beginning to feel overwhelmed. Charlie wanted desperately to get out of the chair and run away, but he stood firm and gripped the arms of the chair. He opened his mouth, but no words formed, and he shut it again.

He gripped the chair tighter and clenched his jaw. He tried to remember his sins again. Why couldn't he remember them? He wrote them out for practice just before getting in the car on his way to confession, but he forgot to bring it with him in his excitement and now his list was eluding him. He squeezed his eyes shut and gripped the chair so tightly, he swore he heard a seam rip. He could feel his cheeks reddening as he started to think about Alex and how cool he had been about everything. *How did he do this? How does anyone do this?* Charlie was hyperaware of everything going on in the room—everything from the small thread in his sock that rubbed irritatingly against his ankle to the flickering light from the candles casting shadows on the priest's face as they burned. Charlie was dying on the inside, and he couldn't come up with words to express the guilt he felt.

"It's okay, Charlemagne. This is often a very hard thing to do." Fr. Brian stood up and walked around the altar. As he knelt in front of Charlie, he nudged Charlie's chin up and said, "He wants to forgive your sins. Try again."

Charlie's eyes were burning from holding back the tears, which he couldn't hold back anymore. He cried—no, he sobbed silently in the cold, drafty, and dimly lit room. Fr. Brian was used to this happening at a rate that was becoming more and more alarming, but as it increased, he became more understanding. Everyone understood. Whether or not they were religious, people understood the psychological strain the technological world had placed on their bodies. Normal people were overly anxious, depressed, irritable, and tense when nothing was happening, and felt more comfortable when they were connected to entertainment media, news, and with their friends online. There was no telling what someone might do when they were put under additional stressors, and keeping the secret of practicing an outlawed religion was tough for a nine-year-old.

Following this logic, it was obvious why the State had revoked the Second Amendment and outlawed any unofficial uses of the internet. Only research institutions, school systems, medical professionals, and government agencies had access to a filtered intranet, where regulations and restrictions made it impossible to access anything without permission from an authorized party member.

These changes happened so quickly that it led to mass hysteria, which in turn led to both a revitalization of family and religious life as well as many group suicides and shootings. Hanging parties, as they were called, claimed more than a hundred people on a typical occasion. The biggest one on record was January 1, 2097, when 833 people tied their own nooses in a forest outside of Portland, Oregon. Shootings happened despite firearms being illegal, which in turn led to increased raids and unwarranted searches under suspension of habeas corpus, in effect removing more amendments from actual practice and straying further from liberty. Congress extended the suspension of habeas corpus indefinitely, which gave policing authority the all-clear to simply arrest anyone or seize anything if they thought it was justified.

As much as the elite rich were empowered in this system, many feared for their own wellbeing and emigrated out of the country. Almost all of them left for Australia or Canada due to a shared culture and language. The intensity of this emigration was comparable to when the Nazis started taking control of Germany in the 1930s or immediately following the first Islamic Revolution in 1979 Iran—all who were under threat and could get out did get out.

The legislature had been deadlocked for so long in the 2000s and early 2100s that nobody thought it would be possible to achieve anything like this, but once the Civil Liberties Party entered the political spotlight in the mid-2070s, liberals and conservatives alike met closer to the center and were capable of incredible legislative speed. This ultimately led to the rise of several presidents who stripped away the power of the courts via executive orders that went unopposed in the House and Senate. The Supreme Court's rulings of unconstitutionality fell on deaf ears—nobody in power cared, or they were afraid to lose their reelection bids and their status among the elite ruling class. Everyone in the middle and lower socioeconomic classes, as they were called at the time, focused more and more on self-preservation and watched as others' rights were stripped away—and when the middle class was targeted, they were powerless to actually resist. No number of protests, peaceful or otherwise, were capable of stopping injustice in its tracks.

This caused a short-lived devotion toward family and religious life similar to the pandemics of the mid-21st century. As people were forced off the internet, they found that their time was better spent with family and were devoted to whichever god they believed in. From the mid-2080s through the early 2090s, many agnostic Americans found that hope in a god had purpose, whether or not they were convinced of any god's existence—they felt that there was more out there in the universe than sheer chance and randomness. In the minds of the religiously pious, it was God who had used this tragedy to pull in his people, much like the plagues of ancient Egypt. However, any passive reader of the Old Testament would know that humans always find a way to mess up good things sent by God. This time was not different.

In a matter of a couple of years, the ruling class noted that religious organizations had too much power to coordinate with one another and could possibly form a political faction, which was exactly what happened in the 2084 election cycle. That year, the independent religious parties took more than ten percent of the popular vote, gaining twenty seats in the House and four seats in the Senate. The next election in 2086 saw another fifteen seats flip in the House and seven seats in the Senate. The legislature took swift action before the next presidential election took place by barring any religious member from holding office. In subsequent years, Congress passed the Religious Tolerance Acts. These effectively made all religious organizations pay taxes, outlawed citizens from having a religious activity performed outside of a private home, and gave the Federal Communications Commission the authority to approve regulations that removed all religious content from the airwaves and televised media due to its "inappropriate content." Charlie was living in this world and knew nothing about it—he was only a kid.

Charlie collected himself and let out one last pathetic whimper before pulling out a tissue to wipe his eyes and blow his nose. He felt that his composure was returning, and he would be ready to start his first Reconciliation.

"There you go," Fr. Brian said, patting him on the shoulder and standing up. He made his way back to the chair on the other side of the altar and adjusted it before sitting back down. Then Fr. Brian noticed that one of the candles had burnt out and pulled out another small, thin white beeswax candle. Reaching toward the closest burning candle, he lit the one in his hand and placed it in the empty candlestick.

"Would you like to try again, Charlie?"

For the next couple of minutes, Charlie recounted his sins and asked for forgiveness. Charlie first started by talking about several times in the past couple of months that he had disobeyed his parents. One such time was earlier in the week when he was told to do his homework before he took President Barkley out to play. Another sin he told Fr. Brian was about the time he shoved everything under his bed and pretended that it was all done when he was supposed to clean up his room. After that he confessed that he had lied to his friends Gregory and Juan about not being able to play with them after school, when in reality he was still depressed about losing his brother. Charlie didn't know what depression was, but was able to convey his sense of helplessness and lack of happiness to the patient priest. Charlie had to pause for a few moments after crying again at that point in the confession—the wound was still fresh for the young boy.

Charlie relived the events leading up to the planting ceremony and described missing his brother so badly, even though it had nothing to do with confessing a sin—he just needed to talk with someone about it—not a psychiatrist. Robert and Claire were unable to help him cope with the pain because they themselves were still reeling from the loss. Charlie knew that he couldn't talk about it with François either for two reasons. One: At the funeral service François didn't say a word to Charlie, nor did he bring it up since then—clearly, he was uncomfortable with it. Two: Charlie would have broken down in tears in front of his best friend at the lunch table or on the playground and that would have been social suicide for an eight-year-old. Fr. Brian was the first person that Charlie had the opportunity to talk with who would understand.

Fr. Brian heard the pain in Charlie's voice, which sounded like that of a wounded animal trying to find help or a fawn looking for its mother who mysteriously disappeared. The priest's heart sank as he listened silently while the boy wiped his dripping nose and dried his eyes with his shirt sleeve. Once Charlie had caught his breath, he went on to explain another sin. He felt guilty over switching his art room stylus with Andromeda's a couple of days ago because hers was so much nicer and he knew that she wouldn't notice any difference.

Fr. Brian patiently listened to the young child and offered his counseling as both a worldly adult and a priest. Fr. Brian took it upon himself to mentor Charlie to the best of his ability because he sensed something different in the child. He sensed a profound wisdom from someone so young and felt that Charlie deserved just a little more attention than every other kid. Fr. Brian could also see that Charlie was, in fact, unique—just as Robert and Claire had mentioned to him several years ago. He noticed the genuineness and the tender, loving nature that Charlie had, and saw how his mind was leaps and bounds above any of the other children he had ever hosted in confession.

"See? That wasn't so hard now, was it?" Fr. Brian said after he absolved Charlie from his sins. "Go and do your penance. God has forgiven you." Charlie started to stand up, and the priest was moved as he felt a great weight coming off Charlie. Charlie didn't feel anything yet because he still had watery eyes and couldn't see very clearly. Once the sobs and tears subsided, Charlie felt a great relief. He didn't feel that he deserved it.

After the child had left the room and rejoined his family in the hallway, Fr. Brian prepared the room for Mass. This would be an amazing day for Charlie. He was going to receive his first Communion as well.

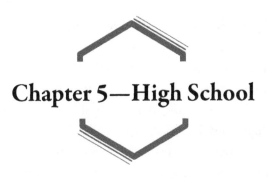

Chapter 5—High School

The year was 2113 and many things in the past hundred years had led the world to the Western age of depression. Charlemagne Prescott, who went by his nickname, Charlie, was in his second to last year of high school when he first learned about the Great Nuclear War, despite it lasting for nearly fifteen years and destroying the greater part of the Northeastern United States just before he was born. This deceit was customary for education practices at the time, and the DoESS kept information back from nearly every student to protect the youth from brainwashing. Ironically, brainwashing was exactly what the school system did. Since Charlie was a citizen first class preparing to start his career as a civil engineer, just like his father before him, this was the prescribed time to learn about the GNW. In fact, all citizens first class children who were pursuing jobs within the government were authorized to learn about it. No citizens second class were allowed to know.

Other than what was expected to be a tough semester in school, life was perfect for Charlie and he didn't sense a need to pray to God or a higher power for anything. However, this year's world history class changed his mind forever as the truth of the world unfolded for him.

"Now, class, the government has deliberately kept this next subject from many of its citizens due to its sensitive nature," Mr. Kadeem said to the class while distractedly reading something on his desktop screen. Mr. Kadeem was a highly educated citizen first class from a party family, but instead of joining the party himself, he decided to enter the world of academia. Many universities accepted him because he was Arabic and half black, without even opening his transcript, which showed that he had graduated as the valedictorian of his high school class. Now, as a doctor of history, he was teaching at a private high school for citizens first class.

"Just as when you learned about the solution to the hyperinflation, you will be preemptively sworn to secrecy, understood?" The entire class nodded aggressively in their collective excitement. Some of them looked concerned, others eager, still more were merely anxious, and the rest wanted to leave school completely. The room only sat fourteen students due to Department of Education and Scholastic Screening regulations and historic concerns over communicable pandemic diseases. These same regulations did more than limit the class size; the subjects taught in class were also regulated. Even the most privileged citizens outside of the DoESS simply didn't know the extent of the censorship.

Presently, Charlie sat in the second row of the classroom at the far-left side closest to the faux windows. He looked at his friends—Gregory Fredericks, a neighbor whom he had known for years, and Juan Kennedy, a friend who lived on the opposite side of town where Spanish was the popular language. The three hung out during church programs and prayer groups. Unfortunately, Gregory sat across the room and Juan was behind Charlie, so they were not able to talk during class. Charlie and Gregory both rolled their eyes.

The last time they had been sworn to secrecy was because the United States Treasury moved a decimal on its currency values to stop hyperinflation in the 2080s, which subsequently caused nearly all citizens third class to tumble into deep poverty and even pushed some citizens first class onto state supplemental incomes. What serious revelation would they learn about in history class now? Mr. Kadeem had the class stand up and face the rear of the classroom, where the Oath of Scholastic Secrecy was printed on a poster large enough for all the students to see. Instinctively, the class stood rigidly, balled up their left hand, and placed it across their chest—the current military salute.

"Begin," instructed Mr. Kadeem absentmindedly while he continued to manipulate his screen.

"*As a Citizen First Class of the United States of America, I will safeguard all information which has been deemed too sensitive for Citizens Second Class and lower by the Department of Education and Scholastic Screening, Department of Defensive Land Warfare, and the President of the United States. Under penalty of political prison and death, I will report any violations of this oath to State police regardless of time or place.*"

Afterward, the class turned back around and sat down. Charlie looked back at Juan and shook his head. Both of the boys and many of their classmates thought that the oath was ludicrous, but they knew that failure to recite it while being recorded in the classroom would result in punishment. Occasionally, police and school administrators would drag a student out of class and give them a reprimand for failure to wholeheartedly recite the oath, which would later go into the student's academic file and follow them for the rest of their life. Once there was a girl who was actually expelled for an outburst and her family was given the choice between being stripped of their citizens first class status or forced relocation to another state. Charlie never knew what happened to her or her family.

Mr. Kadeem made his way back to the front of the classroom and tapped on the wall to bring up the presentation. The screen on the wall came alive and moved all of the different notices, notes, and otherwise irrelevant items off itself to the edges, before bringing up a deep red screen with white lettering: "The Great Nuclear War."

"The Great Nuclear War, commonly referred to as GNW, contains a great amount of information and can be quite hard to digest. The entire fall semester will be dedicated to this topic." Mr. Kadeem began, "The earliest critical part of this 'road to war' began in the early 21st century, nearly eighty years before the first battle even took place. The world was in a unique state in the early 21st century, and nearly the entire Middle East was at war with one foreign entity or another. The United States had been perpetuating this instability for decades." He shot a glance at the camera mounted in the corner of the room. He was both nervous and defiant as he spoke; any misstep would result in imprisonment for corruption of the youth.

"The only nation that was not physically damaged during that time was known as Iran. This was due to its nuclear program and rich history of well-trained armies and paramilitary organizations, like the Islamic Revolutionary Guard Corps, or IRGC, as it was called. It was a well-known fact that the United States wanted regional instability but simply did not want to mess with Iran's military power. After some escalation in the 2010s, Iran allied itself with Russia and formed the Iran-Russia Pact of 2022. This sealed the deal, since the United States would not go to war with Iran and Russia at the same time. Funding to the Department of Defensive Land Warfare, also called the DoDLW, had been cut, recruiting rates were low, and domestic issues diverted popular support from the armed forces. Fighting would have been suicide." He looked up again and wetted his lips.

"Despite this deterrence," he went on, "the United States continued to meddle in the Middle East and caused unrest, death, destruction—you get the idea. Iran had enough. The Iranian Navy shut down the Persian Gulf at the Strait of Hormuz and destroyed all Western presence with the help of Russia. By 2028, Iran sent their IRGC into Iraq, Kuwait, and Syria, slowly growing their empire to historical proportions. The United States did not commit its forces in fear of a full-blown conflict because of the Iran-Russia Pact. That being said, the U.S. Cyber and Space Force effort during the first three years of the war was the primary war effort. The U.S.'s weak attempt at modernization was undermined by the Russian state-sponsored hackers and Armed Cosmonaut Corps. If Russia was not as effective a deterrent and had the U.S. waged a full-scale war, the U.S. would have ended the war quickly and Iran would have been kept to its mid-1800s size and strength. The Russian effort essentially neutralized U.S. intervention and support of regional governments, which fed into the strength of the growing empire. Oddly enough, the two Cold War enemies allowed a sleeping giant to emerge.

"In 2035, Iran was officially declared victorious in the Tehran Accords and the politics of the region were dramatically changed. For instance, Iran declared that it would be called Persia once again and the conquered areas were subject to Sunni laws. Between 2035 and 2050, there was a period of great unrest in Persia, which ultimately resulted in the annexation of all the –stans, equating to the approximate size of the historic Persian Empire under Cyrus the Great."

THE NEXT FEW WORLD History lessons with Mr. Kadeem went into further detail about the assassination attempt of the Supreme Leader of Iran, technological development in the world, and Persia's ultimate success in conquering Pakistan, Kashmir, Israel, the Sinai, the Arabian Peninsula, and everything in between.

After several quizzes, tests, and essays (which were all mandated by the DoESS), the subject shifted from Iran to North Korea. Charlie was not the only one surprised that the class didn't shift directly to the GNW as the timeline would suggest. Mr. Kadeem addressed the class one morning by saying that this, too, was essential for understanding how the Great Nuclear War both started and ended. He went into detail about the 'hows' and the 'whys.' It was actually irritating to see how condescending he was during that class as he spoke down to them as if they were to blame for all the secret keeping and all the problems with the U.S. government.

At one point, Mr. Kadeem brought up the fact that most of the class would never make it to a university because of the way the state lottery worked, and none of them would qualify for admission to a university based on their academic merits alone. He was so arrogant, yet so passionate about the subject that he felt compelled to prove to the class that history was important and should not be forgotten, even if he thought none of them would amount to much. In fact, he was close to breaking several of the oaths he swore as a Public Educator of the Youth of New Boston during these classes. His own higher education from Clemson afforded him certain knowledge at the doctorate level that his students were not authorized to know yet. Clearly, Mr. Kadeem disagreed, and on more than one occasion he had sent home research topics about the day's lessons for the express purpose of having the students realize that the information was restricted.

"Class, this next section will cover the 2033 North Korean Revolution, and the ensuing chaos in the Far East." Mr. Kadeem was still so high on his speech about history that he didn't notice his olive skin turning red or the sweat stains under his armpits after giving such an impassioned talk. He walked over to the wall-mounted screen and allowed the next presentation to come up.

"Pyongyang was booming after the Treaties with America in 2022, but a large portion of the Supreme People's Assembly was disgusted with Kim Jong Un's rule. They believed that Western civilization was evil and that there was no trusting America, something that Kim did not agree with. Kim managed to make trade deals with Canada, England, and France in the 2020s, and even openly traded with the United States for some time. Since the treaties removing all of the United Nations sanctions in 2025 and the beginning of South Korea's open trade with the north, North Korea began to experience a period of revitalization. Just enough revitalization that the Supreme People's Assembly believed that their secret nuclear capabilities developed deep underground in the Rangnim Mountains were strong enough now to persuade any adversary to think again. Then in 2033, as Kim was walking to address the Supreme People's Assembly, each member of the Assembly stabbed him.

"This was poetic irony, to imitate one of the greatest Western tragedies of all time. Did you hear that—a Western tragedy! This was in a culture that hated the West but loved being known as a shadow nation. There was no leader, their god had been killed, the remaining bloodline fled. Despite this dramatic shift in power, there was no further death—just Kim Jong Un. Through the 2030s and 2040s, nobody knew how to liaise and negotiate with North Korea. There was no officially recognized state. All that the rest of the world knew was that if you flew over their airspace or sailed into their waters, you could count the crew as dead."

THE VERY NEXT CLASS took a dramatic shift toward the Americas. "The United States' diminished world status and ongoing immigration issues led to very harsh criminal punishments for all first-generation immigrants," Mr. Kadeem started. "The United States border wall and security systems were intensified and effectively stopped all immigration. The flow from Central and South American countries still continued northward, trying to get into America, but they simply couldn't. Immigrants decided to stay in Mexico, which stressed the food supply and medical services. The weak and corrupt Mexican government was incapable of coordinating with other governments for assistance. Mexico defaulted, suffered from a long-term depression, and collapsed outright in 2034. Naturally, there were several adversaries to the U.S. that were highly interested in funding a revitalized Mexico without taking it by outright force. The Iran-Russia Pact saw this as a way to strip down the strength of the Americas in order to limit their recovery efforts and dry up a good portion of their tax revenue after the end of the U.S.-Iran conflict in 2035. The common theory behind the Iran-Russia Pact's support of the Mexican territory was to keep the U.S. focused on domestic affairs and leave the rest of the world to the new world power—Persia."

The class was getting used to Mr. Kadeem's lecture format. They were frantically transcribing all the additional notes onto their school-issued screens, because as helpful as the displayed images were, they lacked information depth, which their teacher enthusiastically provided. Midway through this particular lecture, Charlie got a cramp in his hand, and as he massaged it briefly, he looked out the window toward the old playground that he and François used to play on and daydreamed for a moment about how happy he had been when he was blissfully unaware of the government keeping secrets from different classes of citizens. He eventually snapped back to reality with a slight smile on his face and sighed as he continued to copy down more notes.

"Naturally, this Eastern European and Middle Eastern influence drastically changed Mexico. The principal changes included the Islamification of Central America and religious persecution similar to the first time Islam spread throughout Africa and the Iberian Peninsula. Christians were slaughtered on sight and the provincial government in Mexico became the first of many official Muslim countries in the Americas. To add to the difficulty of understanding the situation, Mexico was more or less a colony of Persia by 2050, and the religious fervor became a tool which aided in the recovery of the Mexican economy. New immigrants avoided funneling through Mexico to try and enter the United States because it was nearly a death sentence if they failed to convert to Islam."

Charlie absentmindedly stopped taking notes and stared into the middle distance as he thought about conquistadors like Cortés and Pizarro who destroyed the Native American culture in the name of God. He couldn't help but feel sorry for all the injustice that had happened in the past. Looking at the clock and seeing that there was still over a half hour left in class, he closed his eyes and inhaled deeply. He picked up his stylus and twirled it in his fingers for a moment before mentally returning to class.

"Well, Persia and Russia were nearly successful in keeping the United States from directly entering the war for some time. The U.S. government decided that merely increasing the number of Border Patrol agents on the southern border would be sufficient to completely eliminate all remaining immigration. It was difficult to cross illegally since border defense was seriously overhauled in the 2020s with huge walls and deep dry moats, but now the Border Patrol were armed with drones and authorized to shoot on sight. It was a very cruel measure, but a successful one. This let the United States focus all of its attention on its next biggest threat—China."

THE REMAINDER OF THE semester was about the Chinese Civil War from 2051-2072 and a small bit about India. Mr. Kadeem didn't seem to care all that much about the Chinese Civil War and gave incredibly vague information and details.

"Ever since the North Korean Revolution, they began harassing China. North Korean aggression was actually so strong that many in the Communist Party of China, also called the Gong Chan Dang, saw that simply giving North Korea fertile territory from China would stop the aggression. The Gong Chan Dang was directly at odds with a joint faction of several older political parties, which realigned under the title of the Chinese Nationalist Party, called the Guo Min Dang. The Guo Min Dang sought to build an army strong enough to knock Persia and Russia out of alliance by simply hosting a military parade so large, it would intimidate them into submission. After all, China was the only remaining power in Asia that was still independent.

"Unfortunately for the Chinese people, and fortunately for the several other world powers, China went into civil war under this hard division. Fighting was fierce and bitter, as with any civil war, because brother was pitted against brother. Generals who knew each other for decades outmaneuvered the other simply because they knew every weakness. There was no honor left in the Chinese society, which is saying a lot. If you were on the wrong side, in the wrong territory, during any part of the day, you were killed. If you weren't so lucky as to be killed, you were sent to the political work camps for reeducation and retraining, as were your children. And when their children's children were born, they too were political prisoners."

The class murmured amongst themselves. The idea that someone would kill children was inconceivable, let alone imprisoning multiple generations for the crime of not supporting the government. Sadly, some of the boys in the front of the classroom bought into the idea of indoctrination camps and started to socially distance themselves from the rest of the class from that moment forward. It was clear to Charlie and his group of friends that those boys would be the rising members of the local government in the coming years. It shook Charlie to the core just thinking about having bigots and racists in charge of the country. But later that week, he realized that it wasn't just the next generation of bureaucrats and party members who were bigots and racists; it was also those already in power. The class slowly quieted down and allowed Mr. Kadeem to continue his lesson.

"In fact," Mr. Kadeem said flatly, "it is believed that there are still political concentration camps in operation today with the third generation of children approximately your own age." He peered at the camera mounted on the wall, shook his head, and let out a deep sigh before he continued with the lecture.

"In 2072, the Chinese Nationalist Party declared victory and set up the Chinese Provincial Government, or simply put, Provincial China. The best comparison to Provincial China would be the now-defunct European Union, where there was free trade and travel agreements—an interstate system, if you will, with the national government holding nearly no power. The resulting change led to negotiations with North Korea and all other bordering nations to return Chinese territory back to historic ownership. For instance, the different cultures of Beijing, Sichuan, and Mongolia all speak Chinese, but their accents are so different because their culture is so different. They wanted to revert back to pre-empire China—the civil war allowed this to happen. This process led to China being divided into many countries, and the wealth and power of its army—or what was left, at least—was distributed appropriately and proportionally to governments who took ownership. In other words, China was no longer a threat to anyone because they weren't a unified force. Their army was so disjointed and dispersed that they were ineffective after Provincial China was formed.

How on earth did China fall into such a mess? This makes absolutely no sense, Charlie thought to himself, finding this one of the weirdest instances in history that he had ever learned in high school so far. He tried to find more information on the subject in the school's library after class that day, but there was almost no available text on China with information after the 20th century. The librarians said that they didn't even know if any recent books about China existed and looked at him like he was crazy. Several of them had concerned smiles and encouraged him to read about ancient China instead. It became obvious that the school system did not want their students to learn anything more than the sanctioned classroom instruction. Modern history was still being rewritten.

The next block of instruction in World History focused on India and the socioeconomic issues caused by regional instability. India was experiencing troubles of its own. The Muslim population shift in the mid-2040s nearly wiped out its entire status quo and left the country incapable of functioning on the world stage. All of its engineers (both electronic and physical) fled to Persia or Russia for their own livelihood. Consequentially, this left India handicapped economically, in a complete reversal of the previous century. Charlie's father knew some missionaries working in New Delhi and the messages he received were very grim indeed. It seemed that India had been in despair for literally over fifty years.

That was the end of the semester for World History. Charlie anticipated that the next semester would be far more exciting, because the Great Nuclear War was next chronologically, and he expected the alliances and axis powers to provide a great well of knowledge. Stunning victories and terrible defeats. Charlie idolized the great generals of World War II and wanted to learn about new heroes that might still be alive!

SPRING SEMESTER STARTED like every other year. It was snowing when Charlie arrived at school, and he met some of his friends in the courtyard where they normally met before he headed into the classroom. The small open area was surrounded by the classic brick school buildings on three sides, several shallow fountains—all of which were frozen over, and black cherry and black oak trees with absolutely no leaves left for the winter. The area was calm in the morning as the different citizen classes formed into their cliques and groups with the occasional citizen second class hanging out with a group of citizens first class. The teachers recognized that those were the individuals likely to be granted a waiver and allowed to become citizens first class. In fact, each year the school was allowed to award one student that privilege if they felt it was prudent.

Charlie and his friends talked passionately in the courtyard about their winter break and the vacations they had gone on to visit family members or to different mountains and other citizens first class privileges. The crowd didn't even notice their citizens second class classmates' solemn and bitter faces when they entered the buildings—they were not authorized to travel outside of the region they lived in. Charlie, however, took time to say hello to François for a brief moment, as they had not seen each other for a couple of weeks since the last Mass.

Charlie said goodbye to François, who then walked down the hallway with his fellow citizens second class and gave a small wave goodbye to Charlie, Juan, and Gregory. The rest of François's high school classes were most likely going to focus on vocational training because he was not eligible to attend college. This system of technical schooling was not unlike how Japan, Germany, and Korea screened their students for eligibility to attend college. Charlie didn't think about it at the time, but François would likely never know the true history of the Americas unless he was invited to renounce his family and undergo an exclusive program to change his citizen class status. Instead, Charlie thought about the emotionally complex struggle that his friend would likely be facing in the coming months with regard to how the rest of his life was being funneled into a job he had no interest in. François was a talented student who was interested in both medicine and physics, and had he been born in a different time, it was likely that he would have been a lead researcher in new and emerging fields of science. Charlie waved back and walked up the stairs to his classroom with Juan and Gregory.

The first few days were fairly pointless as both the students and the teachers got back into the rhythm of school. Mr. Kadeem summarized where they left off in the fall and finally got to the new material about the Great Nuclear War.

Charlie had been so curious throughout his entire break and tried to get his parents to talk about it, but they flatly refused. There was an odd, dissociative nature about their responses and Charlie couldn't imagine why. It was just another war, but he had seen monuments and memorials all throughout his city—on the sides of buildings, in parks, and even emblazoned onto city sidewalks, similar to the Hollywood Walk of Fame. The war must have been a great event, so why had he not been told about it before? Little did he know that his parents knew more about history than they let on, but they felt that he needed to be properly introduced to the subject before telling him further truths.

"Please stand and recite the oath," Mr. Kadeem instructed and the class obeyed anxiously. After the last students settled back into their seats, Mr. Kadeem manipulated his desktop screen and swiped the display to the screen on the front wall. "The Great Nuclear War" was shown across the entire wall again.

"We are now ready to start talking about the Great Nuclear War," Mr. Kadeem said. He pushed up his glasses and sighed. "I think that you are all too old to just now be learning about it, but the State would rather wait to tell you about it because they want you to feel safe and secure in the great United States." He looked up at the camera and gave an exaggerated toothy smile.

"The fact is, the GNW is still happening." The students looked around at one another and he continued, "What's wrong? Didn't you know that there was a war being waged in the United States?" The class began to murmur and Mr. Kadeem patiently allowed it.

After a minute of them talking to one another, he subtly shifted the display to the next graphic, a map of the United States. The entire New England area was highlighted in a light green hue with a radius measuring approximately 500 kilometers around a center identified as Allentown, Pennsylvania. The names of many major cities were bolded in a bright red. The class started to notice the new graphic one at a time, and Gregory pointed at the screen, catching Charlie's attention.

"This is where the first strike took place in 2079, the hundred-year anniversary of the first Islamic Revolution. Persia hit us with several different types of nuclear bombs and launched a high-atmospheric electromagnetic pulse, or EMP, and effectively shut down all infrastructure and created chaos. They didn't directly hit Washington, D.C., but some of the most heavily populated areas in North America saw death tolls in the millions and were sent back into the pre-electricity age. Our government scrambled to protect the coastline from invasion and placed all relief efforts on the back burner. At the same time, all federal government activities were relocated to Nashville, Tennessee.

"If you remember, this was around the time that the United States was suffering from hyperinflation and the citizenship status categories were further divided, with the final resolution creating a citizens third class category. Economists believe that the Great Nuclear War forced politicians to make a tough decision to focus the federal effort on war defense rather than restoring the areas that Persia bombed. The Navy was called and they stationed their ships off the coast of Maine, New York, and Virginia. An entire five years had passed, and then the second round of missiles came in and hit secondary cities and naval ships. To cap it off, Persia launched another EMP. The U.S. had to start all over again. Then, five years later, it happened again and different cities were leveled. The attack became so predictable that by the fourth round of nuclear strikes on northern cities, the Navy pulled their ships out of the area when the time drew near. This saved many of the naval assets and billions of tax dollars, but the territory became so irradiated over time that nothing could live in a vast majority of the region and the U.S. erected a shield to contain it. Essentially, the fallout never dissipated. Does anyone know what this looks like?"

A couple of students looked around at each other. Andromeda, a thin and shy girl with Greek ancestry, slowly raised her hand. Mr. Kadeem raised his thick graying eyebrows, indicating for her to speak.

"It's the green we see at sunrise," she said, her beautiful brown eyes looking at the floor. "My father told me about it, he's an engineer for the Party."

"Very right you are, Andromeda!" said Mr. Kadeem excitedly. "He would surely know about it and why it was there." Then he turned to address the entire class. "Have you ever sat on a bench along the shore of Lake Adams in the morning?" Several hands went up in recognition. "Well, we are close enough that we can see it in the distance, and when the sun reflects off of it at the right angle, we get a bright flash of green. The engineering behind it is complex and even I myself don't fully understand it, but I do know that no one passes that radiation shield and comes back. Apparently, the nuclear drift was strong enough that it began seeping into the groundwater and was spreading to areas that were not bombed. The people who lived northeast of that shield became cut off from the rest of America. The government abandoned the northeast completely.

"The new powers given to the president allowed her to close off the area and officially remove those states from the Union. There are no longer fifty-two states. This caused an uproar from surviving senators, representatives, and governors from across the country. They, in turn, pushed for a new alignment of power. Thus, the regional governments were formed."

A new graphic was shown on the wall. The United States was divided by thick black lines into five distinct regions. The Northeast, from where the shield was erected and northward. The Southeast, from the shield southward and westward to the Mississippi. The Southwest, from the Mississippi River to Arizona and from the Mexican border to the parallel edge of Oklahoma. The Northern, from the Mississippi River to Nevada and Idaho and from the Canadian border to where it met the Southwest region. And the Western, from Utah westward and from the Mexican border to the Canadian border. Alaska and Hawaii joined the Western region, although it was merely a geographic formality. Other annexed islands and territories like Guam were returned to original local ownership.

"The assault on the southern border came after the third bombing in New England in 2089 and placed the U.S. in a situation that it has not known for over two hundred years. We were being invaded by a foreign power. Luckily, the military was combat ready in days and was able to meet the threat head-on. Unluckily, though, the Mexican army was being propped up by the Persian government. It was what we had been doing in the Middle East since oil fields were discovered there. Many in the regional governments saw this as a sort of payback for the historic imperial actions and shrugged it away as a natural human response. Many remaining federal government officials in Nashville committed suicide, thus weakening the power structure even further. Since 2094, the war has mostly been a stalemate. Sure, smaller battles have changed the front lines, but nearly half of Texas, New Mexico, and Arizona were taken back under Mexican occupation. Southern California was largely unaffected; the Mexican government had the opinion that the rampant disease in the southern part of the state was not worth fighting for, so the Mexican army merely bypassed southern California and is letting it rot."

Mr. Kadeem shook his head in disgust as he called to memory a time when he visited San Diego in his youth and saw that the government was failing to provide help to its people. Disease was sweeping the area, which also became a hotbed of drug and human trafficking.

"Today's map looks like this." Mr. Kadeem pulled open another map, where a solid green line representing Mexican territory was pushed northward through Corpus Christi, Austin, and Phoenix in a sweeping arc. The land from that line to the traditional Mexican border was gray and marked as "disputed territory."

"The war is still ongoing, bombs are still dropped in the Northeast, and the federal government is nearly powerless. The only reason a central government still exists today is to provide a military. The regional governments are stronger and tax more effectively. Not to mention that the national debt of the federal government has caused it to default anyway."

Mr. Kadeem paused for a moment and surveyed his class. This lecture summarized what he hated most about the regional governments—they gave up on reuniting the country after only a decade. He kept recalling the famous drawing by Benjamin Franklin, *Join or Die*, and it always frustrated him that this was the only instant in his teaching career where he could even discuss this topic. Just then, he saw a hand go up. He acknowledged that there was a question:

"Does this mean we might go to war?" said a soft voice in the middle of the class.

Part II—The Army

Chapter 6—The Letter

Charlie's world had changed ever since learning about the Great Nuclear War. His perspective on his childhood was shaken to the core, and he realized that his family was directly involved in treasonous activities. He felt betrayed, but he couldn't tell where his betrayal lay. It felt like his parents were criminals and he was an accessory to their crime. But what if it was the other way around? What if it was the government that was so corrupt that he had been fed lies since birth? Either way, he needed more answers after he learned about this intentional deceit.

The close of his junior year was marked by mixed emotions swirling inside him. Every junior across the country was feeling likewise. Some of them practically knew the truth already, like Andromeda, while others outright rejected it, and still more embraced this realization in extreme ways. There were news stories occasionally where families involved in illegal activities were turned over to authorities by their own children. The kids were old enough to know right from wrong and the government played on that knowledge to their own interest. In withholding the truth and framing the curriculum in such a way, the DoESS effectively brainwashed the youth. When it came down to the truth, the kids had to decide for themselves why their parents hadn't told them about the world. Were their parents actively trying to deceive them—or were they trying to protect their children? Typically, the kids tried to rationalize that the deception was out of love and was for their own good. Sometimes, though, the kids thought that it was cruel to keep the information from them when sixteen and seventeen was considered the age of comprehension.

While the news stories about renegade students were rare, suicides were common among sixteen- to eighteen-year-old Americans. The struggle with the new knowledge created such an intense internal conflict that suicide became a regular occurrence, and society embraced it by honoring them with vigils and proud proclamations in Congress on a monthly basis where names were read like they were being inducted into a cult.

His new knowledge aside, Charlie needed to decide what he was going to do after high school. After all, in the fall semester he would be testing for college placement, trade schools, or government party work. None of that was appealing to him, and therefore he didn't pay too much attention to what he needed to study. His aspiration to be an engineer like his father was his only motivation to pursue higher education. Charlie's childhood had been full of anxiety, so he expected an anxiety-ridden life anyway; college was just an additional stressor. Rather than worrying about what would happen in the fall, however, he decided to relax and take life easy for a change.

This summer, he planned on spending time with family and rereading his favorite books: *Blended into the Twilight*, by Lot Knowles; *Podium*, by S. Hammer; and *Submit Today*, by Anon. Other dystopian books whose authors had been forgotten to time or wished to remain anonymous also filled his family's hidden bookcases, and he would probably read those too. He felt that despite the authors being born hundreds of years ago, they got their prophecies correct, and literature in general had only declined since then. For the past few years, Charlie had read those books many times and also enjoyed other government-blacklisted books just to see what the State was keeping from him.

The government had approved classics such as *Canterbury Tales*, most of Shakespeare, works by Victorian-era authors, and even some technology-era authors. The public would have rioted if the State banned them because they were such memorable books. Culture is hard to change. Naturally, Charlie was familiar with all of the government-approved classics because the public and private school systems made it a point to show that the government was "rational" and "generous" by providing reasonable fiction for students to learn and enjoy reading. Ironically, the government rejected religious freedom in the name of tolerance, and many books with strong morals also met this unfortunate end.

Despite the best-laid plans of mice and men, Charlie never got a chance to enjoy his summer. About a week into his vacation, he received an official government letter through the actual mail. Nobody used the mail system anymore except the government, because private sector instantaneous delivery systems, such as Bowers&Godfrey, denied governmental use of their proprietary technology. Essentially, the second a letter or package was placed into a drop-off location, it was transported instantly to the designated delivery location. This took a lot of investment in infrastructure for the program and funding from several billionaires—Genevieve Okafor, a fashionista who was best known for the now-famous Parthegon waistcoat and the style of side buttons; Jerome Winston-Marlboro, the self-proclaimed savior of tobacco through his reimagined clean-smoking cigarettes; and Philibert California, a savant guitarist who refused to allow consumers to purchase recordings of his music and only offered live performances. Together, the three made it affordable for the average American to purchase reception boxes of various sizes.

Mail bombs were a major concern that came to fruition merely a few days after the system went active. A couple dozen packages were sent to high-ranking officials in the party and twenty-three of them died. It shut down the teleporters for a couple of days while screening procedures were upgraded to refuse teleportation of hazardous materials. Ultimately, though, these reception boxes directly replaced mailboxes, and in turn, the U.S. Post Office eventually went bankrupt and stopped all nongovernment mail services in 2084, a few years after hyperinflation had decimated the economy.

This version of correspondence was so archaic in the 22nd century that Charlie didn't even know what it was. Even Robert couldn't remember the last time he had actually received a letter. Still, Robert recognized it as bad news because several acquaintances had received similar letters a couple years ago and they were served Bills of Repossession for some of their assets resulting from improper communication with citizens second class. Robert didn't know the exact topic of said bad news in the letter his son was now holding; he just braced himself for the inevitable issue.

"What do I do with it?" Charlie asked, holding the unopened letter in his hand extended toward his father.

"You open it." Robert was amused at his son's confusion.

"How though? I don't see a button or anything. It's glued shut on itself." Charlie turned it around and inspected it thoroughly for about the tenth time.

"You cut it open." Robert was smirking at Charlie as he pulled off his baseball cap and reached into his pocket. "Here, use this." He handed Charlie a small folded knife that had belonged to Alex and set his hat on the kitchen counter. Charlie recognized the knife as the very same one that he had used out in the woods to make spears, kindling for fires, and once used to free a deer from a rabbit snare. Charlie opened the knife with a smile, then looked at his father with confusion.

"Just give it to me." Robert took the knife and the envelope, slid the knife through the seal, and pulled out the letter. Charlie rolled his eyes and let out a little chuckle.

"That's really how mail works?" Charlie was amused by the simplicity of standard mail and its rudimentary packaging technique. "Now I know that I'd rather work for the government so I can fix this nonsense. Beats being some corporate stooge."

He looked down at the thin paper, which was folded in half with a staple in the top left corner. It was only a handful of pages long, but the header was enough for Robert to know that the time had come to lose another child.

Date: 24 May, 2113

From: Department of Defensive Land Warfare

Attention: Charlemagne Adam Prescott

Subject: Military Draftee

Salutations, fellow America-loving Patriot! We are happy to inform you of your upcoming obligation to serve our superbly splendid citizens. You will join us on June 24th, no later than 1300, to perform your mandatory medical screening and testing for duty placement. It is your honor to report with all of the belongings you wish to keep with you inside of a readily available government duffle bag, for purchase from all government point-of-sale locations. Ensure you have one with you regardless if you pack anything in it or not.

The following pages included information for families and friends. One page had the mailing address where carefully screened packages would be sent, and the next page included the enlisted terms of service which Charlie was legally bound to even if he did not consent. Charlie read over the letter several times and flipped through the pages nervously, not understanding what was happening. No one he had ever known had been drafted before. Was this some sort of sick joke?

"Dad, am I. Am I?" He couldn't put a coherent question together.

"You've been drafted," Robert said flatly. He reached over and hugged his only living son as if it were the last time he'd see Charlie.

Robert had grown colder since the loss of Alex, but it was difficult to tell in average daily interactions. In the day-to-day, Robert appeared to be his cheerful self, but at night when everyone else was asleep, he often sat awake in his library looking at old pictures of his kids and praying silently in the natural light from the stars and moon. It would be drastic to say that Robert was mentally unstable, but it was clear to his closest friends that he was still hurting. Even after nine and a half years, Robert was still in pain.

Claire would get up sometimes in the middle of the night when she couldn't sleep or when she noticed that Robert wasn't in bed. She would find him staring out of the office window or sitting in their garden and go to sit with him. She wouldn't have to say or do anything to express a mutual sadness. They supported each other and understood one another on a spiritual level better than most married couples did. Neither one of them shared these experiences with anyone else, but it was what kept them focused and gave them purpose.

The hug Charlie found himself in was more than a typical hug; for his father, it was reliving a nightmare that had been replaying in his head nearly every day for the past decade. Alex was only a couple months older than Charlie when he was taken. Robert knew he couldn't survive losing another son. He didn't want to let go. He couldn't let go. The hug was silent; there was no crying. It was a soft and loving moment, which Charlie intuitively felt. Charlie knew that his dad needed this and that it would last as long as his dad needed it to.

Charlie couldn't ask his dad about what he needed to do with his letter; Robert wasn't ready for it. Instead, he would talk to François at the next program. Until then, he would give his dad hugs every time he thought about it. While this hug dragged on, Charlie considered simply not going to his designated appointment time. He felt that it would be better to be a fugitive than leave his family in a quasi-voluntary manner. Later that day, though, he decided to follow the law and his own moral code by performing his duties to the best of his ability.

IT WAS NOW JUNE 20TH, and the Prescotts had just closed the door to a familiar basement below a restaurant located on Lake Adams. The basement of the restaurant had a false wall, allowing passage to a network of tunnels and chambers for both illegal religious services and inter-class romances. The basement itself was fairly well lit, since it was a pantry for the restaurant above, but the hallway through the false wall was nearly pitch black, as electricity was an unnecessary luxury. At this point, though, everyone who used the underground passages knew them in the dark. Depending on how far you were going and what you were going there for, you could pretty much count the stones on the walls to get where you needed to go, because each smooth stone was equally spaced apart by ten rough stones. Each branch in the tunnel was a hundred meters apart from the next branch, and the main hallways split into T-intersections, which in turn continued on for a hundred meters each. Charlie hadn't gone any further than that before. He used the tunnels for church only. Robert had scared it into him that it would lead to terrible outcomes if they used it too often or for recreation. It was safer to stick only to the areas they needed to go to.

There were other entrances that the Prescotts knew about, but the one under New Horizons Café was the easiest cover for them. They simply enjoyed a private meal in a back room every Sunday for the past nine years. They decided to sponsor the entrance point in the café when they discovered that the restaurant owner, Javad Tehrani, was a citizen second class Muslim who wanted to help those in need. It was perfect. The restaurant owner had a vested interest in secrecy not only because the owners received favors for their service, but also because they too were religious. How you prayed wasn't important to the Tehranis, but the fact that you worshipped was more valuable to them than their own lives. They would most definitely be executed if they were caught. Mr. Tehrani fully accepted the risks.

By now, Charlie had counted the smooth stones and turned left with his parents, then went another hundred meters before turning left again. Just a few meters away was a bigger hall with about a hundred candles illuminating the entire area. The candles gave only a soft glow so as not to hurt night vision in the underground hallways, but it was more than enough to function in a crowd of thirty or so. After the past several years, it was clear that this network had not only become more popular, but the decorations and altar adornments became far more familiar to elderly churchgoers—more gold, fancier and more prestigious robes, chalices, ciboria, and even newly printed Bibles.

Robert and Claire met some of their friends and struck up a casual conversation while Charlie went over to where François was talking with Gregory and Juan to say hello. The three other boys got quieter and the tension between them grew uncomfortable. They knew about Charlie's letter already and were trying to act like it wasn't a big deal. In all honesty, they felt that they weren't prepared to lose someone they had known for most of their lives. Unsure of what to do or say, they stared blankly at each other's feet for a while before Charlie offered a slight smile in the corner of his mouth. Juan rubbed his neck nervously and tried to be tough about the bad news. Charlie could tell that he was holding back tears and couldn't blame him. This was miserable for the small friend group. Sure, they didn't really have the chance to meet up with one another after school, but they were still very close friends. It was a bitter pill for them to swallow and they handled it as best as any group of teenagers could—by ignoring the topic as long as possible.

Eventually, they cracked a few jokes about school and their summer before their families started moving to their seats. Charlie shook each of their hands in turn as both Gregory and Juan avoided making eye contact. *That's ok,* Charlie thought as he saw their misty eyes, *I understand.* The Durand family usually sat in the tenth row and the Fredericks family sat right in the front. Today they sat in the same row next to the Prescotts, about a third of the way back. The symbolism of solidarity wasn't lost on Charlie and he felt a welling of emotion, which was so overpowering that he sat between his parents with watery eyes and couldn't focus on the beginning of Mass very well.

The priest focused his sermon that evening more on the virtue of servitude than the readings for Corpus Christi. Charlie felt everyone's love during that moment and knew that he was being well taken care of. He found refuge in the fact that his entire community would be keeping his safety in mind.

He reached over with his palms sweating and grabbed both of his parents' hands. They both gave him a gentle squeeze. He looked at his mother's face, then his father's face, and saw the swelling of emotion in their eyes and the firmness of their resolve—they were letting their last child go out into the cruel world all alone for the first time in his life. For the first time in years and the last time ever, Charlie saw his mother in a vulnerable state of fear for her son, pride in raising an outstanding young man, and the deep sadness of a mother sending off her son to war.

Chapter 7—In-Processing

"You need to take this with you to the next station," the lady behind the old office desk said. "Once you get there, make sure you tell Rhucha that you are a 2A and need to go through dental, optometry, and audiology immediately. She will take care of you."

"Yes, ma'am," Charlie said. He began to wonder what the previous visits at those doctors were all about if he was being sent back to them. He recalled that nothing was remarkable about any of his exams at any of his doctors. The dentist said that his childhood cavity fills were in good shape and that he needed to floss more. This was after prodding his gums with sharp dental instruments, of course, and despite the fact that he actually did floss a couple of times a week, his dentists always recommended more flossing.

Charlie walked out of the office and the woman who was helping him from behind the old desk cleared her throat. When he turned around, she pointed to her right. Charlie smiled, gave a slight nod, and made the turn down the hallway. As he rounded a corner, he saw the sign labeled "Station Two," where both the words "station" and "two" had clearly been replaced at different times by poorly trained craftsmen. Charlie looked at it inquisitively as he raised his eyebrows and gave a slight sigh. By now, he had gotten used to the military procedure of waiting in lines and therefore intuitively stood behind a red line in front of another old desk. This desk was in worse shape than most and the veneer had long since chipped away, while paint from a couple of years ago had already worn through in the heavily trafficked spots.

As the woman behind the desk was filling out a form and referencing a screen mounted on the wall next to her, Charlie looked over his printed audiology report and marveled at holding a printed text such as this before he actually read the document. All of it was annotated as within normal range. The notes section of the sheet stated that the test was done in a group environment under ATE-R2 guidance and was in compliance with the joint military regulations for medical screening. There was nothing hinting at any concern with his hearing or dental.

Now the woman got up from her squeaky desk chair with an exasperated exhale as she saw another person in line.

"I'll be back in a minute. Go ahead and start filling out one of those," she said, indicating the stack of archaic photocopies on the front of her desk. She didn't wait for Charlie to respond before she turned around and waddled over to a safe even older than the desk. Charlie watched her try to lift the handle by squeezing it, pushing it up, pulling it down, smacking it, and swearing at it under her breath. Finally, the safe yielded with a cringey screech, and then slowly, painfully slid open.

Charlie grabbed the form and began filling it out absentmindedly with standard biometric and personal identifiable information. At this point into in-processing, Charlie had written out his date of birth, national ID number, and family sequence number about a hundred times. While he did this, he thought back on his eye doctor visit. The optometrist was perfectly pleasant and wanted to both be polite as well as fast. The little conversation he had with her about his eyes made him think that his eyes were in great shape. Just under 20/20 vision, but not quite worth getting a prescription to correct. She did, however, prescribe the prescription shooting glasses, which were corrected to 10/20 vision to make targets appear sharper to his eyes, allowing him to be more accurate with his aim. She had told him that it would feel very unnatural, but ever since the army had made the change for shooting, nearly all of their soldiers qualified with their assigned weapons on targets over 500 meters away with over seventy percent accuracy—an increase from thirty percent. She said that this was clearly a program that worked, and any little advantage was worthwhile in regard to military power.

Charlie didn't realize that he had finished the form until he was returning it to the lady behind the desk.

"Ma'am, I was told by the lady down the hall to tell Rhucha that I was a 2A and I needed to see some doctors immediately." There was some hesitation in Charlie's voice, hoping that this middle-aged woman would see his file and disregard whatever the other lady said.

She raised her eyebrows and took the form from Charlie. Turning to the screen, Rhucha navigated to an input field and punched in Charlie's data, then asked, "What service were you volunteering for?"

"Army, ma'am." Charlie was irritated that everyone in the building was treating him like he wasn't drafted into the military. They kept calling him a volunteer. Charlie did, however, think it was funny that they also acted as if he had a choice as to which branch he was going to serve in. All of the forms he received during his first day indicated that he was going into the army and would be in service for no less than four years, which could be involuntarily extended.

Rhucha inputted the information and then referenced Charlie's electronic files for some more data before her eyes widened. She leaned in closer to the screen, adjusted her glasses, put her finger under the on-screen reference number, and wrote it down on Charlie's paperwork. She then glanced up at Charlie, down to the paper again, and finally back to the screen.

Everything began to move quickly. "Hey, Carlos," the woman said, pressing a button on her screen, "we have a 2A here. Are you ready for one?" She did not remove her eyes from Charlie the entire time that she was speaking.

"A 2A? Really?" Carlos said with a rough, deep voice through the screen's speakers. The screen was a little bit archaic and matched the wear and tear of the other equipment. Based on Charlie's assessment, the thing must have been at least as old as he himself was. However, it was obvious that the actual touch surface had been replaced recently due to over-manipulation. The speakers were still magnificent and Carlos's voice sounded as clear as day.

"Yeah, we really do have one here. Sitting right in front of me in the flesh." Rhucha let go of the button and waddled back to a filing cabinet sitting beside the safe. She fumbled with a keyring for a minute before dropping it. No one was used to working with physical keys anymore as biometrics had largely replaced traditional locks. She took a wide stance to attempt reaching them and failed several times. When she did manage to pick up the keys, she struggled to actually unlock the filing cabinet. "Do you have any idea what a 2A is, young man?"

"Not yet, ma'am." Charlie swallowed impatiently as he waited for her to answer him. Charlie shifted uneasily in his seat and felt that the small of his back had begun sweating through his shirt. This made him more anxious, and he noticed that his cold, clammy hands began to shake slightly as he tightened them on the arms of the chair he was sitting in. "Ma'am?"

"A 2A is a state secret military position. Carlos will be here shortly to brief you on the cover duty description as well as what you will actually be doing." Rhucha finally found the forms she needed and turned around from the filing cabinet. She returned to her desk as quickly as she could. As she took several exasperated breaths and mopped her forehead with a towel, Rhucha noticed that Charlie's face was pale and actually a little blue. "Don't worry, baby, this is all absolutely normal. In time, I'm sure you will be thankful you got this opportunity."

"Yes, ma'am," Charlie said intuitively. By this point, he had already become accustomed to answering anyone with any capacity of authority with yes sir, no sir, yes ma'am, no ma'am. He wasn't at peace or thankful. In fact, he was more concerned than ever. A couple of minutes went by and Carlos, a hulking tattooed figure, came to escort him across the facility to another location. Charlie was concerned when the man went through a doorway and down a staircase that was clearly going underground, but he followed anyway with an internal shrug. They twisted and turned through several corridors and finally reached a small room. They both entered. The room was unnerving, and Charlie began to feel that he made a mistake walking underground with this huge man.

"Just lean back, Private Prescott. Relax, this won't take long," Carlos said, indicating the chair in the center of the dimly lit room. The chair was reminiscent of a dental chair, but the lighting made Charlie think of both an x-ray room as well as a torture chamber. Along one side of the chair was a stool, presumably where the dentist, or torturer, would sit, and the other side of the chair had several empty trays. Other than that, the room was completely bare except for a lamp in the corner opposite the door and a closed cabinet against the back wall.

Carlos himself wasn't exactly a relaxing person to be around, either. The man was probably 195 centimeters tall and weighed more than the car Charlie's family drove when he was a child. Carlos had a thick brown mustache and tattoos up and down his body. The fact that this mountain of a man with the voice of an old-timey Hells Angels member was telling him to relax was more unnerving than being led into a torture chamber. Charlie let himself slide back into the chair and felt the familiar adjustments of a dental chair as it laid him completely flat on his back. Above him, a panel in the drop ceiling was retracting and a screen turned on, displaying the image of a waving American flag.

"Here, you'll need these," Carlos said, handing Charlie a set of over-the-ear headphones. The tattoos on his knuckles read, "no future." Carlos continued, "Just listen to the audio and I'll be completely set up by the time it's done." Charlie watched Carlos exit the room and then shifted his attention back to the screen. The image began panning out from the flag.

The audio cut in during the end of the national anthem. The on-screen images began to change into a documentary-style slideshow, showing warfighters from historic wars like WWII, Vietnam, WWIII, and the first few space battles.

The narrator began by introducing himself in a fairly retro fashion. He was sitting in a director's chair in front of a backdrop of several fake plants and dim lamps from the late 21st century. Charlie recognized the age of the lamps because they were the only décor from that era that actually survived into the 22nd century. Most people had a few of them still because they were symbolic of what it meant to be a true American patriot, seeing as the lamps were the last item completely sourced in America, made in America, and explicitly sold only in America. The lamps were also useful. They had wireless connections to the internet and were controllable from nearly any interface, including voice commands, which were popular before physical movement cameras took hold. Technology-age lighting was controlled by merely pointing at it with a finger while also looking at it. The cameras were sophisticated enough to actually coordinate multiple movements of eyes, hands, and user intentions. These older lamps reminded people of simpler times and the sensation of privacy, while also boldly declaring that they were true patriots—regardless of citizenship status.

"Good morning. I am Keith Burrow, liaison between military medical sciences and the Department of State. I wish to congratulate you on this bold step forward and also explain a few things. However, as you were most likely already told, this briefing is a state secret and we will recite the pledge before we get into details. Be mindful that this is being recorded and monitored for cooperation. Failure to heartfully respond will lead to your unfortunate detention for the remainder of your enlistment."

Charlie felt his heart beat a little faster as he swallowed nervously. *Was this guy serious?* he thought to himself. He realized that his mouth was dry and wished he had something to drink. *Maybe I could just get up for a minute and get a drink from the sink in the bathroom. What would happen if I got up? They would probably just play the video again anyway.* All of this flashed through his mind in an instant before the oath showed up on the screen. As soon as the official party music started playing, he snapped back into focus and really wished that he had some water right then. This desire was so strong that he nearly convinced himself that he was going to suffocate if he didn't get water soon. Nonetheless, he pushed those thoughts aside and was ready for the oath.

"*As a Citizen First Class of the United States of America, I will safeguard all information which has been deemed too sensitive for Citizens Second Class and lower by the Department of Education and Scholastic Screening, Department of Defensive Land Warfare, and the President of the United States. Under penalty of political prison and death, I will report any violations of this oath to State police regardless of time or place.*"

"Good. By now it is certain that you have said this with such strong conviction and vigor that the individual monitoring you accepted it without reason to question your integrity," Mr. Burrow stated as he gave a large fake smile and crossed his legs in an awkward and forced way. He reached for a pocket on the side of his chair and pulled out a small book. He opened it and adjusted his glasses to focus on the undoubtedly small text of the page.

"Now, it is my distinct honor to explain to you what you have been selected for and how seriously you need to take it." He flipped the page. "1. You have been selected for sensory enhancements including but not limited to auditory, visual, time, and balance. Each of these enhancements will be accompanied by detailed training and proposed uses. The developers themselves will be your instructors and they will answer all of your questions."

He flipped to the next page. "2. As an enhanced service member, you will be assigned to special forces in critical shortage situations and therefore your standard training will be shortened in order to facilitate the defense of the nation in as condensed a timeframe as possible. The standard twelve-week combat training will be forgone as you have no social or public infractions, are a citizen first class, of good family history and family party registration. It has been determined that the disciplinary training is unnecessary and the skills you will develop will far exceed that which your unmodified counterparts will have."

Mr. Burrow licked his thumb and turned to the next page. He cleared his throat briefly before continuing. "3. These enhancements are still in the experimental phase and therefore all medical expenses incurred following these treatments will be covered by the federal government, unless your state of residency is deemed responsible for payment."

Charlie struggled to take in all of this information as it was coming at him. He was going to have enhancements on his senses? *What did that mean?* He was going to be special forces without military training? *How was that possible?*

Mr. Burrow flipped through several pages as he was reading. It looked like he was about halfway through the small book he was reading from. "4. This will not be without pain. The medical professionals on your team will make sure you are as comfortable as possible during the integration processes, but they must complete all phases no matter your pain level in order to not leave you dead, blind, or physically disabled. The goal of your medical team is to complete the surgeries within three hours so as to minimize your pain. Once complete, you will be in recovery for several days, depending on the severity of your reactions and whether your body rejects any enhancements."

He flipped to the next page. "5. Upon your recovery, you will be retroactively promoted to the rank of second lieutenant. Your official birth records will be modified and you will not be permitted to contact any previous family or friends during the duration of your duty. You will be briefed on your new biographical information at a later time. Upon discharge, you will receive additional briefings on the matter."

He reached over to a cup of water and took a sip. Charlie licked his lips and wished that he had the water in his hands. Mr. Burrow continued, "6. To reiterate your oath of secrecy, you will be severely punished for disclosing any of the information you have thus far been briefed on and you will be disciplined for discussing any military mission or information of any kind, including uniform, duty locations, techniques, tactics, or procedures."

Charlie thought that he was grasping what was going to happen when he joined the military, but this was not what he expected. This anxiety was beginning to overwhelm him, but he had already committed to doing exactly what was just briefed. Regardless, he was drafted and didn't have a choice in the first place. One would say that he was stuck between a rock and a hard place and didn't know which was which. It was an odd feeling, understanding his helplessness. Clarke's mounting anxiety made him want to do anything but sit in the reclined dental chair.

The video wrapped up with a quick salute to the men and women in uniform, and Mr. Burrow gave a thank you to the viewer in a very desperate and forced sort of way. Charlie was unsettled by not just the seeming nonchalance of the brief, but also by how Mr. Burrow was reading from a book. Nobody outside of the underground did that anymore, especially since digital media was cheaper and easier to manipulate. The little pamphlet he read from must have been printed fairly recently too. Charlie began constructing hypotheses for why the book was printed, why it was read to him, why the medical liaison to the Department of State read it to him, and why it was a video.

He came to the conclusion that the video must have been made a state secret and that the doctors were not authorized knowledge of what their procedures were for. Charlie also realized that if he had been given a book to read it would be out of a controlled environment where anyone could access it. That was the trouble with printed material—anyone could get their hands on it. By this time, Carlos had opened the door and made his way back into the room with a cart loaded up with various medical equipment. On the other side of the cart, a different technician assisted him by lifting it up over the threshold into the room and across several power cables.

Charlie just realized that this room really wasn't supposed to be for whatever they were about to do, but it was about to happen anyway. The two technicians clipped several Wireless Attached Bio-Magnetic Universal Vital Status Scopes, or WAB-MIVSS, onto Charlie's wrists, ankles, neck, and chest, the data from which transferred to screens on the cart when audible pops connected the devices. Then Carlos started a hep-lock on Charlie's arm closest to the wall and attached a bag of saline with a steady drip while breathing heavily over him. His neck tattoo was an eagle centered on his Adam's apple with the wings reaching around the man's neck.

"This is just regular fluids to keep you hydrated," the second technician said. "It might taste a little funny because of the additives to enhance water retention."

Charlie gave a puzzled look as he tasted what flowers smelled like and both of his medical providers gave a small smile. The second technician was a woman in her forties and had a very motherly demeanor. She said with a half smirk, "I tasted how Mozart sounded to me the first time I heard him, what did you taste?"

"The smell of dandelions," Charlie said and gave a chuckle. "Tech-age medicine confuses me so much."

"I can't get past biological nanobots, honestly," Carlos said, then pulled out an audio scope, various pliers, cotton swabs, a scalpel, and a small black bag. The black bag was smaller than a cotton ball and was vacuum sealed. The audio scope screen was secured over Charlie's head in a manner that the operator could easily manipulate it without straining. Unfortunately, this placement took up nearly all of Charlie's field of vision and made him feel like he was back in his mother's suitcase before the traffic stop nearly fifteen years ago. He started to breathe heavier and then closed his eyes. He had practiced controlling his anxiety and calming himself down, but using it in such a stressful situation was new to him.

"Sorry to do this to you, soldier, normally you would be asleep for this kind of screening," Carlos said. "The doctor tells us that keeping you awake is just her preference really, and the DoDLW sides with the doc. I don't get it."

"No problem, sir. I've already signed away my right to complain anyway. So long as I don't die in combat, the army doesn't want me to even get a paper cut and risk infection under their watch."

Both of the technicians laughed slightly as they finished prepping the room. They made minor adjustments after conferring with one another and a screen on the cart. When they had finished, they turned to each other and gave a little sigh before Carlos left. The women turned to Charlie, smiling as she reached for his hand.

"You will make it out okay. Just remember that no one has died in this procedure."

Charlie couldn't muster up his voice for a response. Instead, a little squeak escaped as she left the room and the bright LED artificial light from the hallway disappeared as the door closed behind her. He was terrified at hearing those words. He swallowed again and realized that he still hadn't had any water. Although the IV was providing him with fluids, Charlie was deprived of the psychological comfort in the simple act of physically taking a drink.

He must have only been alone for a couple of minutes until the next person came into the room, but he still felt that it dragged on for hours as his anxiety mounted and the sensation of claustrophobia set in with the machine hovering overhead. Charlie quickly turned his head when the hallway light was cast onto his feet as the door opened. He saw a name tag that read: Dr. Goosh, Audiology.

"Good afternoon, soldier," she said, "and bla bla bla, other party references, salutes, streamers, and pomp." She smiled and continued, "I'm Dr. Goosh, your audiologist and Father's messenger." She gave a wink.

Charlie picked up on the coded message by responding with a message of his own. "My Father is truly wise and kind to send you. I concede that my life is in His hands as well as yours," he said and gave a subtle thumbs up.

This type of coded messaging had been so well engrained into Charlie that it was second nature at this point—he barely had to think about an appropriate response. In his youth, he stumbled a few times and actually was told by his mother to stop trying it and simply touch the center of his hand with his opposite middle finger. This gesture was obvious enough for anyone sending a message, but subtle enough that it otherwise would go unnoticed. Claire had told him about it when he first started asking about Alex's death. Apparently, she thought that it was time to teach Charlie about communication safety and keeping secrets. Nearly ten years had passed since then, and Charlie had grown fast in his knowledge of these codes and subsequent eagerness to be involved in the Church. He matured so much in the first few years after his brother died that on more than one occasion, several elderly neighbors mistook him for Alex completely. One time, Mrs. Quinan actually asked him as a twelve-year-old to chop up some firewood. Despite the fact that he was still just a teenager lying in a military dental chair, he behaved as if he was well beyond his years in culture, wisdom, and eloquence. Those facts might be why he was in the predicament he found himself in.

Dr. Goosh smiled again in a shared understanding that she wasn't going to let anything bad happen to Charlie. She sat on the stool and set to work unpackaging sterile equipment and modifying the positioning of some of the instruments. Charlie felt his anxiety being swept away because he was in the company of an ally who comforted him. He quickly prayed a prayer of thanksgiving and several Hail Marys while Dr. Goosh went about her equipment. After a minute, she got Charlie's attention by gently rubbing his shoulder.

"I am responsible for embedding top-of-the-line auditory enhancement implants into your head," she said. "This is what they want me to put in you," she held up the small black bag, "but it has several tracking mechanisms which will never be deactivated. In fact, this implant and more importantly—this implant," she pulled out an identical black bag from her coat pocket, "cannot be removed without causing you to go deaf."

Charlie gave a nod of understanding before she continued, "We only know that it causes irreversible deafness because we've tried to remove a few, and obviously were not successful. Anyway, the most important thing is that this one," she held up the one from her pocket again, "will not track you. Essentially, once it's installed without the tracking capabilities, the government accepts the loss because all attempts to remove it will make you useless to them."

"Thank you." It was all he could come up with, until he thought for a moment while Dr. Goosh began opening the small black bags. "Excuse me," he said, "how do you know who I am? And why are you helping me anyway?"

"Some things are best left unsaid," Dr. Goosh said. "Besides, word travels fast." She gave him another wink and a kind smile.

"Thank you," he said again, feeling like he should say something else. Clearly, this woman was doing him a great favor by letting him know about the tracking capabilities of the original device, but she also went out of her way to disable a different one entirely for him. He really didn't understand the significance at that moment, but would grow to appreciate it in just a few weeks' time.

"Now," Dr. Goosh said, "this is not going to feel good no matter how we do it, but it will go much faster if you are fully awake. You have the option of being knocked out completely, drugged up so high you won't know your name, or just dealing with it. What will it be?"

"Whatever you suggest," Charlie said to emphasize that he trusted her.

"Wide awake it is!" she said with a grin on her face. "Most people don't know that it's nearly painless if you rub your tongue on the roof of your mouth while it happens." Then she whispered, "Also be sure not to moan, wince, or otherwise make noise from your vocal cords, because that will delay the process."

It was not painless, or even remotely manageable. Within minutes Charlie was sobbing and clenching his jaw so hard he actually pulled a small muscle and loosed a tooth. Dr. Goosh wasn't concerned, though, and finished up the procedure in under ten minutes. The screen with Charlie's vitals stopped flashing red and beeping quickly thereafter and his heart rate normalized.

"That was better than being asleep?" Charlie said, exasperated and still breathing heavily.

"Actually, yes," Dr. Goosh said, "if you were asleep, then I would have had to open up your ears more and dig around for the proper, uh, 'wires,' if you will." She air quoted wires to keep it simple for Charlie. "If I messed one up while you were sleeping, it would seriously have messed with your hearing and balance when you woke up. Instead, I knew right away when it was wrong because it hurt you. Is the pain gone yet?" she asked.

Charlie was too caught up in the moment to realize that he actually wasn't in any pain—well, except for his pulled muscle, which was really his own fault. He raised his eyebrows at the doctor in a puzzled look and searched her face for answers while feeling the sweat roll off his eyebrows and down the side of his face.

"I told your brain to ignore it essentially," she said. "It will hurt in a couple hours. Like you got smacked across the head."

"Great," Charlie said, "so what now?"

Dr. Goosh explained the primary use of the auditory enhancements and said that he would need training to actually use them, but his brain was in control of the range of frequencies he could hear. Then she gave the state secrecy oath once more to remind Charlie that it was serious and he should remember not to say anything, to anyone.

After the formalities, the same process occurred with the optometrist and the dentist. All three doctors were members of the underground who knew that Charlie was going to be a 2A and risked their lives to best preserve and keep their brother safe.

The contact lenses were little computers inserted beneath his retinas to increase his visual perception, and dye was introduced into his cornea to increase light sensitivity. Charlie felt that after his procedures he pretty much got super hearing and super vision. Excellent advantages for a soldier. He would now be able to hear an enemy a kilometer away breathing in his sleep, and subsequently find him in the dark from that same one-kilometer distance and successfully end his life without moving so much as a meter closer to the enemy.

The dental enhancements didn't really make sense to him at first. They were there to detect poisons and served as signals for his health. No matter how many questions the dentist answered, Charlie couldn't understand what the implants did. Eventually, he would learn how to use them more or less like a radio receiver. Charlie was thrilled to learn about his lifelong abilities during training. Or at least he was excited until the pain hit him like a truck. He was wheeled into a recovery room not unlike inpatient rooms at typical hospitals. That's when Charlie knew that his life had really changed. He started to hear things while he slept.

Chapter 8—Recovery and Training

After his recovery time, Charlie received blocks of instructions that taught him how to use all of his enhancements properly. He received his own screen that he had the option of wearing on his forearm or more traditionally carrying as a notebook. The screen itself was flexible, very thin, and fairly translucent. All commands were intuitive and if it was used regularly enough, it actually anticipated commands. This was a fairly recent development and was explained to Charlie as an algorithm that merely made very highly educated guesses. In total, he spent fifteen days in training before he was assigned to the 24th Special Forces Group out of Fort Powell, Minnesota.

He was notified that he would receive traditional orders via the U.S. mail, but that would be irrelevant because it was already uploaded into his personnel files. In the meantime, Charlie was instructed to get some uniforms and a haircut.

After he was issued his uniforms from the central issuing facility, Charlie headed to the medical facilities barbershop. He was sure that he would be forced to cut his hair to nearly skin, but when they scanned his screen, they gave him several options which were far less conservative. He settled on a technology-age standard style—part down the middle, off slightly to one side. While he had his hair cut by this frail Hispanic woman, he browsed his screen to locate his personnel file. He then discovered that he didn't actually exist anymore. Well, not exactly that he didn't exist, but that Charlie

Prescott did not have a record in the entire database he had access to and not even his national ID number generated any results. He then scoured the State news websites for his name and found it in the obituaries. Nothing noteworthy was in the brief entry. It just had his name, his birthdate, his parents' names, and his death date, which was last week. Charlie Prescott was legally dead. He was curious what his parents knew. They already had connections that aided him, so maybe the message got back to his parents and they simply carried on knowing that he wasn't really dead, or at least not dead yet.

As his haircut was finishing up, Charlie was thinking about how to inform his parents. He was sure that if he sent a message directly to them it would be blocked—and when he did try later that day, it was blocked. Regardless, he sat in the barber's chair and puzzled over his personal problem.

The government had me officially listed as dead, he thought to himself. *They can do anything to me if they wanted to, I'm their property now.* The sense of helplessness again set in, but this wasn't an anxious sensation anymore; this was more of a depressive feeling. He could do nothing to improve his situation and it felt futile to even try. Sometimes during his training, he would disassociate with the instruction and completely miss the point of the lesson. Realistically, though, this was normal and more or less expected. Either way, he snapped back into reality when the Hispanic woman spoke to him.

"How is this, Lieutenant?" the barber asked with a subtle accent. It was clear that she was a citizen second class and was at least second-generation American. Charlie's friend François spoke French at home and only learned English for school, so Charlie was thrown off when the barber spoke as clearly as she did because nearly all non-citizens first class primarily spoke languages other than English, resulting in a biased accent. Those who were American during the reformation and ratification of the 33rd Amendment were grandfathered in and allowed to speak English; however, their children would not be allowed a formal education nor be allowed to take grammar lessons. This would ensure class stability with relatively small exceptions for superb members of other classes—like François. The government saw this clause as a way for upward mobility, but put outrageous stipulations on its possibilities.

Charlie took a quick glance in the mirrors and noticed that there was a small patch of hair left uncut behind his right ear.

"Ma'am, you forgot this spot," Charlie said, indicating the little patch of hair. The barber put on her glasses and inspected the area Charlie pointed at.

"Ah, yes. I'm sorry, sir. You have very good eyes to catch that. It was under the top layer!" She was both impressed that Charlie found the piece but also disappointed that she missed it herself. She had noticed recently that she was beginning to slip away from excellence. She was old, fairly malnourished, and had degenerative diseases wrecking her hand-eye coordination. The only thing that kept her good at cutting hair was that she had been cutting the same haircuts for nearly thirty years. She felt that she could do it in her sleep. The only difference from a couple years ago was that now she needed to focus and move more intentionally.

Charlie felt bad for calling attention to the uneven hair, but couldn't help it. His eyes had been naturally drawn to imperfections ever since his classes on pattern recognition. It was incredible how much of his brain wasn't being tapped into until his enhancements. One of his tests was to find the errors in a sudoku puzzle from twenty meters away. He had played the number puzzle a lot in his youth and got pretty good at it. From a twenty-meter distance, he never made a mistake.

As she finished recutting Charlie's hair, he got a message on his screen. It informed him that he needed to report to the hospital for immediate processing. Charlie had his screen scanned and the proper amount was transferred to the barbershop. Charlie then rushed back to his recovery room and was greeted by a government official in a sleek suit with several party pins on his lapel and a bold ring that was more a status symbol than anything else. Charlie saw that the man also had a slight tremor as he reached to shake Charlie's hand. Charlie deduced from the clues readily available that the man was in his thirties, separated from his wife, and very wealthy.

"Good afternoon, Lieutenant, I am the military medical czar responsible for the 2A program. I am here today to brief you on who you are." He gave an uncomfortably forced smile, revealing his effervescent teeth, and Charlie noticed that the man's tremor also affected his lips and eye.

"You are now Lieutenant Clarke Anicius, son of military parents who both unfortunately died when you were only fifteen years old during the Siege of San Antonio." The czar recited this well-rehearsed monologue with next to zero emotion, and after several minutes explaining backstories and extended family tree, he paused as if he were waiting for something.

Charlie took a moment to realize that his name was now Clarke. He didn't exactly know how to react to that, but internalized it unnaturally quickly. So, Clarke took the long pause as a cue to recite the information back. He did well as he attempted to repeat it verbatim. The man seemed very pleased and Clarke waited to see what else would happen.

"Sir, you did not have me recite an oath of secrecy. Am I authorized to share this information?"

"Well, of course you can, it's your own biographical information. I don't see why I would have you swear anything to keep who you are a secret. You already know what you are not allowed to disclose, and this is permissible." The czar abruptly stopped his tremor and reached into his suit pocket to pull out his screen. He called up a file and put away the screen as it started to play. To the naked ear, it would seem like they were standing there in silence, but Clarke heard the quiet and muffled sound through the man's jacket.

It was a soft voice saying, "We know that the military has taken you away and that you have been kept safe in the hands of our allies. Please know that we will not be able to send any more messages, but we love you and know that you will be safe in their hands." Clarke couldn't be happier to hear his mother's voice and he memorized her message. The czar's tremor kept rattling while they said their goodbyes. Clarke thanked the man and asked how he could contact him if he had any questions or special requests. Clearly, the man understood from Clarke's sunken-faced reaction to the recording that he had heard the message and was referring to speaking with his family.

The czar smiled and pulled out his screen. He subtly navigated to where he could record audio and placed it back into his pocket. Clarke didn't hesitate to speak, but he didn't know what to say. "I love you all so much. I will send you messages at every chance I get." Then he looked at the floor, pausing for a moment, and shook his head. He didn't have anything else to say. The czar gave a short bow, picked up his hat, and his tremor continued as he left the room. The entire encounter had only been about ten or fifteen minutes and was the weirdest moment of Clarke's life so far, including being medically enhanced.

The rest of the afternoon was spent wandering the hospital and browsing through shopping networks on his screen. He was given information on his pay scale and realized that he would have quite a lot of money to spend. The first thing he looked at were sunglasses, because the glare from light was pretty intense outside. Clarke ended up falling asleep early that night and had a dreamless sleep.

The next morning, Clarke woke up to several messages on his screen. The first few were trivial advertisements and appointment reminders, which he had long since gone to, and the rest of the screen was populated with all the other messages. There were also two urgent matters at hand: assignment briefing and travel briefings. Clarke already had his orders for the 24th Special Forces Group and knew that he was heading to Fort Powell, but otherwise he had no clue what he was supposed to do or how he was supposed to do it.

Well, first things first, breakfast, he thought to himself.

The hospital's cafeteria wasn't exactly spectacular, but it was better than the private sector. The government had finally spent tax dollars where it counted, although it could be argued that this was a tad bit on the wasteful side. They served steak burritos, fresh caviar, and even had their own livestock on the opposite side of the parking garage.

The concept of farm-to-table dining had really destroyed the transportation industry in the past fifty years. The United States had gotten to the point where instantaneous delivery was expected, and food items were not an exception. Before the nuclear bombing, farmers grew crops and raised livestock in the middle of nowhere and relied on traditional modes of transportation. Slowly, farmers shifted from trucks to the Bowers&Godfrey model of industrial and personal instantaneous delivery platforms, eventually cutting the traditional transportation industry out of the process, which ultimately led to the collapse of the trucking industry. The problem with teleported food, though, was that the processing degraded organic products, and the increased cost of using teleportation made it cheaper and healthier for food to be locally grown. Oddly enough, the GNW was a blessing in disguise—some might even say divine intervention, because the disruption it caused in the agricultural industry led to some serious innovations, which increased healthy food consumption practices and affordability for quality ingredients, in addition to bringing jobs to the local economies once more.

All of that taken into account, however, steak and eggs at a hospital was still a bit lavish. The government could afford this, though, with the tax reform of 2085 under the Carter presidency, in which the budget was not only balanced for the first time since 2001 but also led to a surplus. Naturally, the surpluses went into development and the defense industry, with the military hospitals receiving a healthy bargain from the iron triangle between veterans' groups, pro-military or faux pro-military politicians, and the medical providers themselves looking for a little kickback. The policy led to some substantial changes in food for troops under the ruse of soldier health, but in reality, it was geared toward giving hospital workers, Department of Defensive Land Warfare employees, and Veterans' Affairs civilian staff members more extravagant food choices.

So that was how Clarke found himself eating fresh eggs Benedict and a mixed green salad and picked his own grapes off a living vine while sitting in a dining room fit for most European royals. The ambiance was beautiful, with classical music being played live by a violinist for the first twenty or so minutes, followed by a pianist for the next hour. The room was the size of a small church cathedral, capable of seating two or three hundred people comfortably, with high arched ceilings and orange-tinted oval windows overlooking a highway system. Small fiber optic chandeliers provided light for the room. It was the single most elegant room Clarke had been inside and he cherished every meal there.

The waitress came up and asked if there was anything that she could get for him.

"I'd love another one of these drinks, ma'am," he said, pointing to a cup of coffee, "it's delicious, but what exactly is it?"

"This is specialty coffee with herb blended milk from our house garden," she said before walking across the room to get a fresh carafe of coffee. She returned momentarily and spoke again in a sweet and innocent voice, "It's made with supplements and medicinal blends to balance the bitter taste of traditional organic coffee and to stop any irritations that are common among frequent coffee drinkers."

"This is coffee?" Clarke asked in amazement, pointing at the light-brown liquid. "I can't believe that. I'm so used to my family's coffee that I would have never guessed that."

"Some people like it and others hate it!" she said in response with a polite and shy smile. Clarke couldn't help but notice that her smooth, slender fingers and narrow wrists were several shades lighter than her dark-tan forearms, as if she frequently worked in the sun with gloves on. There was an odd strength to her, showing she was more than capable of taking care of herself.

"If there is anything else, please feel free to indicate so and I will be just a few seconds away."

"Thank you, ma'am," Clarke said as he watched her walk away. The waitress was in her mid-twenties and was fairly short at about 160 centimeters tall, with dark-tan skin and classically beautiful curves. Clarke was weak for girls like her, whose genuine smile and soft jawline reminded him of the way a new mother cradles her baby's head in the crook of her elbow. She wore a professional shirt and pants with the hospital apron around her narrow waist, but was clearly a student—her college-issued screen was a dead giveaway.

Clarke also thought that she was a student based on her tan lines where she regularly wore her screen on her left forearm, the several highlighters in her back pocket, and the overexplaining of hospital coffee. Her knowledge and expertise indicated that she was likely a student of agriculture or something of the sort at New Boston University. The school was only a couple miles away from the hospital, and despite it being known as a feeder school for doctors at the regional hospitals, it was also a remarkable agricultural school. He remembered looking at her hands as she poured the coffee just a minute ago, noticed that she wasn't wearing any rings and thought about how manicured they were with pastel yellow nail polish. The fact that her hands were strong yet soft was perplexing, but the tan lines didn't lie—she worked in the sun a lot. Since she wasn't an intern or something more related to hospital business, it was a pretty good guess that she was at New Boston University for horticulture or the like.

Clarke noticed himself smiling and staring at her as she walked through the doors to the kitchen and he shook himself hard, feeling embarrassed. He wasn't that kind of guy and he felt ashamed of himself. He knew better and didn't consciously stare at her, but he still felt bad. He quickly looked around the cafeteria to see if anyone else noticed, but no one was nearby enough to have paid it any attention. Just him and his conscious now. He quickly recited a prayer of reconciliation in his head and looked upward for a moment of atonement. He knew better than to stare at someone with that kind of lust.

For the rest of his breakfast, he put his screen on the table in front of him and reviewed the documents he had received for in-processing. Nothing made sense and he couldn't find any information on Fort Powell, Minnesota. It seemed to be in a vacuum of information, which he chalked up to being a result of government censorship. Clarke took a long drink from his cup of coffee and a bite of French toast before turning back to his screen. He sat back in his chair, took off his baseball cap, and ran his cold hands through his fresh haircut before letting out a long exhale.

"Mind if I sit with you?" a fellow second lieutenant asked while holding his tray. He had short curly black hair and playful dark-brown eyes. He was fairly short but obviously muscular, with the body type of a natural athlete who never made it to a professional league.

Clarke looked over and said with a smile, "Absolutely. I'd be upset if you didn't." Clarke reached over and pulled the chair out so the other lieutenant could sit across from him. "The name's Clarke Anicius."

"Lewis Abubakari," the other lieutenant said, setting his tray down quickly and reaching out to shake his hand. "Pleasure to meet you."

"The pleasure is mine," Clarke said calmly and removed his hand as gently as he could. Lewis had a very firm grip that made Clarke want to wince, but he prevented himself from showing that sort of weakness and had simply squeezed Lewis's strong black hand even harder for a second. The formalities they exchanged were typical initial greetings between citizens first class, and the ice was broken once they started talking with one another. They had both been unsure when Lewis first sat down at the table, but they quickly opened up as they realized they were both enhanced and already had a shared experience even before saying anything beyond hello.

"What are you here for? I'm about to leave for my first duty station shortly," Clarke asked.

"Same, actually. I got a letter about two months ago telling me I had been drafted! Me, a soldier? Yeah right. My father lost his mind and my mother was distraught," Lewis said with a fake little laugh, showing bright white teeth and a prominent gap in between them. He raised his arm out and gave a short nod, which cued the waitress again. Clarke, still feeling embarrassed, struggled to keep his eyes off her. As she hurried across the room, he noticed her hair had been ironed flat and cut in a faddish way, which, in Clarke's opinion, detracted from her natural beauty. First her shoes, then her hips, her hands, and eventually her eyes. He was beginning to feel that his eyes were a curse rather than a blessing. As he looked at her eyes, Clarke could see each and every freckle on her face. Her deep amber-green eyes with punches of dark brown were intoxicating to him, and he felt his heart rate increasing.

"Hello sir, how can I help you?" she said to Lewis with a coy smile.

"I'll have what he's having. But could you bring me a double serving?" Lewis asked with a playful wink.

"Not a problem, I'll be right back," she said politely, before offering a small bow and a genuine smile.

"Thank you, Roxi," Lewis said with an ear-to-ear smile.

Clarke's head wheeled from Roxi's face to Lewis, his own face going from a neutral and impassive appearance to a puzzled expression. "You know her?" Clarke said as Roxi made her way across the room.

"Well, yeah. She's been working nearly every breakfast I've had." He looked down at the table between him and Clarke. "My, uh, recovery was a bit slower than they anticipated. I thought it would be better if they knocked me out, but practically every nurse I've talked to said that it was a really bad idea to be unconscious during my, uh, procedures."

Clarke already knew that his new friend was a 2A, but didn't exactly want to give away that he knew it, so he opted for a more subtle way to confirm it. "So, I'm going to leave for my first assignment soon at Fort Powell. My orders are for the 24th Special Forces Group. What about you?"

Lewis looked back up from the table and his smile returned as if nothing had bothered him a moment ago. "So, you're special forces too? I thought they only had one opening; clearly I was wrong, though."

"When are you supposed to report?" Clarke asked.

"Tomorrow, 14 July, no later than 1700 their time," Lewis answered.

"I'm supposed to be there next week. I guess they just want to make sure I'll be okay with all the new gadgets they gave me," Clarke said as he reached for his coffee, "but my orders don't say how I'll be getting there."

"You haven't gotten a travel briefing yet?" Lewis asked. "You better not miss your appointment—those ladies are unforgiving." Lewis grabbed an apple from a cart, which was being wheeled past the table. "Didn't you get the message on your screen?"

"Yeah," Clarke said, "it just said before 1200. Figured I'd go there after this. What's wrong with that? What did they tell you?"

"You and I both know that I can't tell you anything about official travel," Lewis said, rolling his eyes. It was true enough. Likely the travel briefing was covered under the state secrecy act and Lewis was specifically told to stay quiet about any and all information, regardless of whom he came across. It was possible that Lewis might be thinking that Clarke was an imposter, or even that Clarke might not be a citizen first class and therefore not of the same status as himself. Clarke was embarrassed that he had asked the question, but also felt a bit clever because Lewis didn't outright admit that he knew Clarke's status.

At that moment, while Lewis tilted his head just a second longer than natural, Roxi came back from across the room. Clarke resisted watching her come up this time. He not only felt guilty, but he was also worried that Lewis might notice his gazing. She set the dishes on the table very gracefully and gave a short little curtsy with the server tray under her arm before turning and walking away silently. Clarke was starting to admit to himself that she probably wasn't a citizen first class and that any hopes of a relationship with her would be impossible.

"How long have you been here?" Clarke said to re-break the ice. "I was admitted a couple of weeks ago, but really I've been in therapy after some surgeries for most of that time."

"Just a few weeks!" Lewis nearly shouted. Nobody in the cafeteria cared or bothered to look at them. "I've been here for a few months. God, I should have just stayed awake. I was in a coma for about a week—don't worry, it was medically induced to keep me from losing my mind, although I'm not so sure it worked. I had the weirdest and most lucid dreams. It was like reliving parts of my life that I forgot about really. Anyway, after that, I was nearly deaf, dumb, and blind until my therapists worked out the problems. Trust me, that took forever. I think that's what made me accept my fate as a soldier."

"Wow. I couldn't imagine that. I'm sorry to hear," Clarke said playfully. "It's a shame you weren't prepared to die before then."

"You should get to your appointment," Lewis said with one of his big smiles and a small chuckle. "Leave me your access number and your coffee. I'll send you some information that I found by myself and, uh, maybe Roxi's access number," he said scratching his neck absentmindedly.

Clarke smiled and looked in the direction of the kitchen door. "It's that obvious?"

"Like a werewolf under a full moon," Lewis said.

"Whatever," Clarke said as he wrote down his access number on Lewis's screen, "just don't embarrass her, please."

"Scout's honor," Lewis said, placing his hand over his heart.

Clarke stood up and collected his trays into an orderly pile for Roxi to come grab in a moment. "I'll see you then."

"See ya, pal," Lewis said while reaching for a key-lime pastry on another passing cart.

Chapter 9—Reporting for Duty

C larke was sitting in the small lobby of one of the buildings adjacent to the hospital proper, waiting to be called back to get his travel briefing. This room was similar to the first one he was seen in before he had his enhancements done. That initial building and the one he was currently in were clearly older than the hospital itself by well over fifty years. The layout of the older buildings suggested that the hospital had previously been an open field or some other structure. Little did Clarke know, however, that the hospital actually used to be the site of a cathedral and the old buildings were office spaces owned by the church prior to government confiscation. Naturally, the tall spires, decorative towers, belfries, and—generally speaking—the architectural style were unacceptable for government buildings and were therefore torn down. The smaller buildings were simply converted by a thorough renovation to remove all artifacts and statues from the inside, but it just wasn't feasible to do that with the cathedral itself.

Over time, as the population of the local area increased due to the mass Northeast United States migration southward resulting from the Great Nuclear War, the demand for medical care skyrocketed. The nuclear fallout killed thousands, left millions sick, and drove the pharmaceutical industry berserk seeking new and improved treatments, which, of course, came with through-the-roof prices. The State decided that this location was primed for conversion to a hospital, and thanks to technology-age engineering, it was built in record-setting timeframes—under two years from groundbreaking to fully operational ORs, ERs, and pediatric care, orthopedic, EENT, dental, maternity, NICU, and chemotherapy centers.

Despite this lack of knowledge, something stirred inside Clarke as he sat there. He felt comforted in the worn-out seating and natural light from the windows lining the waiting room. He could tell that the space wasn't always used in this way because of the unnatural position of the counter that nobody bothered to reposition. It sat tired in the middle of the room with chipping paint and a grimy black buildup on the baseboard from years of being mopped with dirty water. Clarke looked over at a digital bulletin board that was at least twenty years old judging by some of the ads. He looked closer at some of the ads just to stay busy and noticed that one of them, an ad for an attorney's office, was paid in advance until Clarke turned fifty.

Clarke closed his eyes and thought back on the strange government visitor he had the night before and smiled remembering the message he had received. He replayed his mother's voice in his head over and over again, before his memory shifted focus from the recording to the czar himself. Clarke recalled that the man was wearing a golden half-circle on his lapel and a ring with an eagle perched on an olive branch with arrows clasped in its beak. Clarke was amazed that he recalled such a small detail well after the actual meeting. Apparently, his enhancements helped him focus his memory more than he consciously could, and he discovered that he was able to remember things that he had missed while the events themselves happened.

"Second Lieutenant Anicius, Clarke to room two-oh-four. Lieutenant Anicius to room two-oh-four," a voice over an intercom said patiently yet monotonously. Clarke remembered what Lewis had told him at breakfast and grew weary. Clarke felt his palms start to sweat as he stood up and he instinctively rubbed them on his pants before he rounded the corner into a hallway, looking for room 204.

The room was another small office space tucked among dozens. It must have been smaller than the average bathroom, with barely enough space for a little desk and a visitor's chair that poked out into the hallway a little. The porthole-sized window behind the desk was a poor attempt at making the room feel bigger than it was and incidentally caused there to be less usable wall space, a fact that Clarke picked up on because nearly every spot on her walls had something posted on it. One wall had a large screen with digital notes displayed, including a calendar the size of a doormat. The opposite wall had postcards from family members visiting different national parks—a perk of being a party member. One of the laws that had been passed before Clarke was born prohibited average citizens entry into national parks as a way of keeping the environment beautiful for the elite.

Clarke liked the look of the printed postcards because they were tangible. They could actually be held and cherished. Electronic mail wasn't so, and it would never be so unless you dedicated a portion of a screen to it. For instance, his parents had memorialized a note from his brother in their hallway by purchasing a small screen and mounting it to the wall. Clarke had the little note memorized ever since it was put up next to Robert's study. He spent hours sitting in front of it, crying at first, and then over time sat there just to be closer to his brother. He must have been there for a couple hours a week just reading or doing homework with his brother's memory.

The little screen read, *Hey mom and dad. I'll be out camping in Doe Woods this weekend. I'll be sure to have a nice strong fire you'll be able to see from the upstairs windows. Love Alex.*

Clarke sent a similar message just before he left for the military processing station: *Hey mom and dad. I'm going to be gone for a while but I'll be sure to keep sending you mail when I get the chance. Love Charlie.*

Clarke was sitting down in the cramped office of the notorious travel lady, taking in his surroundings, when she walked up behind him.

"Good morning. Lieutenant Anicius, I presume," she said, slightly scaring Clarke with how close she had gotten before making any noise. "I'm pleased to see you here during your allotted time." She was actually thankful for his tardiness because it had allowed her to take care of some housekeeping things for her office. She was smiling as she said this and pushed her full-framed body between the wall and her desk, as she had clearly done hundreds, if not thousands, of times before based on the even wear on the wall where her backside sanded off the paint. Her desk very intentionally didn't have anything resting on the first couple of centimeters on that side so she could pass without knocking things off. She herself wasn't a large individual, but her Brazilian heritage definitely showed physically by the landscape of her body. She wore full-frame glasses and a frilly blouse with loose cuffs, standard business professional attire of the time, and her hair was cut in the faddish half-up and half-down look of a twenty-year-old, not the more conservative braid or bun of the forty-five-year-old woman she was. It was obvious that a previous life was trying to break through via her wardrobe, as she wore a blouse that would be considered popular for college girls, not a mature woman. Clarke avoided making eye contact with the her. He was nervous to begin with and didn't want to be even more intimidated by the mysterious travel lady.

"Just a moment while I locate your document," she said while tapping the screen on her workspace with a colorful pointer finger. The screen came to life and projected a three-dimensional file storage system. She flicked through several rows and found the 2A cabinet. After indicating it, the screen scanned her eyes and Clarke's eyes before it opened a list of names and dates. Some of the dates went back as far as 2055 but stopped periodically, probably coinciding with active war and peace times, but Clarke noticed that there weren't any people on the list aside from himself, Lewis Abubakari, and Analyn Zheng in the past fifteen years.

All Clarke knew about previous wars was that there were always covert and clandestine operations that shaped public opinion and ultimately decided the outcomes of the wars. He thought back to how the Defense Strategic Operation Protection Cell, formerly the Central Intelligence Agency, was responsible for the assassinations of foreign leaders in Vietnam, and how Julius and Ethel Rosenberg took the fall for other spies during the Cold War. No espionage from the 21st century was declassified yet, and it was unlikely to ever be uncovered given the current political climate, despite laws and international agreements. Classified data was more likely to be destroyed than lawfully handed over to any journalist—if any of it really existed anymore.

Clarke then wondered why there were so few people on this list. Although Clarke knew about the war with Mexico from the government's weekly reports, there was something unnerving about the gap between Lewis, Analyn, and himself with the last group. Maybe he would learn more about his situation in the coming weeks after getting to know his teammates.

Clarke knew Lewis already, but according to the list, Analyn had arrived prior to either of them. Clarke assumed that Analyn must have already arrived at Fort Powell some months ago. He also understood that the drafts had always been in teams of three based on the historical data in front of him and therefore judged that it would likely just be the three of them: Lewis, Analyn, and Clarke.

The travel lady picked up Clarke's file and sent it to a screen above the wall she had just scuffed up in getting to her desk. It was his orders, no surprise there. She began skimming the document for something unknown to Clarke, but after a minute or so she must have found it because she selected a portion of text and pulled it back over to the workspace on her desktop. The cabinets previously opened on her screen were sent to the periphery as they stacked up and consolidated their data as three-dimensional icons. The only projected cabinet left in the center of the screen was one labeled *Travel*.

"This is just a fancy way of making sure that only *I* can get your information," she said while the massive data files were filtering in. "Essentially, we take your orders and code them in a way that's unique to your authorizations. Naturally, this takes a lot of processing power and can end up on the longer side of data mining, but some of us know what we are doing." She stood up and leaned around Clarke to look as far down the hallway as she could manage before continuing, "Unlike the government, I, for one, think that all of the technical aspects are run by the underground." She quickly mimed an 'X' on her forehead, lips, and heart.

He didn't know how he was so lucky, but he definitely wasn't going to complain. He motioned a quick sign of Jesus as naturally as he could before scratching his chin and sniffling a little. He heard the sound of short stubble and thought to himself that he probably should have shaved that morning. He snapped back to the current conversation with a visible shake of his head and cleared his throat.

"I guess that you just need to know who is working for whom, right?" Clarke said coolly and gave a small smile. He was relieved to see her smile in return.

"Your colleagues, Lieutenants Zheng and Abubakari, will have already left Fort Powell before you get there." She laughed a little to herself and then continued, "it's just so typical that they would give you enough time for in-processing but then immediately ask you to deploy."

"Deploy?" Clarke said out loud a bit louder than he intended. He caught his little outburst before it had really begun and quickly apologized, "I'm sorry, I guess I thought that I'd be in training still by this point. It's just that I only left home for the first time about a month ago and you just told me that I was deploying." He was overexplaining himself but he couldn't help it; it was his personality. A couple of months ago, he had been sitting in his armchair in his parents' upstairs hallway, reading a forbidden copy of *American Author Classics*, and now he was an enhanced soldier getting ready for deployment to God knows where without actually being trained in combat. It all was happening so fast, and he wanted it to slow down. His heart rate was picking up and he started to feel that he was hyperventilating. A cold sweat broke out and his hands started to get clammy.

"I—I just don't know what's going on completely and I'm hoping that you could explain a lot of it to me so that it makes sense," Clarke said rapidly after a pause in their conversation while the data continued to load.

The travel lady peeked over her glasses and said with a wide grin, "What is it you would like to know?"

"Well, I guess my biggest question is, what is a 2A and why was I selected for it?" Clarke said bluntly. His tone wasn't the kind that would come off as disrespectful, but rather one of confusion and mild panic. The travel lady pinched the bridge of her nose and closed her eyes for a moment.

"You really don't know?" she asked.

"No, I really don't." Clarke's voice was nearly silent. He sunk in his seat just a little and lowered his head. Feeling defeated, he sank deeper into his seat, his neck hanging so low that his head was nearly resting on his lap. His mind went from anxiety and paranoia to a more futile concern as he absentmindedly played with a stylus for a minute. Clarke looked up from his hands in his lap and noticed an internal struggle playing out on the travel lady's face. She grimaced, smiled, furrowed her brow, and rubbed her eyes, all while moving her lips in extreme positions. Finally, she let out a deep sigh.

"Do you understand what I am about to show you is highly classified and I could be imprisoned or worse for telling you?" She was whispering but Clarke could hear her perfectly.

"Yes," he lipped.

"A 2A is not just a special forces soldier; you're an intelligence collector," she started in near silence. "But really it means you are a spy. You were selected because of your ingenuity in hosting secretive meetings as a child. The government knows what you were able to keep secret and with whom you shared information. It's all here in your file." She motioned to the desktop screen. "Your family has been followed for a very long time, but the State can't get anything concrete against you. Since all of your family are party members, they meet the stringent screening criteria for the most sensitive positions."

Clarke's eyes widened when he heard this. The State knew about him hosting secret meetings and his code among friends? Did they know about the church too? Of course not; if they did, then all of the congregation would be murdered in the streets—unless the State wanted an underground, that is. None of it made sense.

The rest of the exchange was rather trivial as she sent Clarke several files, including the details of his travel itinerary and his authorization to not wear army uniforms. Instead, a badge and credentials would be the only indication that he was military. In other words, he was to wear civilian clothes, grow whatever facial hair he wanted, and he didn't have to worry about physical fitness. Clarke was particularly keen on his permission to grow one of the trendy mustaches and was also thrilled about not being required to run or do any sort of physical activity. The way the orders read was that the army wanted him to be as non-military as possible so the average soldier and the average civilian would mistake him for any other civilian.

Clarke thanked the travel lady and bowed himself out of the room. Relieved slightly, he took in a deep breath, raised his head toward the warm sunlight, and smiled.

This won't be that bad after all, he thought to himself.

The rest of his day was peaceful. He grabbed a hefty afternoon snack and returned to his hospital room and packed the rest of his belongings. As he closed his small duffle bag, he couldn't help but feel he was forgetting something, but instead of worrying about it, he pulled out his screen and switched it over to some entertainment channels for a couple of hours. He had been forgetting a lot of things recently and decided to occupy his mind with mind-numbing entertainment in lieu of analysis.

Clarke got hungry around 1800 and put away his screen. He paused for a moment thinking about inviting Lewis but realized that he undoubtedly would already be gone based on what the travel lady had told him, and he hadn't met Analyn yet, so Clarke simply went down to the cafeteria by himself, expecting to be a bit lonesome.

Being alone was bittersweet to Clarke. He liked solitude and enjoyed the ability to simply be at peace with himself by not worrying about others, but sometimes it got depressing. He longed for social interaction and a meaningful connection with someone else. He struggled to qualify these feelings and oscillated between content and depressed. Several times in his life, he felt that he was at the point of depression, but after a quick talk with his dad, Clarke felt refreshed and ready to take on the world. He could no longer talk to his dad, though.

Clarke adjusted his gray and neon-yellow baseball cap and walked slowly down the hospital hall. He was looking out over the amber-hued sunset and blissfully glided to the central staircase, which he descended slowly in order to really embrace the craftsmanship of the handrails and overhead lighting. It was magnificent. Finally, at the bottom step, he looked around as if he expected something to be happening and slowly turned to the cafeteria at the end of the hallway.

Clarke entered the beautiful room and sat at the table he and Lewis had shared earlier that day. He pulled out his screen and accessed the dinner menu by selecting several items that intrigued him. While he waited for his server, he thought again about Roxi. Her skin looked so soft and her smile was intoxicating. His own subtle smile scrunched into a deep frown as he pushed the thoughts out of his mind. Clarke knew that what he was thinking was going to lead down an immoral path and he fought hard against the temptation. He prayed for this temptation to leave his mind so he could continue living a pure life. He also prayed that he would find his spouse sooner rather than later because he was longing for that blessing. After a moment, he opened his eyes to find that his waiter was starting to set down several small plates of food.

"Sorry," said Clarke, "I've been having some terrible headaches recently; my eyes are sensitive to the light." As true as the light sensitivity was, it did not cause headaches, but it was at least a logical statement to explain why his eyes were closed for so long. The waiter didn't care, of course, but Clarke felt embarrassed anyway.

"Thank you," Clarke said as the waiter bowed himself away from the table. He felt like this sort of embarrassment was starting to happen more and more as he was getting older. Maybe it was the increased stress from becoming an adult, or maybe it was just dealing with how awkward he actually was. Regardless, Clarke zoned out of reality for some time while he stared absentmindedly at some toast and took a sip of his sweet iced tea.

After a while, he snapped back into reality when he got a message on his screen. It lit up with a soft pastel blue and pink and gave a subtle pulse on his wrist. Clarke glanced over and saw that it was from Lewis.

"Almost forgot. Her access number is 209309021011. Good luck!"

Clarke thought for a moment while he grabbed a strawberry from another plate. Was he really going to be the guy who awkwardly sends messages to pretty waitresses? Other than being creepy and weird, it would definitely be pathetic. He looked back at the message and read over it several times. Lewis was making it harder to just get on with his life and forget about her.

God must be telling me something, Clarke thought to himself as he let out a deep sigh and took a sip of tea. *Well, I trust in You.* He then proceeded to draft a message to her, but he couldn't send it. Something didn't feel right about doing it. He was embarrassed and nervous; after all, he had never done anything quite like this before. She was clearly not in the same citizenship class as him and that was a serious problem.

The next few days filled him with overwhelming anxiety as he thought about sending his message to her. Finally, on July 20th, Clarke made his way to the airport, which was just down the road. The government-operated magnetic-propelled transportation was behind the times, but it was still the cleanest mode of travel available. Clarke actually thought that the car might flip over as it rounded a corner going in excess of 160 km/hour. The trip itself did nothing to calm his anxiety. Needless to say, he also felt a good bit of stress in the entire process of going to the first assignment of his compulsory military obligation as an intelligence collector. So much had happened in the past couple of weeks that he had not taken the time to really digest how drastically his life changed. Clarke no longer had the lifestyle he grew up with. His silver spoon was replaced with a cloak and dagger—and between the dread and guilt there was an inkling of excitement.

The government had done terrible things, of course, but nothing bad had come his way; rather, the opposite was true. The State actually improved his life. Now he could literally hear a pin drop from across a crowded room, he could see said pin, and he could process the complex pattern of it bouncing off the floor faster than anyone he ever knew. It seemed that his status as a member of a party-related family had paid off. Despite being drafted, the government had done him a favor. Clarke wanted to question why, but he pushed that out of his thoughts and decided to simply enjoy what was going on in his life.

After he had checked into the airport, he went through security screenings and a brief interview with the Air Flight Authorization Agency or AFAA, by which point about four hours had passed since he had arrived. Now that he had boarded his flight, the anticipation of flying for the first time paused his anxiety and concern for a while. Not everyone was allowed to fly. Nearly everyone who did fly was a citizen first class with official party business, or inversely, was a prisoner going to another facility.

Regardless, it was nice to see the city from above, and the plane ride was fast and nearly silent. The perpetual vacuum that provided propulsion also acted as a noise cancellation device, which was channeled throughout the plane. Although there were studies that showed passengers felt more comfortable when there was sound from the plane, the engineers felt that the technological advances in airstream navigation that led to nearly zero turbulence for high-altitude flight paths with incredible speeds made the actual flight feel like just sitting in a lounge. In fact, it was far more comfortable than the magnetic tracks of public transit, which had nearly killed Clarke just a couple of hours ago. The flight itself covered nearly 2,000 kilometers to Fort Powell in northern Minnesota and the total duration was just over an hour. Clarke felt that this sort of speed was outrageous, but also fantastic. *No wonder wars end so quickly*, he thought to himself.

Chapter 10—Travel

Touchdown came and went smoothly. As Clarke was making his way to the baggage claim, a sign caught his attention. It was a soft blue with yellow lettering, like so many of the other public notices he had seen in parks and public areas throughout Alabama. But what caught his attention wasn't the sign itself; it was that the words were written in a different language. This language was cursive with dots and swirls and flourishes—maybe Persian? *That can't be the case,* Clarke thought to himself, *writing in other languages is a felony.* Felonies were punishable by death because they showed an absolute disregard for the State and therefore could not be tolerated.

Clarke pulled out his screen and put it on his wrist, then paused for a moment in contemplation. *Would this make me stand out as military? I mean, it does mark me as at least a party member, which is a benefit, but is there a downside? Nobody told me not to do this.* After a moment, he came to the conclusion that it wouldn't matter much since he clearly just got off an airplane and anyone who saw him leaving the airport would know he was a citizen first class. Having the screen out for the rest of his travel would be more convenient anyway, so he went ahead and formally attached it to the port on his wrist and threw caution to the wind.

By this time, he was standing in the line for his baggage. In the queue, several waiters were offering drinks to the travelers and one was performing a complimentary cleaning for personal screens. The man quickly made his way down the line, clearly unhappy with this job. He wiped down the screens of a man and woman standing directly in front of Clarke. Clarke really did not want his screen touched at all. He couldn't explain why, but he was just uncomfortable with it.

"No, thank you," Clarke said to the man before he could spray the screen down, "I've only just gotten it, it does not need to be cleaned."

The man nodded with an irritated face, as if Clarke had spit on him. It was then that Clarke noticed the black armband with a subdued red 'X.' In fact, there were a lot of different armbands with a lot of different colors. Some were black with red, like the man Clarke had just dismissed, and there were others in blue with a yellow 'II,' and still more in green with white chevrons. Clarke noticed that he was the only one in the room without one on. What was going on? Clarke immediately pulled up his orders and tried to make sense of it all. Page after page yielded no results. His eyes were flicking through information furiously as his heart rate began to climb. He felt his armpits begin to sweat and his hands get clammy again as he pored over more information. There was nothing in his orders about this—absolutely nothing.

The line was moving forward as the baggage claim attendants with the black and red armbands returned luggage with solemn faces. They were courteous, but they were silent and did their job with precision. It was very mechanical and forced, like they'd rather be doing anything else but didn't have a choice—slavery, to a degree. Clarke couldn't help but feel bad for them despite his paranoia about being hauled off somewhere for not wearing an armband. Another couple steps forward and Clarke abandoned his search for information and relied on his obvious status as a party member to get him through. Scanning the airport terminal for more information about what was going on, he saw an information desk by one of the exits to the transport parking lot. Another step forward and he would be able to see what was behind several columns that were obstructing his view.

He was nearly at the front of the line by this point and nobody had taken note that he was clearly out of the ordinary. Was the whole armband thing unnecessary and merely a coincidence? Clarke looked around the room again just to make sure, and yes—everyone had an armband of some kind, including the janitors, the clerks behind the information desk, the police officers, the passengers in line with him, those walking around the terminals—everyone had one on.

He looked back around the column and finally saw the sign again. It was the same sign he had seen when he disembarked the plane, although here, the message was repeated in several languages. Clarke recognized the French, German, and Spanish, but then there was some kind of character writings, Chinese perhaps? Finally, as he skimmed down the list, he saw the English:

Please be sure to keep distance from citizens of differing classes.
Superior classes will wear pre-authorized armbands:
Black with Red X= State Laborer
Green with White Chevrons = Police and Civil Order Personnel
Blue with Yellow III = Citizens Third Class
Blue with Yellow II = Citizens Second Class
Blue with Gold I = Citizens First Class
Blue with Gold I and Laurel Wreath = Party Member

"Excuse me, sir," a young woman said to Clarke after he had loaded up his luggage onto a little cart. Clarke felt his heart skip a beat in panic, closed his eyes for a second, and took a long breath before answering, "Yes, ma'am?"

"The transport to Fort Powell is this way. I forgot to tell you when you took your seat on the flight over." It was the flight attendant from the plane he had just disembarked. She appeared slightly embarrassed as her pale cheeks turned red and she clasped her hands low in front of her. She was fairly short and wore the standard forest-green formfitting dress of all flight attendants, with the matching cap covering just the top of her beach-blonde hair.

"Please forgive me," she added. Clarke was taken aback when he realized that her body language showed fear rather than embarrassment. This poor woman was actually afraid of Clarke. He took a moment to process this and furrowed his brow in contemplation.

After a short pause, he responded with, "It's not a problem, just be sure to remember in the future. Not everyone is so forgiving." Clarke remembered a moment from his childhood when his dad had to act tough, yet forgiving.

CHARLIE MUST HAVE BEEN about ten years old when he was playing in his backyard greenhouse and the gardener had accidentally flooded the azaleas so badly that the entire flowerbed was more water than dirt. Apparently, Jacques, the gardener for the Prescotts' greenhouse and lawn, had left the water in the full-on position rather than in the auto-off position. To be honest, though, Charlie could barely tell the difference between the switches because they didn't have a label, and gardening was actually a very difficult job. Charlie saw the flood after a couple of minutes playing and immediately went to get his father. After being informed of the mess, Robert sighed heavily and closed his eyes before calling for Jacques.

"Oui, monsieur?" Jacques said as he poked his head into the doorway.

"Jacques, when did you turn on the water for the azaleas?"

Jacques paused for a moment and thought about it. Then he snapped and lifted his head. "Eet must 'ave bin Frrihday before I leeft for zee weekend," he said with his thick accent. Sometimes Charlie struggled to understand him, but he had grown to appreciate how hard the middle-aged man had tried to learn English.

"Well, you need to think about that a little harder. It seems that it was set for too long and you have destroyed my bushes. I will have to keep you here longer this week so you can fix it. Expect to lose some of your pay as well to make up for the loss. Go get started."

Jacques shamefully took off his burnt-orange knit cashmere hat that had a short and soft brown brim and bowed his head before slumping away to the greenhouse. Charlie watched him sadly walk down the hallway and turned to his father.

"Why were you so mean to him? I don't think it was his fault."

"Maybe it wasn't his fault, but he needs to be reminded about the way society functions. We are on the top, he works for us, and to keep society functioning, we must act this way." Robert paused for a moment before giving an exasperated sigh. "Hey, come here." Robert motioned for his son to join him at the mahogany desk by the bay window, which overlooked the front garden's Divine Mercy bushes and the row of oak trees lining the street. He pulled Charlie into a tight embrace and whispered, "If we are too kind to them, word will get out that we are not worthy of our party status. Without being in the party, we could not afford to employ all of these people. Have you noticed how I only hire refugees and not citizens first class? I know who needs protection. Even if he didn't do anything wrong with the switch, he is still the gardener."

Robert pulled away and held Charlie at arm's length while smiling broadly. His eyes looked tired and were sunken in a little more than usual. Charlie remembered that when he got up to use the bathroom last night, his dad was up late in the sitting room down the hall from the bedrooms. This was during a period of time when Robert was still actively grieving the loss of Alex. During the exchange after Jacques left the room, Charlie felt that Robert was looking into him and he saw his father's eyes start to get watery.

"I'll be sure to get the switches looked at and upgraded. We don't want the same punishment to happen twice, now do we?"

Charlie was pulled into another long and deep hug without noise. Both of them needed this. After a short while, Charlie stood up, walked through the door, and skipped back down the hall toward the garden. What Charlie did not remember was Robert's tears as his father sat silently in his chair, staring out the window at the one oak tree where he had built a tire swing for Alex when he was Charlie's age. The swing had long since broken, but those memories flooded his mind every time he looked out that window. It was then that he decided to take action and save his remaining son. Soon thereafter, Robert uprooted the oak tree that pained his memory and had it moved to the opposite side of the house, in a corner of their acreage where he would only see it in his dreams. He didn't want to get rid of the tree; he just wanted to not be reminded of it every time he was in his office. He used to love watching his kids play on it when he took breaks from drafting building layouts and designs. Now the view constantly reminded him of the son he lost.

CLARKE'S FATHER'S HOLIER-than-thou approach in handling citizens second class was a bit disturbing, but the show needed to be perpetuated for his own protection. So long as he didn't actually incriminate anyone or cause physical harm, he knew it would be okay. After all, he was a party member and that status came with power to influence change—or at least help those in need. *Ironic,* Clarke thought, *I need to be rude to her in order to be kind to her.* Despite knowing that he was doing the right thing, he felt bad. As she led him down the long, vaulted terminal, she quickened her pace so as to keep Clarke a stride or two behind her. This was intentional; she didn't want to speak with him if she could help it.

The walk took them past several long stretches of glass panels that spanned all the way around the pathway in a sort of dome and through several narrower sections that facilitated high-speed train tracks. Along the way, Clarke noticed several patriotic paintings and sculptures of wartime presidents. Classic portraits of Washington, Lincoln, Wilson, Roosevelt, Eisenhower, Bush, Barkley, and Carter hung in a growing crescendo of size and embellishment. In Clarke's opinion, the paintings began to slowly change from a modern and realistic style to a more expressionist and fantasy-like style. Barkley's portrait made him look like a professional athlete, despite the fact that he was nearly eighty-five when he took office and decided to bomb Venezuela. All of it was preposterous. The décor was both elegant, yet gaudy; amazing, yet tacky; impressive, yet underwhelming. Compared to all that Clarke had grown up knowing and seeing, this airport was definitely older, more decrepit, and, well, foreign to him. It felt more like an Orwellian future than New Boston, because Snowball and Napoleon-esk concepts were posted around the entire area for all to see via the extravagant display of patriotism and the security warnings that permitted access after retinal scans as well as other biometric identification measures. Privacy was dead in this airport and the pigs were in control.

The scared attendant brushed between two Chinese travelers in electromagnetic handcuffs and nearly knocked one of them off his feet. *She's showing her power so strongly over them; it must be why she is so afraid of me,* Clarke thought, assuming that the way she showed her superiority over others indicated that she must be afraid of what a superior citizen would do to her if they had cause to do so. Regardless, he was able to follow after her without too much effort because she cleared the path for him. Clarke doubted whether he would have pushed the prisoners the way his escort did if he had to make the decision. This was very good information to digest. Power based on political class and status was very important in the Northern United States region apparently. He had to learn new social norms.

The culture shock he was experiencing was amazing. At first glance, every interaction in Minnesota was chaotic and disturbing, like reading about slavery in the Confederacy or the Reign of Terror in France, or even the class warfare in the 21st-century Americas. Ultimately, class warfare in the past century ended up in a division of the United States based on regions, just as he had learned in class a couple months ago. All of this resulted in a drastic division of laws and human rights. The separation of citizens based on immigration status, heritage, religion, and ethnicity began to take root in the laws as the Constitution of the United States began to crumble. Sure, the federal government still technically existed and they were, after all, still the United States, but the regions began to organize in different ways and the federal government slowly dwindled its powers away and became more like the European Union rather than the nation with a manifest destiny.

Sadly, the nation founded on religious freedom became a land where people were persecuted for their faith, language, and even their last name. Racism and systematic discrimination became normal in some parts of the country faster than in other parts—but that was a secondary concern. For instance, New Boston was more or less an anomaly in how citizens second class and citizens first class shared schools, whereas the Dakotas were on the cutting edge of progress—or entropy—with citizens second class being arrested for entering a shop designated for citizens first class. Nothing Clarke could have done in that instant would have helped the poor Chinese men. Although he didn't know it, it was actually better that he didn't do anything because the local law included public execution for disturbing a party member on official business. There were about fifty people in the terminal at the time the attendant pushed through the prisoners, and if Clarke had acknowledged the Chinese men, all fifty bystanders would testify that the Chinese men harassed Clarke and literally scream for blood.

The attendant made her way through a large open room where vendors sold food, travel items, sleeping pills, and souvenirs. An overhead display projected a sunny sky, with a gentle breeze blowing and speakers playing natural noise, the ambiance reminiscent of a small forest. Clarke saw the archway he was being led to and instantly recognized the status that military members had in the Northern Region. The archway shone with white gold-plated bricks emblazoned with pristine crystals in a stunning artistic rendition of the Arc de Triomphe, showcased as an entrance to the USO reception area. Of course, there was a squad of armed guards with fully automatic and direct-energy weapons designed for maximum lethality. All of the pomp associated with the military made it clear that the wars were being treated very seriously. Another obvious byproduct of the military presence was that no vendors occupied the shops closest to the archway.

The attendant approached one of the soldiers with a large set of silver captain bars emblazoned on his forest camo jumpsuit's collar. The captain was expecting her and beckoned for one of his soldiers to scan her screen for authentication prior to letting her pass. Clarke followed suit as he caught up and held out his screen.

"Good afternoon, sir," Clarke said, addressing the captain. "My orders don't exactly tell me where to report, could you show me where I need to go?"

"I don't know what you are saying. I only speak French," the captain responded after looking at the orders. Clarke was caught off guard. He had never been taught French, but he realized that although he was hearing a different language, he understood it completely.

"Um," Clarke stammered, "one moment." Clarke held up his finger in pause and pulled out his orders, pointed directly at them, and then did an overexaggerated shrug. Even though his enhancements allowed him to understand other languages, Clarke did not know how to speak them. The captain looked down at the orders again and then his eyes sparkled with a glint of recognition.

"You need to go to the reception desk at the far end of the lobby. Go past the dining facility and security offices. You will see an exit to a hangar on the right and a car rental on the left. The reception desk is just past that." He rattled it off in rapid French without pause and was gesturing with over-the-top hand movements as he explained where to go.

"Um, merci," Clarke said, reaching out his hand for a handshake in gratitude. Apparently, this was a bad call. One of the guards standing by immediately shoved Clarke to the ground and sneered with his direct-energy emitter aimed at his chest. The French-speaking captain pulled him away and reprimanded him briskly. He then reached a hand out to Clarke and pulled him up.

"Sorry about that, he did not know you are a party member or that you are an officer. Trust me, he is going to have a bad day now." The captain looked back over his shoulder while a few members of the squad approached the rogue guard slowly and let out a deep sigh of regret.

Clarke merely gave an uncomfortable smile and glanced over at his aggressor, who was now being handcuffed by his fellow guards and led to the middle of the open area between the vendors. The shop attendants left their shops and people began flooding out of the terminals as if they sensed what was about to happen. Soon there was a ring around the soldiers. Clarke felt like he knew what was going to happen and wanted to get out of there as soon as he could. One of the remaining guards ensured that he would not be a witness and ushered him along, under the replica of the Arc de Triomphe and into the USO. There he met up with the attendant, who wore a stone-faced smile with burning hatred behind her Aryan-blue eyes.

No doubt that she knew what happened only thirty meters away at the front of the military wing of the airport and loathed Clarke for his role in it. He saw that her hands, although held respectfully in front of her, were clenched so tightly that the tips of her fingers were turning blue.

The difficult part was that Clarke wanted to stop it. He felt guilty and responsible for it. Why did he reach for the captain of the guard? Why did he show his normal pleasantries? He was taught in his crash course military training to never reach for a superior officer, but rather to bow with his left arm across his chest in salute. It was his fault that the guard was being punished like this. Clarke couldn't blame the attendant for her anger nor her effort to stay as far away from him as possible. It was a survival instinct.

I'd do the same if it were me, Clarke thought.

Chapter 11—Integration

Clarke's reception was simple and uneventful as he scanned in his screen and the reception sergeant processed his packet. He waited for about a half hour for transport to arrive, which carried him to Fort Powell without issue. It seemed that once he was fully engrossed in the military environment, all was well. There was no distinction between citizen classes in the armed forces at Fort Powell, and the only true discrimination was how officers treated the enlisted. Enlisted soldiers were comprised of only citizens second class, whereas officers were only citizens first class.

In history texts, the evolution of officership was fascinating. Ancient warfare displayed commanders and captains as fiefs ruling over their own little fiefdom or as kings over their division or garrison. Then episodes like the Crusades saw more chivalry and a more traditional style of leadership. The first American Civil War saw tactical maneuvers that used both wit and cunning, so sacrificing troops for the greater good was deemed a positive leadership trait. All of the world wars saw a more even playing field between officers and enlisted ranks, so much so as to give true responsibility to the American noncommissioned officers, which is when the concept of teamwork really took root. However, by the time Mexico invaded Texas in the late 21st century, enlisted soldiers were once again treated more like an afterthought and pawns in a fatal game of chess. Today's military was not far off. Now that officers were from a different citizen class, they really were superior in social status, and the compulsory enlistment never afforded a commission to anyone below citizens first class. It was just another way to keep order in the world.

The transport was a small magnetic lane bus that was in substantially better condition compared to the car Clarke took to the airport in New Boston. The theme of lavish and high-quality finishes for the military was becoming apparent. In a demonstration of the economic budget theory called incrementalism, every year the military budget continued to swell. The different levels of command appropriated an excessive amount of money to their units, which ultimately spent the money on frivolous purchases and were compelled to use all of the funding prior to the end of the fiscal year. Each command then claimed that they were effectively spending the money, and they used its complete expenditure as rationale for increasing their funds. When the government spent more money, it was applauded as efficient and effective, whereas the opposite was true in the private sector. The antithesis of efficiency between the private and government sectors bred a sense of mistrust between the government and its citizens. This was a slow process of kickbacks and patting each other on the back over the course of a couple hundred years, culminating in the 2086 Declaration for Voter Representation Act. The DVRA stated that the House of Representatives would no longer be elected from citizens second class backgrounds; they now must be from citizens first class families and thereafter eligible for other political positions. Also, the 2086 declaration rescinded the right to vote for citizens third class, which created an even more complex caste system.

It was ironic how the nation's most diverse political body became comprised of nearly 100 percent white people with college degrees from Ivy League and foreign universities. They were out of touch with their constituency and were oblivious to the problems that America faced, yet were responsible for making laws that defended the country. That was where Clarke found himself—stuck in a world that benefited him at the expense of others. He was drafted into military service, but he had a very good position because of his family status. His father did the best thing in keeping up the charade his great-grandfather had started nearly one hundred years ago when their family earned party status.

The ride came to a stop and the magnetic brakes flipped over to seal themselves completely on the magnetic stripping. Since Clarke was the only passenger on this rotation, it stopped in an actual parking spot and allowed him to exit after securing his bag. The door snapped shut in a quick and precise movement the second Clarke stepped off with his bag, barely letting the duffle clear the door. Clarke looked back in surprise as the transport locked. He put on his baseball cap and twisted it slightly to the side before cautiously stepping forward toward the towering brick building adorned with statues of historic figures and flanked by gardens and large fountains. The gray stone pathway up to the building was very beautifully detailed with intricate cuts and designs paying homage to the practiced masons who worked on the project. The sides of the path were colorful, and birds of a wide variety of species sang sweet songs all around.

Clarke came up to the entrance doors, which opened with a hiss. A gentle voice spoke from all around, "Welcome, Lieutenant Anicius. Please scan your screen at the desk and proceed to the hallway on your left to deposit your luggage. Once complete, proceed to the room marked 1174A."

Clarke was not alarmed by the disembodied voice giving him instruction, nor the fact that it recognized him. He was enrolled in a welcoming database when he started high school and all public venues greeted him upon entry if no host was present. Although it did not happen often, he had become accustomed to it. Clarke did, however, stand slack-jawed for a second as he saw the marble flooring and silver inlaid Department of Defensive Land Warfare emblems in each fifty-by-fifty-centimeter tile. The tiles weren't overbearing, though, as the emblem was subtle, nearly matching the color of the marble itself. The silver in this one room must have been more valuable than his family's entire house. He turned down the hallway to the left after scanning his screen at the tile a few steps in front of him. The voiced thanked him. Then Clarke entered a large room with conveyor belts and the voice instructed him again, "Place your luggage on any of the belts. We will sort out their transportation to your lodging."

Clarke shrugged and placed it on the nearest belt before walking out of the room and continuing down the hallway. The hallway had a slight bend toward the interior of the building and he got the sensation that the building was actually round. It wasn't perceptible, but his eyes noticed that each tile was not an exact square, which indicated that the tiles weren't straight, but they never reduced in size or terminated into the walls. Clarke deduced that the building must be so massive that the average occupant wouldn't ever notice it, similar to the Large Hadron Collider in Switzerland or the replica in Shiraz, which were constructed in a ring but as a nearly straight line so as to make it possible to push protons and ions at the speed of light before they impact to create new and experimental atoms. He marveled at the architectural ingenuity as he walked down the hallway. Clarke slowly realized that he wasn't nervous about being in the military anymore because of the simple act of arriving. Sometimes it's the concern of the unknown more than the actual unknown that causes the most anxiety. Room 1130 was on his left and he continued to walk slowly down the perpetual hallway. As he walked, he said a prayer of thanks quietly to himself. He thanked God for all of the blessings he had been given and prayed for the people he posed a threat to today. His hands felt clammy and he felt the pulse throb in his neck and head when he prayed about the man he undoubtedly sentenced to a horrible public execution at the airport. He knew it was his fault.

Room 1145 was now on his left. He continued walking. *I don't want this. I can't handle this,* he thought to himself. He didn't want any more blood on his hands. Even if he didn't actually do anything, it was still his existence that caused it to happen. After praying for forgiveness and mercy, he realized his anxiety was subsiding because he couldn't hurt anyone while he was isolated in a group of like individuals. Eventually the tension in his jaw slackened and he felt the throbbing pulse in his neck reduce as he knew that God planned this and this period of time was just a trial.

It was a shame that he was a plainclothes military officer. He didn't have the luxury of blending in as much as a normal officer. He was also realizing that it would be hard to keep the enlisted members safe from him because of his lack of uniform. Clarke needed to play by the rules and keep his head down. He prayed for strength. He prayed for courage

He finally got to the room labeled 1174 after a twenty-minute walk down the hallway. He took a deep breath and opened the door. The interior was a small apartment-style suite not dissimilar to an upscale hotel room with separate bedrooms. Fortunately, he seemed to be the only resident at the moment. In the center was a little common area furnished with a leather couch, retracting doors to a patio, and a small kitchenette. Room 1174A was to the left, next to a shower and 1174B. The other side of the suite had rooms 1174C, 1174D, and a bathroom. It wasn't all that much, but again, the military spared no expense. The carpet was pristine white with a self-cleaning vacuum function, the walls were lined with white gold sheets, and each room was outfitted for comfort.

A moment after Clarke toured the space, he got a message on his screen. He sat down in one of the high-backed armchairs in a corner of his room and opened up the message with a flick of his eyes. It was from his commanding officer, Lieutenant Colonel Hudson.

Good evening, Lieutenant Anicius,

I'm pleased to see that you have arrived both on time and without incident. Undoubtedly you have noticed that the Minnesota territory is far different from your recruiting station in Alabama. There will be more to follow when you arrive at my office at 2359 tonight. I've sent you directions to both the security office and my own office after your 2200 in-brief and getting read on to our program. From now on, your screen is considered classified, and no one aside from a general officer or politically appointed citizen is authorized to confiscate it from you. Do not let it be taken from you at all costs. Again, further instructions will be relayed to you via our security officer Captain Strauss. In the meantime, enjoy a meal in your room and be on time later tonight.

Best,

Hudson, Grace B.

Lieutenant Colonel, MI

Commanding

It was pretty clear and straightforward. Clarke was to relax for about an hour and a half and then be at some office tonight. It was interesting, though, that the meeting was tonight rather than tomorrow morning. Maybe he was actually late for something. Could he have had the wrong date put on his orders and was supposed to travel earlier? Perhaps so, but that seemed unlikely. This felt deliberate. There were no other military members on his flight or even at the USO. The few veterans present wore their medals proudly on their chest and were clearly retired by the streaks of gray and white in their hair and their crooked posture. None of them paid any attention to Clarke as he walked by and found a comfortable seat. He had taken the transport to Fort Powell all alone as well.

The entire building here felt empty and sterile of natural life. It was beginning to feel like he was kept away from the general population on purpose. This got his heart racing as he felt an anxiety attack coming on. Clarke swallowed hard as he digested the day's events. It was only mid-afternoon and his entire world perspective had already shifted drastically. What else was he going to see? He put his head in between his knees and closed his eyes. He hugged his knees and took several deep and steady breaths as he prayed for his anxiety to be taken away from him.

After a minute or two, he stood up and exhaled in an exasperated way. *All right,* he thought to himself, *dinner.* Clarke walked over to the kitchenette and motioned for the refrigerator to show its contents. It was empty. He looked at it more closely and saw a little sign indicating that it was set up for delivery, so he quickly tapped on the screen face and it listed out available purchases. Clarke selected a steakhouse meal and sat back in his high-backed chair for a few minutes while it was prepared.

He grabbed the dinner from the refrigerator and placed it on the small table for four in the corner of the common area. Each of the chairs was made of a different kiln dried wood in a fashion reminiscent of the Renaissance, as they were all intricately adorned with different celestial images of angels, constellations, and references to nature. They were beautiful and Clarke would say well-crafted if they were made by hand, but nobody did that anymore. These were likely less than ten years old and literally printed from sawdust, dyes, and glue. Nonetheless, they were fantastic and he liked them so much that he would recall the intricacy later on in his life when he was buying furniture for his own home.

After he finished admiring each chair in turn while he ate, he put the plate back into the refrigerator and it vanished as he closed the door. Food wasn't kept anymore; instead, it was recycled into compost for cropland or condensed and processed for domestic animal food.

By that point, Clarke didn't have all that much time until his appointments so he opened his screen again and accessed the direction to the security officer. The file indicated that it would be a forty-two-minute walk or a ten-minute ride on a transport. He motioned with his eyes to the clock in the corner of his screen and it enlarged to show that the time was 2103; he could walk it.

Clarke did a quick look around the suite to see if he had left anything behind. But before he finished looking around the common area, he rolled his eyes and gave a short laugh to himself for being forgetful. *Of course I didn't leave anything here. I didn't bring anything.* That got him to think about how curious it was for him to drop off his belongings so candidly in a room filled with conveyor belts. He thought to himself that it wasn't exactly the cleverest thing he had ever done, and in fact he didn't even get a receipt for his items. It was a long-practiced military custom that transitioned over into air travel and any other service that collected items or luggage to issue an inventory of the collected or stored items. This was one of the first times that Clarke had ever done it, and, with all the other distractions he had suffered from throughout the day, he forgot to even ask for a receipt.

Clarke pulled up his screen and asked it to show him the location of his luggage. His parents had actually inlaid GPS tracking devices, which were accurate to the centimeter from anywhere on earth. It could tell you the altitude and atmospheric pressure it was under as well. The screen showed that it was somewhere on the opposite side of the building and Clarke sighed with quiet relief. Then he flicked his eyes back to the clock—2105—and then over to his directions. He followed the walking directions to the hallway and then backtracked toward the front of the building, where he was to take an elevator to the B sub six level, or in other words, the sixth floor underground.

As he walked down the empty and glistening hallway, he couldn't help but feel isolated and alone in the sterile environment. It felt like everything around him was manufactured for a silicon-based life-form, not a human. It was too clean, too cold, too precise. He passed the same few doorways on his way back and felt like the hallway was actually longer than when he had come in. A small sense of paranoia crept into his mind and he pushed it back to focus on the mission at hand of getting to his place of duty on time. He quickened his pace.

After a deceivingly long time, Clarke finally got to the front lobby area. He pulled up his screen—2122. He indicated the directions again and a full display was projected above his wrist, showing the elevator location on the near side of the lobby. He didn't see anything that looked like an elevator to him, but he went over there anyway. The walls were smooth and seamless from the corner by the hallway to the back of the room, where a glass mosaic of Mount Rushmore's three remaining presidential heads was located.

Clarke took a step back. He thought for a moment as he looked around. Then he snapped his fingers in recognition. He had been expecting a traditional elevator—not a completely underground one. He realized that the elevator was actually the tiles in front of the wall. It was obvious, really, and incredibly aesthetic. The only real sign that there was an elevator was a thicker grout line on the tiles.

So, he stepped onto the tiles and motioned with his hands to go down. The elevator did so smoothly and silently. Clarke was always intrigued by both old and new elevators because every single one seemed unique. This one had no buttons, no level indicators, no voice recognition nor sound transmission. It was fairly intuitive, actually, as he more or less just counted the levels and motioned for it to stop after it descended for several minutes and passed five floors. It slowed to a crawl and eventually came to a stop when the platform lined up perfectly with the sixth basement level and the magnetic breaks clicked over and engaged.

The time was 2129. Clarke stepped off the elevator and it started to ascend to the lobby again. He watched it go in a giant pillar upward for a moment and then referenced his directions once more. The underground level was not laid out as the levels above. Here the hallways were definitely straight and they terminated at a far-off vanishing point. The symmetry was eerie, and it felt rather odd because of the natural light from the faux windows bringing in warmth despite the sensation of being hundreds of feet below ground.

Clarke went down the corridor to the left and noticed the oddly muted sound of his steps on the hard marble floor tiles. It was a much softer noise and he had trouble placing the source of the dampening effect. Either way, he put one muted foot in front of the other and walked down the hall. He felt like he should pick up his pace but something unnerving made him decide not to. The eerie quiet of the corridor made it feel like there was reason for no noise, so he uncomfortably and silently kept it so.

It was now 2145 and he was still in the same hallway. He had looked at his directions several times because the hallway felt like it went on forever. *This is nothing like the underground back in New Boston*, Clarke thought. In comparison, his hometown's labyrinth looked primitive, as it was hewn from sandstone and made with old-fashioned tools without any power source. It had taken decades to build, whereas this place probably was excavated and outfitted in a matter of months.

He finally came to another open domed area and saw signage inlaid at the entrance that read "West Wing." Each of the other seven wings had cardinal directions at their entrances as well. At the middle of this empty space was a very bright light shining down from an apparent skylight, which was impossible because the sun had set nearly an hour ago. Even the light in the hallways made it appear as if it were midday, so Clarke deduced that this skylight must have also been artificial, despite the accurate sensation of clouds drifting overhead and the warmth it cast on the area it illuminated.

Clarke looked toward his right and headed down the South Wing for a moment when he found a row of office doors extending as far as he could see. *Room 30 should be right down here,* he thought. It took him just a few minutes to walk to the door, and the time was 2155 as he knocked on it. *Perfect timing!*

He pushed the question out of his mind as he heard tumblers click over and allow him entry. The door retracted with a crisp movement to the left and closed behind him once he came in. It moved so swiftly that he felt the breeze it created on his trailing hand. He found himself in a short room with a door located in the opposite corner. Clarke would learn that this was designed to prevent unauthorized access. The small room scanned his screen and retinas before locking the door behind him and opening the door on the opposite side. The same swift closing movement after Clarke entered into the actual office caught him off guard again—it was really fast. When he turned around to look at the room, he saw that it was dimly lit by a red hue coming from screens on nearly every surface. Clarke looked at the room and saw that the space extended to his left for about thirty meters. The wall space was covered with screens, all black at the moment, but seconds before had been littered with handwritten notes, bulletins, reference materials, maps, and targeting information for USHCOM, or United States Homefront Command, which operated in the traditional NORTHCOM area of operations.

"Lieutenant Anicius, please come this way," said Captain Strauss from a back corner. The room was aligned with several tiers of workspaces, all facing forward so as to eliminate the possibility of unwanted visitors accidentally seeing what they were working on.

The partitions between the tiered stations and between each screen were approximately 1.3 meters tall and only completely obscured the rear few rows from view. Clarke, being 180 cm, could easily see the entire front row's desk space.

The office was almost completely vacant aside from a group of uniformed soldiers along the far-left wall who were talking in hushed voices. They were fairly young, like Clarke, and he paid no attention to them. If they were officers, they would introduce themselves. If they were enlisted soldiers, on the other hand.

He made his way up the awkwardly spaced stadium-style steps to the eighth and final tier, where he made his greeting.

"Good evening, sir," Clarke said from the position of attention. He placed his left hand across his chest and gave a shallow bow before returning to attention. "I am Lieutenant Anicius, reporting as instructed."

There was an awkward pause before Clarke continued, "Um, how are you, sir?"

Captain Strauss let out a roar of a laugh and the group of soldiers at the far side of the room turned their heads to see what was causing all the commotion. The captain closed his eyes and continued to chuckle for a moment. He was morbidly overweight, and his uniform was beginning to stretch across his middle and the zipper of the jumpsuit looked like it was holding on for dear life every time he let out another little bellow of a laugh.

"Please call me Dan. None of this sir business," Dan said with a huge rosy smile across his face. "I know that what you were told about us in your training came from the eBook, but you don't need to worry about that here. We're special forces," he said with a slight shrug as he reached for a grimy cup of coffee. "Well, at least you are, and, in fact, it's that we're all in a special forces unit. So, cut out the nonsense and let me explain a few things to you."

Clarke nodded, slipped on a wry smile, and sat down where Dan had motioned for him to sit. Clarke quickly decided that Dan needed a shave and a shower. The man's smell was repulsive and it looked like his uniform hadn't been washed in weeks. Although Clarke sat respectfully, he began intentionally breathing through his mouth.

"You are obviously sworn to secrecy—can't talk about this to anyone else—will be held to said secrecy for all eternity, and your soul will be kept in check after your body leaves you." A smile crept onto Dan's face as he saw Clarke's concern. "Listen, Clarke—you mind if I call you Clarke, do you?" He didn't wait for an answer. "See now, Clarke, the oath to secrecy or privacy continuation, or whatever the hell it's actually called—I forgot what it really is—can shove it. What I need you to do is tell me that you understand what I am about to tell you is classified and cannot be discussed outside of this facility or unless told otherwise by a general officer or politically elected official."

"I understand," Clarke said confidently. He was trying to feign enthusiasm by sitting a little more forward in his chair. In doing so, however, he saw that Dan wasn't wearing his boots, but rather he had a sort of slipper on and his bloated pale feet were shoved so tightly in them that Clarke doubted he had worn anything else for quite some time. He quickly snapped his attention back to Dan's face and pretended not to notice.

"Good!" Dan barked. "Now for the fun stuff." He handed Clarke a pair of red-tinted glasses and nodded, which indicated to the room to return to its operational state. The lights turned on to an intensely burning bright red and all of the screens mounted to the walls were again illuminated. The group on the far side of the room spun around to their work stations in a quick movement and slid on their glasses. Dan pulled his on and so did Clarke. He could see the intelligence data now, whereas the lights before were simply too bright. These sunglasses, or whatever the technical term was, made it possible to see the room as if it were a normal light spectrum.

"These glasses are made as an extra precaution against intruders. Without them you would go permanently blind in about one minute." Clarke looked back over at Dan and now the man's skin showed pockmarks where there weren't any before. "Let me take your attention to the screen directly between us."

He motioned for it to open. It scanned his eyes and Clarke's before rendering a three-dimensional map of the United States. He pinched at the area bordering Mexico where Texas once was and it scaled to view the strip of desert where red flags, green triangles, and hollow lines snaked across the display.

"This is where you will be heading in a couple of days. The blue is us, the green are the Mexican and Persian forces, and the red are the insurgents fighting against both sides. It's like they think they can declare independence or something."

"Wait a minute, Dan, isn't that," Clarke indicated Houston, "still the United States territory?" Clarke was confused by where the fighting was taking place. The way it was portrayed in the news made it seem as if the Mexican-Persian alliance only took the territory up to San Antonio and I-10 westward. This display showed that there was a major buildup of hostile forces in a half moon around Houston.

Dan had a small smile on his face as he said, "That's the official story. For now, I'm going to send you this map along with the factual history of the war. It's really not even close to what the official story is. In fact, most of the people in charge politically don't have accurate information. We tell them what we want them to hear."

He slid his finger from his map to Clarke and then Clarke's screen lit up when the information hit its memory.

"I want you to read over all of that before you come back to me tomorrow at 0400. Be sure that you do read it all. It would be a real shame if you didn't." He gave a very serious face and Clarke could see his chins rise and fall with his shallow breathing.

"Relax, Clarke! I'm only joking," he said with another bark of a laugh. "I just don't want to waste my own time." He let out another short snort and then his eyes went cold as he shifted his attention back toward the display and took a sip of his now stale coffee. "For now, though, I'd like to explain the concerns with actually losing Houston. Look over here." He pointed to the east of the city, where several strongholds had been erected in a fortress-style defense.

"Our aerial surveillance shows that these traitors have acquired interceptor tech. Essentially, they can now stop all small arms fire and everything we have available to expend. Our priority is the insurgent conventional forces, and we are really trying to squeeze them into a pincer between U.S. and Mexico. They just mobilized so quickly and pop up in completely different areas, so trying to corner them in a traditional sense is impossible.

"Your specific task is to infiltrate the insurgency and destabilize them politically, then feed us information on their movement strategy and tactics. We know almost nothing about them because they don't use wireless communication. They don't even use wired tech for communication! I'm pretty sure they solely rely on couriers, and honestly, it confused the hell out of all our analysts. Apparently, our methods don't reach back to the modern age anymore and their methods are proving effective. They always seem to be one step ahead."

"Okay, I think I understand my task," Clarke said with his brow furrowed, "but I assume that I will be given something more specific to accomplish?"

"Bingo." Dan snapped and pointed his oily index finger at him. "You first need to learn your alias and the actual history." He pointed at Clarke's screen again. "Learn it."

The rest of his time in that room was spent as a sponge. Dan discussed demographics, statistics, lethality rates, weapon capabilities, and projected effects of tactical nuclear bombs to include electromagnetic pulse, also called EMP. Several attacks from the Persian army suggested that one high-altitude EMP properly employed above the United States would destroy all electronic devices that were not shielded sufficiently and effectively shut down the military and government. The prospects were frightening. Example literature of early EMPs was largely theoretical, but the few case studies carried out over Hawaii and New Zealand saw that they were effective at causing chaos and resetting the playing field across the target reference identification plus about fifty to one hundred kilometers. The effects were wildly unpredictable, and as such, not used in an actual war. That is, they hadn't been used in an actual war so far as deliberate attacks until the GNW. Even the Persian's fledgling EMPs caused disaster.

With Clarke's mind reaching capacity for new information, Dan recognized the growing fatigue in him. He slowed down his approach and motioned for Clarke to relax. He reached below his desk and pulled out a gritty-looking green and yellow canteen and two glass tumblers.

"Only the best for America's finest," he said, pouring a splash of amber liquid into each glass. "Now, I know that you've been told you are too young for this, but what the heck, you're in the military about to go to war, for Christ's sake!"

Clarke winced internally at his superior's phrase. It was uncomfortable to hear something like that, especially in a top-secret facility hundreds of meters underground that was probably loaded with optic and audio recognition software. He doubted that he had a moment of true privacy since he woke up that morning in the hospital. Either way, he took the glass and took a cautionary sip. His senses told him that it wasn't anything to be concerned about. His dental enhancement seemed to have kicked in and communicated to his brain that it was a mild form of poison—whiskey.

Clarke gave a shallow cough and quickly inhaled as his palate adjusted. Dan didn't even laugh. He just sat back as his wire-framed office chair struggled under his weight and smiled as he downed his own glass in one gulp.

"It'll grow on you," he said soberly. "It'll have to."

Dan then looked at one of the screens on the wall and smacked himself in the forehead for being so foolish. It was already 2330 and Clarke would be late to his meeting with Lieutenant Colonel Hudson. Dan hastened to write a memorandum that it was his own fault that Lieutenant Anicius was tardy to his assigned place of duty and to please excuse him.

Clarke exited the dual doors from the security office and pulled up his screen. He then navigated to the directions from the security office to his commander's office. He was already five minutes late and the estimated walking time to her office had him being there twenty minutes late. Clarke's heart started to beat a little harder and he swallowed with uncertainty as he selected the transport route. It would only take him five minutes. *Well,* he thought, *this is clearly the better choice.*

Chapter 12—Lieutenant Colonel Hudson

C larke approved the directions for transport and immediately a tile popped out of the ground to about chair height. It appeared to be hovering by some sort of magnetic force similar to how vehicles functioned, and therefore there was no kinetic feedback when it was in motion; it simply glided over the ground while in transit. Clarke intuitively sat on it and it instantly and soundlessly careened down the hallway back to the large domed atrium. It slowed on its approach and rounded the corner gently, continuing through the outer edge, and turned again down the south hallway. It picked up speed again and after a full minute slowed to a stop in front of another large white gold-plated door.

He stood up and referenced his screen to confirm the room number as the tile settled down on the floor behind him where there was an empty spot. This technology was intuitive like everything else of the age, and the tile settled back into the floor seamlessly. He was in the right location and had arrived only a few minutes late. Walking, or even running, would have been a huge mistake and he thanked God for the decision to take the risk of using a previously unfamiliar method of transportation.

Clarke steadied himself as he pulled open the note Dan had written to excuse his tardiness. He knew that it had been sent directly to Lieutenant Colonel Hudson but it made him feel better to see it before he entered the room. He knocked on the door and a solid and sturdy click emphasized the lock's release before the door slid open. Lieutenant Colonel Hudson's office was reminiscent of an old library with wall-to-wall bookcases that spanned ceiling to floor. They were overburdened and the shelves were bowing in the middle where sets of military doctrine, leadership, ethics, and historical books rested. Other shelves showcased medals, ribbons, awards, and challenge coins that she had won throughout her thirty-year career. The lighting deliberately accentuated the retro sensation of displaying physical books. Her collection must have taken her entire lifetime to collect and its wondrousness wasn't lost on Clarke.

There were only a few screens in the office and several of them displayed State news channels. Another one showed the military intelligence update briefings from the past hour on a looping cycle, and others showed a logistical personnel management tracker fitted with all the bells and whistles a commander could dream of. Just below a window tucked in the far corner of the office was Lieutenant Colonel Hudson's desk. She was sitting behind her desk and reading a message from her desktop screen, which she lazily put away when Clarke walked in.

"Please, come sit down," she said and pointed to a small leather chair opposite her desk. Obviously, she was tired and not exactly pleased that Clarke was late, but was welcoming nonetheless. "I received Captain Strauss's message and completely understand. He is passionate about intelligence and, albeit an expert, definitely an odd one." She cracked a wrinkled smile, her eyes showing a playfulness that Clarke wasn't expecting.

She steepled her fingers and leaned back in her chair as Clarke sat down. She was older than he thought she would be. There were wrinkles on her skin that were so deep they spoke of a world before the Great Nuclear War. She seemed fragile sitting there hunched over like that and her eyes appeared to have cataracts.

"So, I know all there is to know about you, Charlie Prescott. Or should I say, Clarke Anicius?" She seemed both too tired and too old to care about how bold this direct accusation of a dual identity was as it would normally be a chargeable offense; besides, she probably was the one who orchestrated it anyway. Clarke did a double take at the sound of his old name. Sure, it had only been a couple of weeks since he was officially dead, but either way it was unnerving to be called by a previous name.

"Surprising how fast the memories fade away, isn't it?" She smiled softly. "The fact that you remember at all is impressive given that it's almost been a month since your enhancements were done. I suppose that the technicians modified your enhancements in some fashion in a vain attempt to help you."

Clarke suddenly felt an upsurge of dread as she spoke. Not only did she bring up his old name that he had nearly forgotten, but she also directly referenced the people who made it possible for him to remember it. He feared for their lives now, considering how Lieutenant Colonel Hudson mentioned them. Was he to blame for whatever would happen to them? What could he have possibly done differently?

"Don't worry, they are fine for now. I promise that they are experts and finding replacements for them would prove very difficult." Clarke was unsure whether she should be trusted. An old party trick was to voice a threat, retract it, then subtly say that it could still potentially happen. So far, Lieutenant Colonel Hudson was following this exact scheme.

"Besides that, I think I owe you some information about myself. I am not a lieutenant colonel in the army; I have been politically appointed to this rank and position due to my research focus. I study American history with a specific interest in constitutional amendments."

Clarke was confused. Why was she telling him this? She had already shifted his whole paradigm and destabilized his mental focus in the first thirty seconds of their interaction. This information seemed superfluous and irrelevant. Clarke was trying to remember his past more clearly because of his instant recognition that his memory was going away at an alarming rate. Clarke couldn't care less about her backstory, much like any new soldier at any time cared about their superior's resume.

"It's important to know because I need you to understand what things were like before the war. You need to know the truth. Undoubtedly Dan has given you a lot of reading, but what he says will also be false. I can offer you real history."

What is she getting at? Why can't I just know what's going on? His face must have given him away because she smiled before continuing.

"Much of what you've been told about the world just isn't true. In fact, most of what your schools have told you is a flat-out lie to make everything plausible for you. The war itself is real, no doubt there. The shift in world powers is also real. The United States, though? The United States and everything you believe it to be is false. The regional governments have more power than the singular federal government does now. Sure, there is a president and a senate, I guess, but the justice department is gone. The bureaucracy has made any judge an obsolete tool of government. No longer do those in power need to bother with legality. What they sign becomes law—there is no rebuttal.

"Ironically, the federal laws have become voluntary more or less, and the regents in the Southeast and Central Plains are nearly back to a monarchy with a weak parliamentary-style government. Racism, discrimination, lynching, riots, bread lines. All of it has been happening for decades, not just several years." Her voice dropped. "I remember it. I was there when the police grabbed the woman in line behind me and strung her up on a light pole because she was Middle Eastern." She bowed her head and pursed her lips in disapproval. After a moment she looked back up and stared at Clarke before continuing, "That's when I decided I would do something about it. That's when I decided to use my knowledge to sway political decisions."

Clarke was starting to nod in agreement. She was speaking directly to him about the exact same thing he was feeling so helpless about. He was the cause of at least one innocent person's death. Maybe God had set him on this path for a reason. He knew that he needed to impact change like the saints who ministered to the sick and the poor. This calling was just one of many, he felt would lead him toward ending wanton murder and persecution. At least that's what Clarke hoped for.

He was hanging on the edge of his seat, waiting for more of her story as she grabbed a canteen of water and took a long swallow. She smacked her lips in an exaggerated way, then set the canteen off to the side.

"I became a staff member at the local party office and they quickly saw that I knew what I was talking about with regard to history and political power hunting. They eventually shared me—their coveted resource—with their superiors and I was quickly snatched up. I received praises, awards, and some serious wealth, not unlike your great-grandfather." Her smile was evil, but eerily trustworthy. Clarke saw that she knew he was uncomfortable with the mention of his family's wealth.

She pressed on, "I used my money to hire the oppressed as servants. I gave them good wages, fair bonuses, and treats, and they were safe in my care." She trailed off for a moment. "It was always a shame when one of them had to be fired for some petty crime. I'd rather have just given whatever it was that they wanted than see them whipped in the street or lynched outside the tribunal offices."

Clarke saw her face fall a little and she looked down at her hands in her lap. He couldn't help shake the feeling, though, that she was being deceitful. Something about her felt wrong. What she was saying and doing was not normal and he doubted her; it felt like an instinct he couldn't ignore. Lieutenant Colonel Hudson did everything in a nearly genuine fashion and her body language mimicked that of a sorry old woman who had been desperately trying to solve a problem her whole life.

"Over time, though, I grew tired of it and sent them away, and that's when I was asked to be an advisor to the military." Her head rose again and peered over to a gallery on her wall. "They gave me awards and honors for my work that contributed to their war efforts. Only later did I learn that they were slaughtering innocent people both abroad and at home. I swore to end it. To take swift action. They used me.

"So that's when I asked for command of a unit. Yes, of course they laughed at first, but then they saw the merit in it. I would be their scapegoat if things went sour and they would use me in this dreaded assignment to see if I could make it work. They thought that if anyone could solve their mystery of the domestic insurgency, I could."

Clarke's face grew more and more puzzled as she spoke. This story was ridiculous and sounded overly grand. Surely, this wasn't how she came to be sitting in this room in the command of a special forces battalion. Clarke was weary of her, but recognized that regardless of her truths and lies, he was subject to her commands or at a minimum would be risking his own life.

Clarke never wanted to be a martyr, and he felt ashamed occasionally that he chose to safeguard his own life rather than speak up about the broad injustice in New Boston. He was clearly sheltered, but was it his parents' doing or was it the State? It didn't matter anymore. He didn't know what the truth was at this point and felt so lost that he couldn't even gather enough anxiety to care about it. The army had already taken away his sense of purpose; what else were they going to do?

In those few fleeting moments in Lieutenant Colonel Hudson's office, Clarke clung to his faith in God and knew that the darkest hours haven't happened yet. He knew that his own path was going to get worse before it got better. The sensation of hope was vanishing and the light that shone on him since his birth in that dark cellar passage was fading.

"I started asking for the analysis on weapons and equipment being moved from place to place. After several weeks it became clear that the insurgents were absolutely using only a certain number of vehicles and weaponry but moving it completely undetected. 'Impossible,' I said to myself. The notion that we couldn't find any trace of it was ludicrous. Everything is being monitored by the State and we can see every street corner, every brick in walls, and every blemish on your face, but their movement could not be tracked."

She cracked a wrinkly smile and steepled her fingers again. "That's why they brought me to this assignment. I know about the underground networks so well that they figured I could make short work of it. They made a wise choice, of course, but I know nothing of Texas, Nebraska, nor what's left of Louisiana."

The truth of Clarke's upcoming mission was starting to settle in. He knew where this was going somehow and his veins ran cold before she spoke again.

"I knew that I needed insiders to map out their networks similar to how I did my own. I researched historic special forces tactics and espionage in the age of technology and was delighted to see that this was not only vetted by history, but yielded a very high success rate—nearly eighty percent! About three-quarters of these missions resulted in complete target acquisition."

Clarke felt his icy blood moving through his arms and legs as the fight or flight response took hold. His hands started to sweat and become clammy. He felt sick.

"I needed a team of three to go into these networks and follow proper protocol to map out who, where, and how the insurgency works. You and Lieutenants Abubakari and Zheng were drafted for this purpose. Your families are the only known violators of federal anti-religion laws with suitably aged children. The State allowed it so as to groom you all while children for this mission. We waited. We waited patiently for such a long time for you three to come of age." Her smile felt wicked when Clarke looked up at her again.

Why was she saying this to him? The way she had spoken to him before now implied that his past wasn't important, but now she was saying that his childhood memories were actually important? Clarke was getting more confused as the conversation progressed. He saw her cunning nature; whether her story was true or not, she phrased all her arguments well. He saw her knowing face and felt the Thought Police. He sensed a wicked game being played where his options were bleak and his family was likely dead already. Clarke felt cornered and coerced into this mission.

"You three will not be working directly with one another, but rather for one another. Be sure to know your place and understand that your cover is key to saving lives. The swifter we gather this intelligence, the sooner the conflict will be over and there can be peace again like America hasn't seen in a hundred years."

At this she stood up and motioned to the screen on her desk. The clock icon displayed 0003.

"I believe it is time you go to bed, Lieutenant Anicius. You have a long couple of days ahead of you." She started to walk around the front of her desk with a deep stoop and uncomfortable gait, then reached out for his hand. Clarke quickly wiped his clammy hand on his pants as he stood up and shook her hand gently. Her grip was loose and frail; she was a withering person and would undoubtedly be sprouting a tree in the next few years.

"You will find directions to your quarters in your screen. Good night." She gave another hallow and wrinkled smile.

Clarke didn't say a word as he crossed his left arm over his chest and gave a smart bow. Then he left the room and let out a deep sigh of relief and desperation. He closed his eyes and walked a short way down the hall before pulling up his screen and navigating to his sleeping quarters where his bag was waiting for him.

Chapter 13—Briefings

The next few days were spent reading intelligence documents and attending update meetings with a group of intelligence analysts, who gave Clarke brief after brief about what they knew and the situation he was heading into. A lot of it was speculative given the nature of his mission and they did a fairly decent job respecting the unknown. At first, Clarke felt that the briefings were unnecessary because Colonel Hudson had given a great overview of all the information in his short meeting with her on that first night, but he was greatly mistaken. For example, Clarke had no idea that the Mexican-Persian army had weapons capable of literally tearing five to ten golf-ball-sized holes through the standard issue non-powered body armor. The intelligence analyst who gave that particular capabilities brief, Sergeant McDuffie, did an amazing job summarizing each and every one of the terrifying weapon systems for the multilateral militaries and the insurgency. For the most part, though, the main points of his brief were summarized in the last statements:

"The United States uses nanobot projectiles with low muzzle velocity to deliberately spread from the point of impact to soft tissue and bore holes through flesh. They are a nasty bit of technology; not very accurate, mind you, but highly effective even on soldiers with powered body armor. The nanobots spring to life on impact and recognize their target. If it impacts armor, the nanobots simply go through the cracks. If it is organic material, on the other hand, well, let's just say whatever it hits dies, shall we?"

"The worst-case scenario for a conflict with Mexican or Persian forces is the Syrian shoulder-fired missile weapon. It fires like a traditional RPG but uses either six or a dozen separate small HEAT rounds that keep to a one-square-meter target at 300 meters away. It's deadly accurate and no known body armor can fully resist it.

"The insurgents don't actually have any weapons to be concerned about. They use terrorist-style ambushes and overcome small convoys and patrols with sheer numbers and superb battlefield analysis. They only fight when they are certain of victory, and that's what makes them so scary—they never lose when they fight. The good thing, though, is they don't actually fight all that often. They are more or less a nuisance and something worth mentioning for our own tactical maneuvers against the enemy rather than as a primary threat."

The few days of briefings were very tiring for Clarke. The drug-induced alertness from mixtures of caffeine, nicotine, modafinil, methylphenidate, and several other drugs made him feel like his skin was crawling, and he had out-of-body experiences every once in a while when he felt his blood vessels constrict and his heart start racing. He had never taken anything of the sort and felt his skin buzzing, his vision vibrating, and numbness to the world—medically induced psychosis. This was the trade-off for twenty hours a day for study and briefs. The doctors monitored his heart and breathing patterns periodically through WAB-MIVSS. Occasionally, they would give him an injection, which provided immediate relief without detracting from his overall alertness.

Clarke spent so much time in the security office that the red lights began to feel welcoming. Although he had only been at this massive underground military complex for less than a week, he had spent nearly 150 hours in the security office, the equivalent of a month's worth of work for the average soldier. Dan was present for a good portion of the meetings and provided his input on topics that he felt the enlisted soldiers did not have full purview of. This was despite the fact that some of the enlisted soldiers had been in this same office studying their one topic for well over five years and were incredible wells of knowledge.

At about the midday mark of the briefings, Dan shuffled his greasy and dirty self off to a closet, where he had a cot and toilet set up for himself. The first time Clarke saw the man stand and drag his slippers across the floor, he felt a renewed sense of disgust. After seeing that, Clarke wouldn't have eaten even if the drug-induced lack of appetite wasn't a problem. The man was pathetic and neurotically involved in his work, so much so that he didn't even leave his office to shower in the entire week Clarke was there. It also appeared that the man hadn't even changed his uniform either. The graying of his teeth and the plaque buildup made it clear that personal hygiene was something Dan did not care about.

Map after map was displayed on the battlefield projection and explained with a heavy emphasis on Northwestern Houston. Nobody explicitly told Clarke where he was going, but the overwhelming focus on this area made him feel that no one knew about his direct assignment. In fact, no two analysts were in the same brief because the information was so compartmentalized; however, they all referenced the same buildings, districts, and troops in the region as if they coordinated with each other anyway. Occasionally, a few analysts from different briefs did converge to discuss a secondary topic such as local laws and regulations, but that was really just to speed things along. Clarke drew from the presenters that they had actually come from the Southern region and probably from Houston itself because of the level of in-depth knowledge and their rank. These were kids just like Clarke himself, and he could read on their faces that they didn't study many of these facts—they knew them by heart from physically living there.

Their eyes were filled with emotion when they explained how the police and proxy government military arrested and executed their citizens. The large majority of the victims were citizens third class, but there were some citizens second class who bore the same consequences for insubordination and defiance of the law. The double standards set by this regional government granted citizens first class the ability to literally murder anyone if they felt it was necessary. In fact, one of the laws imposed on all citizens second class and below was the restriction of any firearm manufactured after the date 2100—nearly banning all weapons currently used by the army—and also any weapon capable of shooting more than five rounds. This did two things, the first being that a massive underground arms market emerged, and the second that the civilians had no way of legally protecting themselves with comparable weapons. The police were equipped only with weapons designed to kill and often wore powered body armor on patrol, which made antique weapons pointless anyway. The police state went from the struggle between the haves and have-nots to fascism and a hard caste system in less than fifty years.

One of the junior members of the briefing team, who was Clarke's age, started to cry when one of his comrades started talking about dragging people from houses and leaving their corpses in the gutter for a couple of days like roadkill until public sanitation workers came and composted the bodies. The soldier stood firm, but Clarke could see the boy's chest shuddering, the tears rolling down his cheek, and his bottom lip quivering. Clarke couldn't imagine that being a part of his own life. He felt so sheltered and undeserving of the blessings he had been given—what would he have done if François was murdered? The worst trauma he had endured was the loss of his brother ten years ago, and with that memory, he tried to sympathize with the soldier at the front of the room.

After that specific day, Clarke spent his few hours of downtime pondering his misfortunes and difficulties since his conscription and compulsory service. He slowly became disheartened and depressed. The drugs were wreaking havoc on his body by causing heart palpitations and incessant sweating. By this time, he had clearly lost weight too. The depressive state was distressing him and fed into the problem with his anxiety. Clarke felt that he was helpless in his own situation and could do nothing for himself, let alone anyone else. How was he supposed to, anyway? It didn't make all that much sense how his mission would help people. It was difficult to sleep in this state of mind, so he did what he could do: he thought of the things that reminded him of a more peaceful time. He knelt with his eyes closed and bent his head in prayer, but he couldn't focus. He continued to kneel in silence with head bent low. He gradually set his head on the bed and drifted away into blissful deep sleep, until about three in the morning when his next twenty-hour day began.

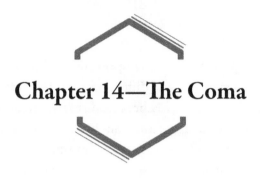

Chapter 14—The Coma

July 29th, the second to last day of his time spent under Fort Powell proper, was far from boring. He was told to sleep and recover from the medicated alertness at his place of duty. The doctors who came to his room and took care of him said that the drugs he was on would likely affect his ability to remember past events with clarity and that they would feel more like fleeting glimpses or déjà vu of a book he had once read. Of course, none of the doctors had any firsthand accounts to share with Clarke, which made him nervous. This was only their third time doing this procedure on a human subject and hadn't gotten enough feedback.

They also told Clarke that he would medically be put into a near coma that morning. One of the doctors, a short and fat man who wore a thick black mustache and a terrible comb-over, hooked up an IV to the port in the WAB-MIVSS on Clarke's left arm and plugged in a couple bags of fluid and medicine. Several nurses came in as well and clipped on an additional WAB-MIVSS to adequately monitor Clarke's vital signs while he was asleep. The machine mixing the different combination of green, black, and clear fluids ticked with several different tempos to ensure the proper mixture before it entered Clarke's body.

Time after the first injection slowed to a crawl as his senses reeled and he felt a quasi-sleep paralysis take hold of him. He noticed that the doctors weren't going out of focus but rather they were just moving slowly as they left the room. Time literally began to stall for

Clarke. The few minutes before he fell asleep had seemed to be hours. Instead of terror of these endless seconds, he started feeling an odd sense of relief to just exist without needing to do anything. Anxiety was erased from his memory.

He remembered the message he had drafted for Roxi sitting on his screen waiting to be sent. His anxiety had gotten the best of him after he had written it, and he had all but forgotten she existed until this moment. The stress from the past couple days and his rigorous study and work had made it all but impossible to focus on anything other than the task at hand. Now that his mind had wandered away from those tasks, he thought about people and things he had left behind. Clarke remembered times long forgotten with his childhood friends Juan and Gregory. He felt that his dog, which only passed away a couple of months ago, was stirring in his lap one more time and giving another exaggerated yawn. He even felt a tear or two start to roll down his face as he remembered when his brother left. Clarke tried to reach up and wipe away the tear but his body failed him. His muscles were behind his brain speed already and it would be only a moment before his consciousness drifted away and his hand would fall limp by his side.

CLARKE'S DREAMS WERE reminiscent of both his childhood and several of the State-sponsored propaganda shows displayed on town park screens and at other public gathering areas. The former brought the sensation of a good and calming dream of fond memories; the latter, not so much. In his coma, Clarke's mind flashed back to when he was about fourteen years old and his Aunt Perpetua brought her daughter over for an afternoon visit. Jo-Ann, Clarke's cousin, was a couple years younger than him. When they were younger, they would play all the same things, but as they got older, she started becoming interested in more stereotypically girly things like painting her nails and makeup, whereas Charlie started finding his interest in the girls themselves.

So, neither one was really interested in playing with the other during the visit Charlie was remembering in his dream. As their parents got along in the sitting room, the two kids were told to go find something else to do. Charlie sighed, rolled his eyes, grabbed his cup of tea, and pulled his baseball cap down over his eyes like any other teenager would do. After Jo-Ann gave an exasperated sigh and gulped her last sip of tea, they left the room and went upstairs, where they sat in one of the spare rooms littered with toys. Charlie reached down and grabbed one of the Russian dolls and smiled.

"I remember when you gave this to me," he said and held it for Jo-Ann to see. "I had all of them for a while. Then President Barkley got into them and ate several." The dog was an absolute terror when it came to leaving things on the floor. Jo-Ann smiled and took the small doll from Charlie. She held it close to her face and really took it in.

"Did you ever open the smallest one?" she said with a playful grin.

"I think so." Charlie didn't feel so confident when he answered. "But you know what, I actually don't know." He shrugged and chuckled a little.

"That's a shame. Daddy said it would have been nice if you figured it out on your own, but I forgot to see if you did." Jo-Ann looked over at Charlie and said, "I can show ya if you'd like to know her secret."

"Well, sure. We're not doing anything really exciting, I guess. I can spare a minute." Then he sarcastically pretended to pull up a calendar on the screen nearest him and flip through pages. He thought it was so funny when his dad did this to him, and apparently it had the same effect on his cousin. Jo-Ann giggled and put her hands on her hips while playing along.

"I'm sorry, but if you can't make time for me, I'll have to cancel your appointment." She pulled open another calendar on a different screen and they both started laughing.

After a moment of prolonged silence, the projected calendars vanished between them. Jo-Ann locked eyes with Charlie and asked for the Russian doll back. Charlie kept her gaze for a minute and held the doll out of her reach but eventually relented. She knew it was him just playing around and was still smiling despite being teased.

"So, each Russian doll represents something important." She started unstacking them. "These dolls are all saints, but the smallest one isn't a solid piece like most Russian dolls are." She had laid out most of them on a small table and Charlie recognized several, like St. George and the Dragon, St. Abigail and the bees, and St. Thérèse of Lisieux, the Little Flower. "Instead, it's more like a puzzle. You need to press on the top and twist it like an old plastic medicine bottle, ya know, like before they were teleported in biometric containers. It's not hard to do, but if you didn't know that it was there."

She had laid them all out and held the last one in her hand. This one didn't look like the rest and now it was pretty obvious. There was a thick ring notched out around its middle and the sides bulged a little bit. Jo-Ann made exaggerated movements and presented the object like it was some long-lost holy relic. Then she indicated how to actually open it as if she were explaining it to a child.

"I think I can figure it out now," Charlie said as he snapped it out of her hands. He brushed off her utter disgust at how he had taken the thing and rolled his eyes. He slowly applied pressure, squeezed the sides, and began twisting it counterclockwise. After about a quarter turn, the two halves separated and revealed a small and tarnished golden semicircle pin. *No, it's not a semicircle,* Charlie thought to himself, *this is too oblong.* Nonetheless, he had seen this before. He knew exactly who was wearing it down to the exact color of the man's eyes. Charlie sat down on a small table and pulled the pin out of its hiding place. They were both quiet for a moment and neither one wanted to break the tension.

After a minute or two of Charlie staring dumbly at the small thing hidden in a child's toy, Jo-Ann meekly said, "I never knew what Daddy put in it before he gave it to you. I don't know what that is, but I can tell that it's important or else Daddy would never have done that."

HIS DREAM BEGAN TO fade and he felt the room he was resting in return for a brief moment. A doctor was shining a very bright light of some kind directly into his eyes and recording something down on his screen. *Click.* The doctor released his lids and Clarke found himself back in darkness. He was back in his dream world.

THIS TIME HE WAS REWATCHING a screen in a public park where summary executions took place about five years before he was born, following the temporary lapse in communication as a result of an EMP during the Great Nuclear War.

The Persian army had successfully launched a high-powered, high-altitude EMP, which shut down all communication equipment in the eastern United States. Fortunately enough, all transportation and creature comforts such as air conditioning and running water remained intact. The internet, radios, and even telephones were rendered completely useless, though, and the subsequent chaos lasted for about three months until new phones reached the end consumers and networks replaced their disabled infrastructure.

The video on the park's screen showed how the slightest shift in stability resulted in absolute discord. The message itself was blunt and straightforward. The screen rotated from displaying somber captions like, "Class status is social refinement," and "We all have our struggles," to disturbing footage of looters being led out from citizen courts in hand restraints and quickly executed by firing squads. The weapons from that era were particularly violent. Back then, a standard home weapon was the MatrixAgeer, a plasma charged round that uniquely curved upon impact to create maximum damage and high mortality rates. Today, the same company provided a laser-based weapon that seared a half-inch hole into most anything non-armored. The intent of this design change was led by a false sense of compassion. A single shot from the old weapon systems was 100-percent lethal, whereas the current weapon was only fatal if the target was hit in the head, an artery, a major organ, or multiple times, because it cauterized the wound and did not lead to hemorrhages. The technology aspect behind the changes was beyond Clarke's understanding even after the briefings he received this past week.

The screens flashed between violent images of classic news footage from the public domain archives reaching as far back as network news had record of. In fact, some of the clips came from the assassination attempt of President Ronald Reagan and the pandemic of school shootings in the early 21st century. At first, the simple threat of violence was enough for elected officials to disarm the citizenry. Then a libertarian backlash occurred, which led to a drastic re-arming of the citizenry with compulsory government firearm issuance to each citizen first class household across America and optional purchases with rigorous background checks for citizens second class. Citizens third class were never again eligible to own firearms.

This program ended up costing approximately ten trillion dollars in 2089 money, but no one was counting the national debt anymore. The taxes for the elite flattened as the classes were further divided. Those with lower incomes began to see a steady rise in wages, but an equal rise in taxes levied against them. The systematic discrimination became so apparent that the DoESS and other federal agencies actually forced this topic to become a national secret and citizens third class were simply not told about it.

Of course, activists had their say through social demonstrations. The classic protests on the National Mall, which were likened to the Million Man March, the March for Life, and so many other groups, were actually permitted but not televised or shared in any way. Thus, freedom of peaceful assembly was not infringed upon, but its impact was diminished via censorship of the press and the stripped-down First Amendment.

The screens in the park continued to flash horrible incidents of Hispanics being rounded into shipping containers, which were then hoisted onto cargo ships heading to Panama and Venezuela. The imagery boasted that in doing so, "the American way of life is safeguarded from those exploiting the law." Human rights groups had shown up to this particular park regularly, all of them from citizens second class or citizens third class families, and defaced the park with obscenities and flags from so many different countries. Their efforts were in vain because most of the government-owned screens were capable of shedding their imperfections during a daily syncing.

The screens simply cycled through several scrubbing mechanisms and returned to pristine condition, causing the vandals to make frequent and increasingly bold trips out to the different city parks to deface the screens as often as possible. Despite several of them being caught every instance they went out, there were too many willing participants to adequately stop them or even identify them for later arrest. Occasionally, these occurrences would be deadly, as a security guard, police officer, or State military unit would open fire on them. These events were not televised, obviously, and it only furthered the divide between the haves and the have-nots.

Charlie, seven at the time, stood in front of that vandalized screen with a wide-open mouth, gazing at the obscenities he did not understand. He was simply too young. He then twisted his oversized baseball cap and walked with Alex down to the next screen before pausing. This one he had seen before, but didn't know what it meant.

The screen had the staunch and serious face of a man with a bold mustache. His eyes were focused in the middle distance and portrayed a powerful presence. Clearly, this was not the first time this particular artist had rendered the image in spray paint—it was well done. Although Charlie did recognize the image, he had no clue where it was from. He had seen it only in places like this—public transportation buildings, park benches, and town halls. They were never in places under constant surveillance for obvious reasons. He finally decided to ask his big brother what they were all about.

"Hey, Alex?" Charlie tugged on his brother's shirt.

"Yeah, what's up?" Alex said as he turned and looked down at the top of his brother's baseball cap.

Indicating the picture of the serious face, Charlie asked, "What's that?"

Alex took a deep inhale and pulled Charlie's chin up so he could look into his eyes. "I'll tell you later, it's not safe to talk about here."

The two continued down the row of public screens scrolling through their various images, videos, and other propaganda. They made their way back to the teen-car Alex was allowed to drive. Teen-cars were virtually accident-free vehicles and functioned similarly to internet firewalls. The car was practically on autopilot and the driver could only pick the roads they would drive on. The positive thing for the driver was that they had the independence to get from place to place on their own without taking public transportation. Ever since Alex had turned fourteen, he had a driver license and went everywhere he wanted to go within reason. He didn't really like going into the city because it was a disaster and incredibly uncomfortable to be in, and besides, he liked camping and the wilderness more anyway.

As they drove in the car back to their house, Alex turned on the sound system to the State-sponsored public radio. Just like the screens in the park, these stations invariably played the same sort of message.

"Tomorrow marks the thirtieth anniversary of the Tragedy of Sierra Vista, where the Mexican insurgents slaughtered all residents in the small military town in the southern region of Arizona. Memorials are taking place throughout the disputed regions under Mexican and Persian occupation, with demonstrations in major cities including Tucson, Phoenix, Los Angeles, and San Antonio. Firmly controlled United States cities in the nearby region are urging their citizens to stay inside and if possible, seek underground shelters, as this date has historically been associated with major battles."

The radio droned on and Alex turned the volume up. This was one of the best ways to communicate privately without modifying the car and drawing red flags from the Department of State Secrecy and Privacy. The only permitted party members allowed to disarm the microphones in cars were those with reasonable cause based on their job description or political position. Not even the average party member had true privacy.

"That picture of the man is Big Brother," Alex whispered into Charlie's ear. "It's from an illegal book called *1984*, where the government watched everything you did. It really is what is happening today. Even right now."

That was the day that Charlie began his fascination with illegal literature. What else was the State hiding?

HE WAS JERKED AWAKE again and his eyes flittered open. The doctors were pumping something else into his IV. He started to taste strawberries and cherry syrup. It made him want to gag, and if he weren't so heavily sedated, he probably would have leaned over the side of his bed. After a moment of choking on the flavor, Clarke actually did vomit all over himself. He felt bad as the doctor cringed and slid his chair away from the bedside as quickly as he could. The room went dark again. He lost consciousness.

CHARLIE, NOW ABOUT eleven years old, was standing by Lake Adams watching the boats go by and waiting with his parents who were sitting on a park bench. The sun was setting and they were heading to church through one of their favorite entrances. It was a little restaurant called New Horizons Café, which had been in business for several generations on the first floor of a high-rise building owned by Javad Tehrani. The name of the high-rise changed when the father passed operations to his eldest child, so Charlie only knew it as Javad Towers but Robert and Claire knew it as Nader Towers before the elder Tehrani passed away. The Tehranis were avid Muslims, but since they were citizens second class, nobody really paid any attention to them. The Prescotts financed their restaurant and artificially subsidized their income in exchange for access to their basement, where a connection to the New Boston underground was literally dug out.

The underground was painstakingly completed over several years with pockets full of sand or rocks at a time. It wasn't just the Prescotts, of course. There were probably a couple dozen families in the area working on the project from the inside of the already existing tunnel and a couple dozen more working from inside the basement. Charlie had personally been to the restaurant once a week for the past six months. Their ritual essentially went from a nice and slow dinner to a quick trip to the basement for pocketsful of debris before they left for the night. After about six months, they finally made the connection with the tunnel and were elated. They themselves had financed the creation of a new tunnel to the underground. The Tehrani family was incredibly excited and allowed them free meals for the rest of their lives.

Of course, Robert had always paid his bill and then some. It was what Robert knew to be right. He took care of those who needed it. Also, Robert knew the risk his friend was taking was serious and he wanted to at least compensate for the trouble.

Mr. Tehrani was on the same page; he knew what it meant to be party to this operation. If he was caught, it would almost certainly mean the death sentence or life imprisonment for him and his family. Long gone were the days of innocence for family members. The crimes of the fathers were inherited once again. Mr. Tehrani knew this and he only permitted guests access to the basement if Mr. Prescott personally escorted them.

Charlie looked from the yellow-orange sunset over the skyline behind him to the green horizon off in the distance. It appeared in the sky like the aurora borealis as it shimmered and danced in the twilight, but it was only off to the northeastern section of the city. These remnants of the Great Nuclear War that destroyed New England were only visible a couple times each month. The atmospheric conditions generally weren't conducive for this phenomenon, and it usually only happened at sunrise, not sunset like today.

Robert rose to his feet from the park bench and grabbed Claire's hand. She was visibly frailer than the eleven-year-old Charlie remembered her. Maybe it was the light or maybe it was the true concern she had about visiting the underground yet again. Either way, Charlie got up too, twisted his baseball cap to match his dad, and started down the red brick path toward the street behind them. He led the way to the restaurant along the street, running in zigzagging lines from tree to tree and hopping on several large rocks flanking the pathway. He was pretty excited to be going to Mass.

"You need to remember to be calm, Charlie," Claire said and then called after him, "Please come walk next to us."

"Okay, Mom," he called back and jumped off a small ledge. Luckily, he wasn't in his nicer church clothes, or else he might have ripped them when he landed. He was just in jeans and a light jacket because it was autumn and a little too cold for the customary dress clothes. He looked up and grinned a boyish smile, almost saying, *Did you see that!* He sprang back to his feet and walked back a few paces to meet his parents before he turned around and walked alongside them.

"You can't do this kind of running around in public," Claire said, shifting her eyes around nervously to see if anyone had noticed. "The rest of the world doesn't have the right to climb around like you do; don't rub it in their faces."

Charlie rolled his eyes and instantly regretted it. His mother had seen. She screwed up her face and looked over to Robert. "Please say something to him. He always listens to you."

Robert tried to conceal a little smile but did a horrible job. His eyes went back and forth between Claire and Charlie before he said, "Your mother is right, you know? If the rest of the world sees what they are missing they might get angry at you. Instead, it's better to show them solidarity and act just like them." He paused for a moment while they approached the restaurant, then continued, "They may recognize you by your clothes or how you speak, but don't give them more reasons to hate you. It's better to give them reasons to forgive you."

Those words never echoed so loudly in his mind. This was probably the most lucid dream he had ever experienced. He felt like he was actually reliving it, not just remembering it. It wasn't exactly a sense of déjà vu; it was like a virtual reality that was based on his memory. Clarke felt that he was creating a memory of a memory and recalled fresh details that he may not have even noticed the time he actually lived it.

The family entered the tired restaurant and headed toward their private room in the back. They passed several large tables in the center of the room and several smaller booths against the windows on their way. It was nearly empty. Business was clearly not going so well tonight.

"Good evening, Mr. Robert!" Mr. Tehrani said and gave Robert a very big hug. "I was hoping to see you again! As you can see, tonight will be an extra private night. I even sent away the staff because we are so slow."

"Don't tell me that you are turning away customers, Javad. I'd rather take a risk myself than have you lose your restaurant." Robert tilted his head and pursed his lips. If there was one thing Robert actually hated, it was when others accommodated him to their own demise.

"Well, no. Not this time really, Mr. Robert." Javad looked down and let out a little sigh and shrugged with his arms outstretched. "It's just slow, really slow tonight." He picked up a cup from the edge of a small bar and began to polish it with his black-and-white pinstriped apron. "You don't need to worry about us, eh? We will be all right; we have always been." The cup was one of his nervous tells, and even Charlie picked up on it.

"Look, Javad, you don't have to tell me that. I don't think you've had more than three customers at the same time since we started coming in. I know business is bad right now. Your ethnicity is something that people are put off by, especially now. You can't help it—people are disgusting! I'm going to keep you going so long as you let us come in here. I promise to make it work for both of us."

Javad actually started to cry and Robert reached over and gave him another loving hug. Claire took Charlie's hand and walked him back to their private room, where the door to the basement was located. Charlie looked back over his shoulder and saw Javad's deep embrace with Robert and felt depressed for the first time in his life after losing Alex. Ever since Alex's funeral, he saw deep compassion for everyday things. For instance, one time when he was walking up his driveway, he thought about how he was taught that God had created everything, the blade of grass growing taller than the others and the small pebble tucked in the compacted dirt. It was so touching that he actually started to tear up at the beauty of the small miracle. Just an hour before entering the restaurant, Charlie already thought that his dad was the most perfect man on earth, but the care he showed for another person was just so genuine that Charlie began to idolize his father even more.

Claire pulled open the access door near the table in the back room and descended the staircase to the basement, pulling Charlie with her. They soon reached the bottom step and Charlie instinctively brushed the wall to find the light switch but Claire stopped him.

"We need to find our way in the dark," Claire said. "Lights may not always work and we might rely on this tunnel to save our lives one day. We need to know it by touch."

Charlie stood in the dark and gave his mother the most ridiculous face, not believing what she had just said. Luckily, it was dark enough that she couldn't see him, or else he probably would have been smacked upside the head—in a loving way, of course.

"Count the stones," Claire coached gently, "and find the pattern."

Charlie rubbed his hands on the wall and felt it. There was a distinct pattern in the texture of the stones. There were ten rough-hewn stones along the wall, followed by a very smooth, almost polished marble or granite. It was incredible how predictable it was. He counted every section and told his mother that he recognized the pattern. She told him that each smooth stone was ten meters apart, so they had gone into the tunnel exactly a hundred meters when they hit a hallway. Charlie knew that they needed to go to the right and made the turn. Claire was still holding his hand and let him lead her. Apparently, she had another way to keep track of the layout and Charlie was spot-on so far.

After another hundred meters, they came to another intersection and he made a left turn before spotting a light at the far end of the tunnel. He counted out the smooth stones and knew that when he reached the corner where the light came from, he had gone another hundred meters. At that point, he could walk with his hand off the wall.

They approached the narthex of their underground church and heard the quiet murmur of their friends gathering for Mass. There were probably fifty people in the facility, an uptick from the past year by nearly twenty percent. The Catholic Church in New Boston was growing—maybe not at a rapid rate, but growing nonetheless. The congregation recently voted to call their church St. Sebastian's Catholic Community. St. Sebastian is the patron saint of persecuted Christians. The name felt fitting.

Charlie entered the narthex and saw François, whom he hadn't seen in nearly a month. Since Alex died, Charlie's grades started to fall and he was moved down a level to the basic class, which resulted in different scheduled lunch and recess times. Charlie's grades never really recovered, but he did do well in his new level.

"Hey, how are you? Did you see the new entrance out of that old guy's restaurant?" Charlie said to his friend.

"No," François said with a little embarrassed smile, "we don't go out to restaurants a lot. What about it, though?"

"It's super cool." Charlie was exaggerating his hand movements while he explained the stairs and the dark hallway. "And my mom told me that I needed to memorize the tunnels in the dark for some reason."

"Yeah, my dad told me that too. Like just a couple weeks ago." The boys paused and gave each other puzzled looks. They knew that it couldn't be a coincidence. They wanted to talk more but Jo-Ann skipped up to them as her mother, Aunt Perpetua, entered the church.

"Hi guys. Whatcha talking about?" she said.

"Nothing much, Jo," Charlie said, "just about how weird it is that our parents are telling us to find our way in the dark down here."

"Yeah, it's a little scary, to be honest. I don't know why they would have just started telling us to do that," François said and rubbed his hands together nervously.

Jo-Ann tilted her head to one side and stepped closer to them, then whispered, "I think it's because of the war." She paused for a minute and looked behind the boys. "I heard my dad saying that it is getting closer than the State is telling us. He's scared. Like really scared."

Charlie could see the fear in her face. He didn't want her to cry so he reached out and grabbed one of her shoulders and turned her toward him. She looked up at him with watery eyes and quivering lips, then buried her head in his chest. Charlie looked mortified as he awkwardly wrapped his arms around her shoulders and tapped her on the back. He felt uncomfortable and embarrassed, but he knew that Jo-Ann needed his comfort.

It was commonplace to see people crying in public as anxiety was rampant and being depressed was not unusual. The Center for Disease Control actually conducted a study of over 10,000 Americans in 2085 that yielded the results that about sixty-five percent were clinically depressed and taking medication for it, another twenty percent were depressed but not medicated. Simple mathematics told the story that approximately 425 million of the 500 million Americans were depressed and spending money on government-manufactured pharmaceuticals. The State actually tried to exploit depression and perpetuate it, not solve the social problem, because it was an 800-billion-dollar annual revenue marketplace—more than just a drop in the bucket.

Jo-Ann popped off of Charlie's shoulder after a moment and wiped her tears on her baggy green sweater. "Sorry," she whispered and sniffled. "Thank you." She offered a shy smile and then turned around and skipped back to her mother as they started toward the sanctuary. It was like nothing ever happened.

"She's crazy," François said to Charlie, shaking his head.

"Yeah, she is," Charlie said. He was more concerned about what Jo-Ann had said to him, though. Why weren't his parents telling him everything? The State was lying about the danger, but so were his parents. The dream was very disturbing for him and he felt that there was a missing piece still. It was similar to having an answer to a question on the tip of your tongue—frustratingly confusing.

"I'll catch you after Mass, okay?" François said and gave his friend a high-five. He walked back over to his parents, who were talking to another couple with a newborn. Charlie walked back to his mother, who was talking with Aunt Perpetua and laughing for the first time in weeks. Robert walked into the narthex a moment later and they headed into the church toward their pew. The church didn't have missals at this time because printed materials were practically impossible to come by, even though it had been nearly fifty years since the religions started to lose their official status. Printing presses were ancient technology and nobody had the means to recreate it on a large enough scale to adequately create enough usable copies. There were several presses working hard to print Bibles and other material, but missals for every church member was woefully irresponsible and largely unnecessary. Each priest had a copy and the parishioners were able to follow along or ask for the readings and psalms for the mass and the upcoming week.

It was impressive how effective the St. Sebastian's Catholic Community had gotten at disseminating information. They hosted several small group Bible studies and prayer groups, which had members in other social circles who then passed messages as far and as wide as they could to ensure that any warnings or recommendations met the widest audience possible. This would eventually become their early warning system. Another thing Charlie didn't know at the time was that an offshoot of the Knights of Columbus, the largest Catholic fraternity to date, turned into an actual spy network and facilitated evacuations from war zones and brought trained fighters into the field of battle. It was one of the most effective methods of combating the spread of the war and also covertly proving to the official United States government that there will always be resistance to injustice and oppression.

The congregation bowed their heads as a priest new to the New Boston underground, Fr. Ron, gave a blessing at the beginning of mass. Then a lector read Amos 8:4-7 and 1 Timothy 2:1-8. The gospel was Luke 16:1-13. The readings deviated from the normally prescribed Catholic Missal, but were suitable for the occasion. Most congregants didn't mind the changes, while others felt encouraged by the selected readings. By the time Fr. Ron was starting his sermon, Charlie's mind began to drift back to his brother. He felt sad again about what happened and the way it had happened. Alex was his absolute best friend and Charlie missed him every day. It had already been three years since Alex died in that car accident, and every time Charlie thought about it, he still teared up.

Chapter 15—Last Day

The scene faded away as he dwelled on his big brother, and his sleeping quarters began to materialize in front of him. He was alone now and felt very refreshed. Aside from some pain in his joints and several pinpricks near his left elbow, he was back to his pre-briefing state. The door creaked open and a nurse dressed in a set of dark maroon scrubs walked in with a small independent screen not unlike Clarke's. She, however, carried hers in her hand rather than mounting it to her forearm. Upon closer inspection, Clarke saw that she had a silver bar above her name tape that read, "Bear."

"Good morning, ma'am," Clarke began to say, but he couldn't quite get out his entire greeting. His tongue felt foreign to him. He lifted his arm to his face and felt that all of his muscles were incredibly sore, as if he had atrophied since he fell asleep. He looked at the nurse in alarm.

"Don't worry," Nurse Bear said, pulling out a small flashlight, "this is a normal part of the detox process." She proceeded to shine the light directly into Clarke's retinas and observed their constriction. "Your eyes have already recovered. It should be little more than an hour or so until the rest of your body feels normal again."

Clarke attempted to nod stiffly. What else was he going to do about it? Nothing surprised him anymore. He had been enhanced with implants and was legally declared dead, he was technically going to be a spy conscripted for service to an army he despised, and over the past day he relived memories in the most vivid way imaginable. *Sure, my body is just a limp noodle for a little while longer, why not?*

Nurse Bear pulled up her screen to Clarke's head and tapped several icons and a sensation of joy rushed through his body. She just caused an upwelling of oxytocin literally at the click of a button. Clarke felt at that moment that he loved her. The feeling immediately turned into rage as she clicked another button, and then stoicism after another audible ping from her screen. She smiled.

"Please listen to me," she said. "I know that what happens right now will have a lasting effect on you, so it is important that you remain calm." She paused for a minute and smiled softly. Clarke saw her round face and kind eyes look longingly out the faux window in his room. "It's been about thirty-six hours since you were placed into your coma, and I'm the third nurse to monitor you." She paused again. It looked like she was conflicted in telling him something.

"You talk in your sleep, and the other nurses felt that it needed to be reported. Since I'm the last in charge of your custody, it's my job to report it, but I'm not going to."

Clarke's pulse quickened. Did they just find out about the underground in his city? What else could it have possibly been? He still couldn't get his mouth to move properly and just stared at her with wide eyes full of concern.

"What I'm going to do is send you the file and delete it from our records. I think it's a little personal for our uses, and I think that it might make you happy."

Clarke was confused most of the time, but this made even less sense than normal. *What did I say? Why would she think that I should have the file, let alone that it would make me happy? Why would she give it to me anyway?*

"I will leave the ninety-nine to find the one," she said and tapped on her screen again. Clarke felt his own screen come to life next to him, and he wanted to reach down, but was still unable to. He breathed heavily in anticipation, but he was helpless.

Then Nurse Bear leaned over and kissed him on the cheek. She was gentle and soft. Her blonde hair hung around him and tickled his nose. Charlie felt his jaw loosen up and he wanted to kiss her back, not like a girlfriend or anything, but like it was the respectful thing to do. Her kiss only lasted a few seconds, but it was suspended in time. She stood back up and wiped a tear from her eyes carefully so as not to mess up her makeup. Then she sniffed slightly and said, "I know so much about you and I always did things hoping that you would remember me. Please forgive that I just stole that kiss. It wasn't right."

Who was she? Clarke had no idea and he felt badly about it. *Why did she seem so upset and sad?* Clarke himself was barely eighteen years old and she was probably not much older than him, maybe twenty or twenty-one, but he didn't know her.

She smiled softly and tapped on her screen again and said, "It's all in the message I sent you. You are officially discharged as soon as you get out of bed. My charge is done here."

Nurse Bear leaned over, kissed him again, and left. Clarke had no recollection of her at all. She was very nice, but nothing rang a bell. Maybe she was a classmate or a friend he once had? But how was she here at this exact time? And what did she send him? It was killing him to find out.

About an hour went by, and he slowly regained the ability to use his arms and legs. While he was still immobile, Clarke accessed his screen and pulled up his messages. Even more than he wanted to admit, Roxi was on his mind, and he quickly pulled up his drafted message to her and reread it to make sure it still sounded good to him:

Hello. You may not remember me, but I sure do remember you. I was at the hospital for a while in June and July this year for a military procedure. I just wanted to let you know that I thought you were stunning and would love to keep correspondence with you. I'm very interested in life as a college student because that luxury was stolen from me. Maybe one day we could meet again.

From Clarke Anicius

He sighed and wanted to rewrite it but knew that he probably wouldn't come up with anything better, so he simply sent the message as it was. It flashed for a moment in his peripheral vision and then vanished. It must have pinged her screen a second later because the automated response opened on Clarke's screen nearly instantaneously.

Warning, you have just contacted a citizen second class. This action is considered dangerous and should only occur in extreme situations. Proceed at your own risk. For advice on how to appropriately report unwanted contact from a citizen second class please navigate to the help desk. Thank you.

That was interesting. Clarke had contacted François and several other people from his church on his previous screen plenty of times. That could only mean that this screen—the government-issued one, that is—had additional software and firewalls that gave Clarke the unnerving sensation that all of his activity was cached on some government server and that he was actively being monitored. Clarke did his best to put that out of his mind. He had already sent the message and the damage was already done. If the police were going to arrest him, he was powerless to do anything about it. But Clarke did question how Lewis got her access number.

He put that out of his mind for now and pulled open the files that Nurse Bear sent him. They were video files but refused to open. Clarke tried to convert them into different types of video—three-dimensional, projected video, retro flat-screen video, and even just audio. Nothing worked. Clarke screwed up his face and tried to think of a grade seven programming class, where he had learned about different video corruption issues and how to resolve them. The memory was too fuzzy to take the risk of processing the videos. He did, however, remember that if he failed in the process of trying to fix some types of corruption, the files would be rendered useless. Clarke wasn't going to risk destroying the videos—he would get around to processing them at some later point. He decided instead to read the attached message:

> *Charlie,*
>
> *If you are reading this, I know you don't remember me. Over the past several weeks, the medical procedures and drugs you have taken for your conscription have modified your memories. Please try to remember that you have friends and family who are trying to give people a safe life. The videos I sent have a password that is my first name. You know me. When you remember, you will understand why it was you.*
>
> *Stay safe,*
> *Your Bear*

Clarke stared at it blankly. He was both dumbstruck and intrigued. *Who was she?* He sat there with his screen pulled open on his wrist and wondered absentmindedly for a while, before drifting into a daydream about the very dreams he had over the past day. They felt so real and were so clear that now the real world felt less true and less certain. In his dreams he knew what was going to happen, whereas being awake he didn't know what the next few minutes held. He snapped back to reality and tilted his screen back over and reread the message from Nurse Bear.

After the fourth time reading the short note, Clarke stood up uneasily and steadied himself on the bedside. He stripped off his hospital robe and dressed himself in the government-provided bright blue corduroys and simple five-button shirt that he mostly closed, only exposing the top of his chest and collarbone. Clarke also slid on the high laced faux leather boots that he was instructed to wear. He wore them in a military fashion, that is, he tucked in his pant legs. His old baseball cap was taken from him when he in-processed, but since then he had purchased a new one, which was now hanging on a hook above the table where his clothes were resting. Clarke smiled slyly as he grabbed it, crushed the brim into proper shape, and then positioned it as he had always done.

It was a small comfort, but significant. He felt his anxiety lessen with the familiar sensation of wearing his hat and realized he had a new resolve and determination to carry out his assignment as a spy—not for the State, which messed up his life, but for all those whom the State was persecuting. He would use his position to keep them safe with the power he now had.

THE REST OF HIS TIME on station happened quickly. He needed to take the tile-based transportation from nearly every appointment. He went from his sleeping quarters to the dining facility and rushed down to the barber as directed. LTC Hudson told him that he needed a haircut because his hair had grown out of military regulation specifications and he was obligated to get it cut. Luckily, she gave him some leeway and said that she only needed a receipt to hold higher echelons at bay.

Clarke stood up and got off the transport in front of a small underground barbershop. He spoke with the barber briefly about his situation and made some small talk about Fort Powell. Neither Clarke nor the barber were concerned about secrecy because both of them had a security clearance, and they were underground in the world's largest secret military facility, after all. The barber gave him several options and Clarke opted for the classic asymmetric haircut that barely cut anything from one side of his head while the other side was buzzed down to nearly nothing. Clarke had his screen scanned and the money was transferred to the barber, who wished him luck. Clarke then hopped on the transport tile and went to the clinic for another round of shots, his final round for the next sixteen months.

The nurse was kind and courteously welcomed Clarke, who in turn stuck out his screen to be scanned and processed. The nurse walked him to a private room and promptly stuck three, four, five and six needles into his right shoulder and repeated the process on the other side.

"We don't know what is going on in the Mexican army, nor on the streets in Houston right now," she said, smiling sadistically, "so we are giving you all we got."

Clarke felt a little disturbed by the nurse's pleasure in this process and got out of the room as quickly, albeit politely, as he could. Then it was off to a final briefing with the command team and security officer.

Dan sat in his chair and appeared to have shaved for the first time in at least a week and also seemed to be wearing a clean uniform. Of course, it was bulging at the seams of the zipper along his right side and the collar refused to stay flat due to the way his girth was pulling on it. Nonetheless, it was refreshing to see him moderately cleaned up—it was getting close to disturbing before. Clarke inhaled slowly so as to not be overwhelmed by Dan's normal body odor and was pleasantly surprised when he discovered that the man smelled like soap.

Lieutenant Colonel Hudson, as frail as he remembered, sat at the head of the table in a high-backed chair and was actively scrolling through several screens, unaware that Clarke had entered the room. A couple of the analysts looked over at the door when it opened and started to show small smiles and positioned themselves more upright. It was fairly obvious that they had been sitting and waiting for some time now.

The senior enlisted member of the unit, Sergeant Major Columbus, whom Clarke had not met prior to this instance, stood up and motioned for Clarke to come to him. Clarke did so, and the sergeant major leaned over and whispered, "I may be a citizen second class, but I will destroy you if you mess this up for us." He then extended his hand in greeting.

Clarke slipped on a welcoming smile and shook his hand, then whispered in response, "I may be a citizen first class, but I will never let you down."

Sergeant Major Columbus grinned and slapped Clarke on the back. He then sat back down and gently reminded Colonel Hudson that Clarke had entered the room.

Having a superior officer waiting to start a briefing for you was definitely not a normal situation to find oneself in, and Clarke felt awkward, even though—according to his schedule—he was actually a couple minutes early.

"My apologies, ma'am," Clarke said, rendering a salute across his chest, "I must have had the wrong time."

"Nonsense," she replied, "you are on schedule. I myself had nowhere else to be." She smiled widely and her wrinkled old face showcased her false teeth. "But if you don't mind, I would like to start this."

Sergeant Major Columbus pointed at one of the analysts, who maneuvered a screen and navigated it to enter into a three-dimensional presentation. Another analyst stood up and began her brief.

"Good morning, ma'am, sergeant major." She gave a short bow to them, then looked over at Clarke and blushed in embarrassment. "And sir—" then gave another bow directly at him. "I am Sergeant Cortez and this is our current course of action to deploy team member Charlie to Dallas."

Clarke smiled at the irony of being called "team member Charlie." Sergeant Cortez plodded on. "He will be departing Fort Powell at 1800 this evening and be taken to the army air field, where he will board a civilian-owned McDermott-30 with tail number 8337. It is being piloted by one of our own, Captain Coleman. She will use standard civilian call signs."

Captain Coleman stood up and selected the map of the region and magnified it before saying, "This is our flight path." She traced a path across the display, which left a visible trail on the map that crisscrossed several times in a very odd pattern. "We will be avoiding all government airspace and deliberately flying over cities to verify our submitted flight path." She then traced another line in a much more logical pattern from Fort Powell to a small city outside Houston. "Our actual flight path is strange so as to conceal our point of origin. We will be off-loading at two separate airports here." She pointed to two locations on the map. "We will be chartering another civilian aircraft and modifying our call sign to match the new aircraft at both locations." She paused for a moment and referenced her notes. "When we reach this airport and disembark, you will be processed at the airport as normal and I will return back here on the reverse flight path. What are your questions?"

She looked around the room for a moment and was about to sit down when Dan grumbled something under his breath, which she must have heard because she looked livid. Clarke saw Dan grin as he reached for his coffee, which he sloshed onto his nearly clean uniform. He either didn't notice or didn't care as the spot on his stomach darkened. Captain Coleman waited for a moment longer and then the questions started. She fielded them expertly and quickly. It appeared her analyst underlings were aware that she would need some assistance in this portion of her briefing to make her look good, so they asked her obvious questions like airspeeds and expected weather and visibility. Everyone knew what she was doing but nobody objected to it. They would want the same treatment if it were them giving the briefing.

Captain Coleman then turned the briefing back over to the young Sergeant Cortez, who picked up where she left off.

"Lieutenant Anicius will then proceed from his disembarking at his final destination and identify himself as Daniel Polo, a new businessman in town who owns a small factory a couple of hours away. The complete details of the cover are in the data packet you have already received." She looked at Clarke and continued, "All credentials and biometric data have been switched over to your identity, so there should be no issues. Once you are cleared to leave the airport, you will then be escorted by a convoy to Les Misérables Hotel, located at 5417 West Plantation Road. After check-in, you will have two hours to confirm back here about additional requirements using your screen. You will connect to our secure system through a dirty network connection. The proxies and protocol will be available for your review, but I advise you speak with Dan if you have any questions."

Dan raised his coffee cup and cheered the sergeant. He then wiped his mouth with the sleeve of his jumpsuit and smeared another stain across it. Clarke was amazed by this man. *How did he get to his position?*

The briefing continued and formalities were followed, allowing Colonel Hudson and Sergeant Major Columbus to add in their two cents, which carried the meeting for well longer than it needed to be, but everyone sat there anyway and listened. Honestly, it was all valid and meaningful to Clarke, but ninety percent of the other people didn't have to be there at all.

After all the pomp of the moment had been carried out, Lieutenant Colonel Hudson stood up and rendered a salute across her chest and said their motto, "Always in the Shadows," which everyone else echoed. She started toward the door first and called for Clarke to follow her. She sat down on a transport and he got the one next to her. Apparently, this technology knew when multiple passengers were headed the same way.

As the transport began down the hallway, Lieutenant Colonel Hudson spoke. "I must remind you that this mission was carefully designed for you and your background." She wasn't looking at him, but rather straight forward as she sat with excellent posture, her hands clasped. "Everything you report back will be used to ensure people stay safe. If we know where they are, we can maneuver around them and focus on the foreign threat, not the domestic concerns. The statesmen can sort out illegal underground cults later."

Clarke swallowed hard and nodded. He was worried; it felt like she was reading his mind again. He cleared his throat and spoke. "I'm prepared for this. Like you said, I need to be myself." Still looking straight ahead, she smiled as the transport rounded a corner into the massive intersection. "I mean, Daniel, that is."

He cringed at hearing himself say Daniel. Something about it felt wrong. It could have just as easily been the fact that this was his second legal name change in only a couple months and it was getting tiresome. After all, he was barely eighteen years old and was being asked to not just place himself in the middle of a combat zone, but to act as a spy. He would later learn that espionage has been a capital offense in nearly all sovereign countries including Cuba, Soviet Russia, Canada, and even Switzerland since Sun Tzu wrote *The Art of War*. Nobody liked spies; it was playing dirty. Clarke would invariably be put to death if he was discovered by anyone on the opposing forces.

Even though he didn't like the idea of being called Daniel, he did like the name Daniel. It made him think about the Prophet Daniel and the story of him in the lions' den. It oddly was a very fitting comparison for what he was about to do. Clarke needed God just like Daniel did. The transport slowed and he smiled lazily; the story was perfect for Clarke's next adventure into the lions' den called Dallas.

"Ma'am," Clarke said with a salute, "thank you for your guidance. You have made my resolve stronger than ever to help other Americans."

The line was practically obligatory because of the way Lieutenant Colonel Hudson conducted business. Clarke felt that not saying something like this would have been a serious misstep, but it was the best he could come up with. She smiled a last wrinkled smile and gave a soft bow before her office door slid open for her. Clarke turned away and got back on the transport. He looked at his screen to see his schedule and a message icon hovered in his peripheral vision It was from Roxi—she had written back. He had almost forgotten about her and immediately felt a mixture of anxiety and depression as he opened it. He wanted to know what she had written as a response, but he also knew that it didn't matter. He would officially have died a second time in the next couple of hours.

Good Afternoon, Lieutenant Anicius,

Thank you for the warm regards and gracious tip you gave during your visits at the hospital dining facility. I can tell you that this has greatly helped me with getting my books purchased for school. I also would like to let you know that I too would like to correspond with you, but would warn you against doing so because I am not a citizen first class. I'm sure you are aware that I will be summarily executed if you reported me and you would become a political prisoner if I reported you. It is a risk for me just to respond to you, but it would be rude for me to not reply. There was no way I could forget you; you were the kindest person I've ever served.

There was a lot to unpack here. The standard greeting from an underclass citizen and a comment on an act of kindness she had received. Clarke had given her nearly a sixty-percent tip on all of his meals and he knew that it was good business for both of them. She got paid well, and he got even better service. He felt his face redden when he thought about her coming and going to his table, her kind smile, her soft voice, and the curve of her body. He kept reading and was glad that his guess about her being a college student was correct and she was using the money for school. The money didn't go to waste and that made him feel good.

Her next comment in the letter was fairly standard about the inappropriate nature of different citizen classes corresponding with one another. Clarke read it as though she was going through the motions and merely putting it in writing so if it would be recalled in a State hearing against either one of them, she would have evidence in her favor. The following line was definitely unique, though. It showed that she was willing to literally risk death so as to not be considered rude. Clarke was amused by this. He himself ignored the warnings his screen gave him, and apparently she did the same. Clarke's anxiety subsided after reflecting on the message for a moment and he relished in his excitement. The final line made him feel butterflies in his stomach.

That was short-lived, however, as he remembered that Clarke would soon be dead and whatever hopes he had with Roxi would be gone too. He let out a sigh as his transport came to a stop in front of his sleeping quarters. The door slid open as he approached it and closed uncomfortably close to his hands again. He was getting irritated with this door. He smiled as he thought that this would also be the last time he entered his room here. This room had very sour memories, despite him only being a resident for ten days. He had barely had time to sleep, he hadn't unpacked his belongings, and he fell into a coma for an entire day, experiencing memories that he wasn't sure actually existed anymore. Even though he was heading to a war zone, Clarke was happy to put this room out of his life forever.

Clarke sat in the little chair and pulled up his screen again. He started to compose a message. Then he erased it; it was too bold. He started another draft. Then he erased that one too because it didn't say anything and he came off as pathetic. He wrote a third draft and threw that one away too. He just couldn't get his emotions down properly and it was frustrating. He sat for a few more minutes and mused in silence.

He knelt down and prayed for guidance and for several saints' intercession. The urgency for his response message to Roxi didn't really matter because he was going to be a completely different person in the next two hours and Clarke would no longer exist. Clarke knew that it was in God's hands now, and if he was led to an appropriate answer it would be divine intervention. Nothing else would have substantiated his need. He tried and failed to write a good response to Roxi, so he sought guidance from above.

After a period of silent reflection and prayer, Clarke concluded by boldly making the sign of the cross. He knew that they were likely monitoring him, but this was his private dwelling, and no law had yet breached the sanctity of that privacy. Clarke knew that it was a daring move, but the risk thrilled him and gave him a rush of adrenaline. They could cancel his mission right now and have him arrested. Technically, he was already dead according to his biometric data; they would just dispose of his body in some forest somewhere and nobody would mourn him properly or know the full story. The risk was thrilling.

Clarke stood up with a refreshed smile and took a long inhale. He grabbed the few belongings he had managed to unpack—a comb, toothbrush, and razor—and stuffed them back into his military duffle bag. Sergeant Cortez's briefing skipped over the part about his military luggage, but Clarke was confident that it would be sorted out before it became a problem. After all, the special forces had spared no expense so far. Clarke chuckled to himself as he imagined a gold-lined suitcase with dazzling emeralds inlaid into the exterior.

Chapter 16—Travel to Houston

C larke's guess wasn't far off. He was enjoying the pleasant warmth of the late afternoon summer sun while standing at the bottom of the boarding ramp to his plane. Several guards were posted by the boarding ramp and looked all too serious. A lower enlisted soldier, Private Drake, wheeled out a titanium-plated suitcase with gold and silver bands for aesthetics. His name, D. POLO, was etched onto the front and back. He actually laughed out loud when he dumped the contents of his duffle bag into it, and the private looked offended.

"It's not you," Clarke said, "I just imagined my bag to be something like this." Private Drake did not seem to find it funny and his face turned from puzzlement to a scowl. Clarke stopped laughing. He realized that the soldier in front of him was a teenager too. The only difference between the two of them was their citizenship status. Had Clarke not been a citizen first class, he could have just as easily been wheeling out a suitcase for someone else. He cleared his throat in embarrassment.

"Sorry about that," Clarke said, "I wish you didn't have to do this; I would gladly trade places with you if I could." The second it left his mouth he knew he was going to regret it. The hotheaded private spat at Clarke's feet, and two of the guards flanking Clarke grabbed him and flung him into the plane. They slammed the door and he bounced off the opposite side of the small jet in time to climb back over to the little window and hear two loud cracks—gunshots. Assault on a commissioned officer.

Clarke rushed over to the lavatory and vomited. His own apology had just killed another man. The kid did nothing that warranted death; he was powerless and angry about the situation. Clarke embodied everything that the private despised—his hatred was understandable. The division between classes was bad in Alabama, but apparently it was worse elsewhere. The military clearly favored its officers and had resorted to disposing of court martial hearings or other military justice systems in favor of a speedy trial and execution to better support its officer corps. Clarke, of course, didn't play a role in the investigation or trial, and the two guards' testimonies would be sufficient to warrant their subsequent actions.

Clarke washed his face and looked at himself in the polished metal mirror. "What am I?" he said aloud and pressed his forehead against his reflection. The trauma he had endured at the airport before he arrived at Fort Powell not all that long ago was haunting him, but that was a result of someone else's actions, not his own. This time Clarke provoked it. Clarke caused this death, whether it was deliberate or not. He felt nausea come over him and his stomach turned when Captain Coleman gently rapped on the lavatory door.

"You feeling all right?" she said.

"Yes, ma'am. Just a moment." Clarke hurried to wipe his face once more and rinse out the sick from his mouth. "Just a little nervous, is all," he said as he slid open the door, averting his eyes and showcasing a shy smile.

"Look," Captain Coleman said, "seeing that happen is never easy. I was just walking up to the plane when I saw them throw you inside." She was silent for a moment. "Was that your first one?"

Clarke tilted his head in confusion. "My first one of what?" he said.

"The first soldier who you had killed."

"No, it wasn't." Clarke looked down and slumped his shoulders. He was on the verge of tears when Captain Coleman reached out and grabbed one of his shoulders with her free hand; a coffee was in the other.

"It's okay. Seeing it is tough. I hate it, but that's the way the world is, eh?" she said in a friendly tone and smiled. "Here, you can read this." She pulled open her screen, navigated through several menus, and started a search. She pulled up one of her files and transmitted it over to Clarke's screen, which promptly buzzed.

"That is the official guide for dealing with insubordination and assault." She pulled open another document and sent it as well. "And this is the stuff that will make you feel better."

Clarke nodded his appreciation and looked up through his watery eyes. He still couldn't speak after a minute.

"You're lucky," she said, "most of your service will be out of uniform and it's hard to kill anyone that way. I've got another four years; probably another forty of my soldiers will die before I get out." She laughed slightly and then frowned as if remembering someone she lost. "I'll just be up here going through some preflight checks," she said and cleared her throat.

Clarke nodded and watched her go through the small hull to the cockpit after she bent over and picked up a little briefcase. He realized that she wasn't in uniform for this mission. She was wearing classic business clothes: a slightly shorter than knee-length skirt and a bright orange side-button blouse with an off-balance collar. She was carrying a coffee cup in one hand and the briefcase in the other—it was very professional. Clarke felt that she had a very different background from him, but she exuded a trustworthy personality. He would have loved to have the chance to talk with her about her past, but there was no time for that now. She was going to be flying a very finicky plane in a very high-stress situation and should not be distracted.

Clarke wiped his eyes again and sat in one of the seats next to a window on the opposite side of the boarding door, as he couldn't bear to look at whatever was happening at the execution site just feet away from where he now sat. He rubbed his corduroy pants nervously and liked the soothing feeling of the soft, yet firm, rows of fabric. It helped distract him as he remembered the pants his parents used to buy him as a small child, which was only a few years ago really. The nostalgia was a comforting feeling and he decided to meditate upon that comfort by saying several short prayers.

The engines turned on and Clarke opened his eyes. It felt like he had fallen asleep, as he had calmed down so quickly in the seat. He stood, slightly startled, and headed up to the cockpit where Captain Coleman was plugging away at several nobs and annotating some of the readouts on her screen. She didn't notice when Clarke sat down next to her and buckled the lap belt.

"I don't mean to bother you," he said, "is this okay?"

She looked over at him and nodded silently, then returned to flipping switches and toggling nobs. Clarke didn't know much about planes and he wasn't sure how dangerous any of the buttons were. As he scanned the instrumentation panel, though, he noticed that there weren't any actual buttons, nobs, or switches—it was all projected from a massive screen contoured to the cockpit dashboard. He gave a slight look of surprise and she smiled while pressing a final button. The engine's RPMs climbed and the roar was louder than he expected.

"I was waiting for you to notice," she said with a short laugh. "This plane might be old, but you can trust that we have had it retrofitted to today's tech."

Clarke nodded. "I think I'm most confused by how you are actually turning and manipulating some of the data when it's just a projection, ma'am."

"Please don't call me that," she said sternly, "I'd rather you call me Nat. I think that we both deserve a little personal information if we are going to spend some time together. Natasha is my full name, but everyone who knows me calls me Nat."

Throughout the rest of the first flight, they talked about their real childhoods and what they wanted to do with their lives before they received their draft notices. They were both very optimistic as they reminisced about their past and they wanted to impress upon the other that they really were a good person. It was amazing how the current social structure fed into the guilt of inherited family status, similarly to the movement in the early 21st century of white guilt and the pressing issue of reparations to descendants of slaves. They themselves did nothing wrong; they simply were born into status and reaped the benefits of their parents' and grandparents' hard work—or rather, their conformity to party standards. The issue was clearly uncomfortable for the 'haves' and many of the wealthy and influential families wanted to do something about it.

Most of Natasha and Clarke's shared guilt went unmentioned because it was obvious to both of them that they each felt the same heartache. So, they talked about their draft process instead. Clarke was amazed at how eerily different it was ten years ago. Natasha had received her notice via a message on her family screen; Clarke had not. Natasha was authorized a deferment to finish her education; he was not. Natasha was allowed to pick from a list of available jobs; he was not. Clarke became a little bitter at the small luxuries she was given, as he would never know what it would have been like to keep his original name or contact his family whenever he wanted to.

Natasha felt sorry about it too, because it was one of the few things that kept her going so long. She leaned on her family for support nearly every day and was allowed to travel to and from her parents' home in what was left of Florida after the rise in sea level. As an officer, the government conscripted her for fourteen years of service and knew that the suicide rates declined rapidly when the officers were authorized travel at government expense. Hardly convenient, but better than Clarke's situation. They were silent for the remainder of the flight to their first stop.

"All right, here is where it gets interesting," Natasha said as she pulled over her headphones. "TXR Tower, this is McDermott-30, 8337, above open fields ten kilometers, inbound requesting touch and go with information Zulu."

She motioned for Clarke to pull on the second set of headphones, which he went to do, but could already hear the static click of the line before it came up to his ears. He realized that he had tuned into the plane's broadcast frequency—the airport's reply came in crisp directly to his brain:

"McDermott-30, 8337, this is TXR Tower, what is your access number? We have no record of your chartered flight 8337," said a sharp and shrill voice from the other end.

"My access number is 208506240139," she said.

"Stand by."

The line went silent and Clarke swallowed hard as the anticipation mounted. He looked over at Natasha as the time dragged on. Her eyes were widening as she began showing concern with flight control and confusion with Clarke not wearing the headphones she clearly meant for him to wear. She started thinking about how this was a civilian aircraft being flown from a military installation to a civilian airport and any air traffic controller would be wary to allow permission. Natasha was imagining that the guy sitting in the tower probably took note of the call sign and the access number, then ran it down the tower and across the airfield to his superior for authorization. Then they both had to get back up to the tower. It made sense, but it had already been five minutes.

"8337, this is TXR Tower, what is your authorization code?" A new voice was on the radio now. This one was warmer but spoke with authority.

Natasha breathed a sigh of relief. She was waiting for their contact at the airport to intervene, and here he was. She knew that he must have been either a supervisor or someone else on the chain authorized to permit flights to land.

"TXR Tower, this is 8337. My authorization code is Napoleon," she said and smiled at Clarke, who continued to look concerned.

"8337," the voice said, "Tower will take control now and direct you to a predesignated hangar."

"TXR Tower taking control, 8337 out." Natasha pulled off her headphones and was about to explain what had just happened to Clarke, but he cut her off.

"I heard it," he said, pointing to his head, "the enhancements are, uh, really good." Natasha raised her eyebrows in surprise—she knew he had enhancements, but didn't know the extent of them. Clarke noticed that she wasn't really that surprised and he laughed dramatically, "Ha, ha, ha. I'm sorry, I thought you never met a 2A."

Nonetheless, she still went on to explain what was going to happen because the radio transmission was coded to a degree and she noticed that he was completely unfamiliar with flying, so she described it step by step. How takeoff and landing was remotely controlled by the air traffic controllers, and the flight authorization codes indicated their flight path. The exchange was fairly normal except for the part where there was a five-minute-long pause between transmissions. The authorization code was not real, but their contact knew that regardless of whatever code she provided, it would be approved and they would follow the agreed-upon procedure of a private hangar with another aircraft prepared for flight upon arrival. In fact, as they touched down and were taxied to a hangar on the outskirts of the small airport, they saw the small propeller on an old plane already idling.

"Quickly," Natasha said, "We have to get airborne as soon as possible, this taxi is taking the other plane out in just a minute."

Clarke stood up and grabbed his metallic suitcase as he opened the door of the plane and hopped down about two meters to the ground. Natasha sat on the edge of the opening and lowered herself down as gracefully as she could. Both of them jogged across the small hangar to the plane and hopped in as the automated taxi attached itself to the front wheel and began exiting the hangar.

Natasha flipped on several switches as she got her bearings. This was a much different airplane, but it was equipped with the same tech that allowed her to customize the display. Effectively, this turned the controls from any plane to the pilot's preferred method of flight. She tweaked several things to adjust the sizing and space of several dials and gauges, then pulled on the headphones. Clarke automatically did the same, before remembering that he didn't need them. He shook his head and rolled his eyes as he returned the headphones to the console, when the voice cut in on Natasha's headphones and directly in Clarke's head.

"Lancair-600, 3249, you are cleared for takeoff on runway Delta. We will assist you with takeoff and initial exit from TXR according to your prescheduled flight plan Adolf. Do not alter course or disrupt this service."

"TXR Tower, cleared for assisted takeoff on runway Delta, 3249," said Natasha. Then the line cut to a low static. TXR Airport had cut off their transmission intentionally. Clarke was sure that this was to conceal any changes that were to happen after the plane left the ground and immediate airspace.

Natasha explained that this procedure was not employed often, but having assets in regional and local airports assisted in covert operations, albeit seldom. The flight from TXR to TXN was short and they didn't even get high enough above the ground to clear some of the taller buildings on the outskirts of the nearby city. Clarke estimated that they were probably 300 meters in altitude at the highest point of their flight. Then they followed a similar process at TXN airport and continued on their way for the longest stretch to the Houston area.

"You should get some sleep, Clarke," Natasha said. "The next few days will be long for you—I'm sure of it. The underground is a serious undertaking."

He looked over at her and was surprised that she knew what he was actually going to be doing. He sunk into his seat and tried to get some sleep. After a couple of restless minutes, he pulled out his screen and accessed the documents Natasha had sent him. The first was military doctrine and typical governmental response protocol with chapters titled, *Their Fault, Not Yours,* and *If You Give In, They Push Harder.* There wasn't really any solace in these words, and Clarke thought that if they did anything, they merely made it sound okay to let the injustice play out by simply following orders. It was uncomfortable to read and felt like it was part of a satire gone awry.

The second document was far more amusing. It was a short pamphlet filled with political cartoons and actual satire. Clarke instantly knew that this document would be against the law to possess, but he wasn't worried because it came directly from a captain in the army. Clearly it would be okay, and at a minimum he would be able to plead not guilty because he had not consented to receiving the document. He flipped through a couple pages and cracked a smile despite its contents. This did make him feel better, even though it was incredibly inappropriate and conveyed a morally skewed message. After he had finished a couple more panels of the book, he set down his screen and sat more upright in his seat.

"How do you know about my mission?" he asked Natasha.

"It's not all that complicated to figure out," she said with a smile. "The security briefings and battle updates are available to all officers who are engaged in any mission associated with the United States Homefront Command theater of war. I know where we are going just because I'm the one flying you there, and only a handful of analysts who developed the plan know that too. It really is simple to place the two pieces together." She let out a short laugh again.

"I hadn't really thought about it like that," Clarke said and shrugged. "I guess it really is quite obvious from the inside, but what do you think about it from the outside? Do you think the people in Houston will know who I am or what I'm doing?"

"Doubt it," she said, deadpan. "Nobody has ever done something like this before. No offense, but you're not a soldier, you're a civilian with a very unique placement and access. You know how this system works. You can get in there and no one will bat an eye. You belong there."

"What do you mean?"

She turned her head and stared at him for an uncomfortably long time before she spoke. "You were chosen because Colonel Hudson knows your father, Robert Prescott. You could say that she was the person who gave your dad the idea to be a patron of citizens second class."

Clarke's head reeled. "Do I know her? I mean—from before all of this."

"You're probably too young to have met her. It's possible that your dad probably never met her too. People who do that kind of stuff don't exactly try to network or broadcast it; they keep it a secret as well as anything else."

Clarke was more concerned for his father now. He knew that Robert was in a terrible mental state after Alex had died, and undoubtedly he was left in the same state when he was told that his only other son, Charlie, had died too. His mom would be doing the best she could. She probably wouldn't be visiting her sisters anymore because of the effect it would have on Robert. Claire may have been a distant mother but she was a very caring for her husband. She knew that Robert took the loss of Alex very gravely and that he sunk into a deep depression. She recognized that he would need her support more than she needed to have space and time away from all the reminders of her children.

When Alex died, she was the one who woke up in the middle of the night and comforted Robert. There was still deep pain that they both shared from their first loss, and now it would only be intensified. They needed compassion from each other and needed to share the burden of that loss. Sure, their closer friends were likely visiting to check in on them, and even the staff at the house would keep them company, but Clarke was the one who comforted Robert with his hugs. Who would do that now?

Clarke didn't think Robert had any hope left for him after a month without news. He also couldn't believe that Lieutenant Colonel Hudson would have informed his father of the covert mission. It was too risky on both accounts of mission secrecy and a fault-proof cover story. Colonel Hudson came across as a very wise and manipulative person since Clarke's first meeting with her, and after the conversation with Natasha just now, he believed that there was some darker motive still. What had the old woman said that was true, what was half true, and what was a flat-out lie?

"Do you trust Colonel Hudson?" Clarke blurted out. "I mean, she makes sense. It's all logical, but something feels wrong about it. Like, why me? Why Houston?"

"You were in the briefings, not me," Natasha said flatly with indifference, "you would know better than me. But I know what you mean about Colonel Hudson; it feels like she manipulates more than commands. I think that she is just all caught up in being special forces and gets away with so many things that she doesn't even care when it affects someone else's life. She's been doing this for decades, hasn't she? I'm not sure she will still be alive in the next few years anyway; have you seen her? She can barely walk!"

"That's true," Clarke said quietly. "She told me, though, that she was a civilian for a long time and was just really good at politics and getting things done her way. It sounded like she saw the injustice toward the other classes and wanted to fix it." He paused for a moment before continuing, "Well, I'm not so sure about that, is all. She makes me feel like I'm being used rather than actually answering government requirements."

"Clarke, she's been using you since you were born. I don't know what you expected."

"She said that she knew my dad. Not like personally or anything, but that she heard about him and knew that I would be perfect for this mission." He paused. "Something just doesn't feel right. It felt like she threatened my family if I didn't go on this mission, but she never said anything directly about that."

"I don't know," Natasha said, "she's never shared anything like that with me. I just fly guys like you wherever you need to go. The most I ever really learn is who you guys are and where you are going. I think they'd prefer that I never even meet you before the flight so I don't have a chance to get close to you." She furrowed her brow. "So, I don't hear any of this kind of stuff."

Clarke felt like he may have said too much about Colonel Hudson, but it came out of his mouth without his control. He felt compelled to say it, and the past few days made him feel that he needed to share his concerns with someone. Captain Coleman was his last chance to talk with someone who actually understood the situation. Whether she could—or would—do anything about it was yet to be seen, and honestly Clarke didn't care. He felt comfortable with Natasha and she seemed to be a genuinely kindhearted person. Clarke trusted her more than anyone else in his unit, despite the fact that he had only talked to her a collective ten minutes prior to today's flights.

The rest of their flight was uneventful. They talked about their shared school experiences with other citizens first class and the way students who paid their way into a quality education were shunned. This was similar to the antiquated private school systems that created a status symbol for the family that was worth more than the educational value itself. Citizens second class, like François, paid a high fee to be accepted into the prestigious schools for citizens first class, yet they were still taught by the subpar teachers and were not allowed to receive the full education of historic events and real-world truths of the injustice. Ironically, though, many of the families that paid for these upper-echelon schools knew about the discrimination and the power that the governing bodies had to control each of the different classes.

Citizens first class were taxed at a very low rate of eight percent, whereas citizens second class were taxed at twelve percent, and citizens third class were taxed at fifteen percent. Clarke made a point of talking about the fact that citizens second class weren't allowed to know what the rates were on the other classes, but he was told that citizens third class were taught these differences because they were never able to achieve upward mobility anyway. Showing them their discrimination kept them from reaching beyond their status. The forced cycle of poverty was so strong that the poor were powerless to change their situation and the ruling elite literally told them so. Aside from several instances of rioting and violent protests, which were quickly put down with lethal force, there have been no serious attempts to overthrow the ruling elite. Helplessness became a way of life, and citizens third class lived as little more than slaves.

Clarke hoped that it wouldn't always be the case. This was why he tried so hard to do the right thing and treat everyone as a human. His status as a citizen first class was not a privilege, but rather a responsibility. He was learning so much about the real world because of his current position in the army as an undercover agent. The corruption, the lies, the inequity all bothered him on such a deep level that he wanted to understand all of it and wouldn't risk losing his connection to that information even if it meant going against what he believed. He needed to know the truth and he would discover it in the underground efforts in Houston. Undoubtedly, he needed to learn a lot and the rest of the world needed to know it too, but he didn't know how to share what he was going to learn. It seemed like an uphill battle that would never stop. The State monitored all internet traffic and no news agencies would publish anything without the consent of the government—another violation of the Bill of Rights, which was superseded by a mid-2060s sweeping legislative bill that funded dam revitalization, railroad modernization, metropolis magnetic streeting, and—to little surprise—the repeal of freedom of the press. Most of the press was under government watch after the bill became law, and when any anti-government agenda was published, the media outlet was stripped of its status and dissolved as an organization. Over time, only several news agencies survived.

Clarke's school teachers would show weekly updates from the approved DoESS newsreels, which were heavily regulated to ensure that the proper content met the proper citizen class. He told Natasha about how François would have news shown to him about different crops being harvested and the newest loan rates for small businesses. Clarke's class, on the other hand, would be shown world news and important legislative updates from both the regional government in Atlanta, as well as the national government, which was relocated to Nashville.

Natasha thought it was interesting that the school-aged kids in the Southern region saw any news media. In the Western region, nobody was allowed to get State news until they turned fifteen and were allowed to drive by themselves. They both agreed that different regions played a part in how children grew up. The states were becoming more and more diverse as the regional governments' policies began to change further and further. Over the course of a couple decades, American culture was diverging.

Eventually, they started their approach to their destination and called up to the tower. "BMT Tower, this is Zenith-950, 6464, approaching from south-east, inbound requesting touch and go with information Tango," Natasha said, sounding far more comfortable and confident. Clearly, it was the first transition that she was the most hesitant about. Afterward, her nerves had calmed down. Here, she was not going to be conducting any additional maneuvers or anything that could get her arrested by the local authorities and processed under local laws. They were liable to stand trial if they did anything outside of the law, even though they were military. The federal government may regulate the country, but local laws were still enforced.

"Zenith-950, 6464, this is BMT Tower, continue straight in and proceed to hangar Bravo 19." There was a brief pause. "Be advised, your controls will not be taken until taxi begins."

"Continuing straight with unassisted approach and landing, 6464," said Natasha calmly and then hung up her headphones. She looked over at Clarke as if to see if he heard the radio. He nodded.

"Well, this means that I will be doing my first actual landing in about six months. Did you hear that over the radio?" she said with a smirk. Local and regional airports did not have the manpower to support that many takeoffs and landings each day. Some of them were completely overwhelmed with traffic, while some just didn't have the proper equipment or personnel trained to use the equipment. BMT was definitely an airport that didn't have the equipment.

"Will that be a problem?" Clarke asked quickly. "I mean, I probably could have done what you've done so far without any real training."

"Trust me, you couldn't do it without training, and no, this will not be a problem. I've flown and landed hundreds of times. This plane is actually one of my favorite models and I know it very well. We'll be fine."

They made their final approach and landed smoothly. In fact, it felt like a better landing than the other times that day and Clarke was genuinely impressed. She clearly knew what she was doing and wasn't afraid to show off. They slowed to a near stop before the taxi connected and guided the plane to the terminal, where Clarke would disembark and continue his mission as citizen first class Daniel Polo, a young businessman with a new factory outside Houston.

Chapter 17—Welcome to the Underground

"**G**ood morning, sir," the attendant said as Clarke walked toward the gate from the plane. "How was your flight?"

Clarke was prepared for a small reception based on the briefings he had received. In sum, his cover was that he set up his factory while he was still living in Alabama, so no one had actually seen or spoken with him yet. He simply had to step in as Mr. Polo, because the man was not real and the military created the factory for this specific cover. Clarke discovered that this mission had been in the works for months before he was selected to play the part. The cover was incredibly well thought out and simple for him to follow, because it echoed so much of what he was in reality—a young, white citizen first class male from a religiously active underground family with affluence. The finer details were different—for instance, his alter ego was from Huntsville, Alabama, rather than New Boston, Alabama, and he was supposedly twenty-two years old, not eighteen.

"Sir?" the gate attendant said when Clarke paused in shock. Sure, he was prepared, but when it came to it, he was caught off guard.

"Sorry, the flight was fine. I'm just tired," he finally said and continued past the counter toward the exit. Clarke noticed that the display on the counter's screen read 0300 and realized that they had flown eight hours, had two stops, and flew all over the central portion of the United States, only to end up a couple hundred kilometers from New Boston. He smiled to himself as he continued down the small airport terminal. It was a very quaint airport and he appreciated the décor. It had clearly been a much larger airport in the past, but was reduced in size due to the dramatic decrease in air traffic over the past couple of decades. As a result, the bulk of flights in and out were kept to just one terminal, but special or overflow traffic was diverted to a secondary terminal where privacy and upper-class touches remained present. Carpeted hallways in the primary terminal were replaced by traditional hardwood floors inlaid with precious metals for the VIPs. The stone finished walls and archways of the secondary terminal took the place of the cinderblock and square hallways of the primary terminal. The secondary terminal had huge floor-to-ceiling continuous windows overlooking a small forest on one side and the runways on the other side, compared to the primary terminal's small antiquated bay windows only facing the runways to bring in natural light. Clarke was in the secondary terminal despite a lack of air traffic.

He noticed that the terminal was nearly empty. Several people were standing by a small restaurant and a couple of soldiers were posted by the USO. Clarke kept his eyes forward in an attempt to avoid all contact with the soldiers and breathed a sigh of relief when he was sufficiently past them. He passed a bathroom on the right and was glad he used the plane's toilet before he got off because this one looked like it had seen better days.

That's odd, he thought, *everything else is in fine repair, what happened here?*

The appearance of the decrepit bathroom was an eyesore compared to everything else lining the hallway and it disturbed Clarke. He didn't know it, but that eyesore was an entrance to the underground he was assigned to infiltrate. If only he knew how close he was to a successful mission already.

Eventually he approached the entryway of the airport with his bag behind him, reflecting artificial sunlight in all directions. Before he reached the end of the terminal, Clarke saw a small group of people wearing black suits like the medical czar at the New Boston Hospital who had helped him send a message. He didn't know it, but Robert did get his message. It made Robert snap out of a period of mourning because he now knew that his last child was not dead—a miracle.

Clarke missed his parents more than he thought was possible, despite only being away from them for a short amount of time. The longest time Clarke had been separated from his parents before now was only a couple of days. Clarke was thinking about how he said goodbye to his parents for the last time as he came to a stop in front of the group of suits, who in turn stood up a little bit straighter and pulled their hands out of their pockets as a sign of respect.

"Mr. Polo?" one of them asked. Clarke recognized the man as the leader of the group due to the rank on his epaulettes. The man was balding a little, wore a higher-quality suit, and had an expensive screen attached to his left arm.

"That's me," Clarke said naturally. Two of the men behind the leader went forward and took his bag through the exit on the right. Clarke watched calmly and said, "I'm ready to get to the hotel. How far is it?"

"Right this way, sir. It will be about a fifteen-minute ride from here. Forgive the old-fashioned transport, sir, it's a high-quality machine and far safer if we have to leave the roadway."

"Why would we have to do that, Mr—?" Clarke asked, prolonging the 'r' in question.

"Mr. Young, sir," he said. "We would only do so if the fighting came too close to us, but tonight is quiet, so it should be fine." Mr. Young smiled broadly. Clarke was outwardly showing his calm, but inside he felt like he was about to vomit and cry at the same time. He was a minute into his mission and he was about to crack; he felt pathetic.

With his resolve firm, however, he shrugged and reached for a handshake, saying, "I'll trust your decision on this." Then he winked. "I'm the new guy in town and it looks like you know what you're talking about."

"Thank you, sir," Mr. Young said and shook Clarke's hand. "I'm happy to be in your service." He then gave a short bow, revealing just how badly his hair was thinning, and indicated that Clarke should follow the leading suit out the doorway to the waiting convoy of antique up-armored trucks and jeeps. He did so, and the remaining entourage followed behind him. Clarke was beginning to feel that he was vastly unprepared for this region, let alone the actual war. He felt his hands sweating again as he reached for his baseball cap to nervously adjust it. If anybody noticed, they didn't say anything and probably shrugged it off as a spoiled billionaire's son's first experience in the real world.

The first suit, who happened to be a woman, walked directly toward the third vehicle, a dark green Jeep 4x4, and opened the door for Clarke to get in. The other suits went to several different vehicles and climbed in. The strain when they closed the door made it look like it was incredibly heavy and he was glad in this instance that he wasn't going to have to close his by himself. Clarke climbed up and into the back seat of his Jeep and then the suit hopped in after him and groaned as she swung the door shut. Then she climbed over the front seat and sat in the driver's chair.

"How heavy is that door?" Clarke asked with genuine interest.

"About one hundred kilos," the woman said. "It's not the weight, though, it's the damn hinges. No matter what we do to fix them, they won't stay lined up, and it becomes seriously inconvenient to use them."

"How else would you use the cars, though?"

"We normally climb through the tops," she said, pointing upward while simultaneously starting the engine. "We are starting to move out now, though. I won't be able to talk with you while we are moving, sir, my apologies."

"Don't worry about it, I understand," Clarke said as the jeep started forward. Over the hum of the engine, he heard the road underneath the tires. He was both alarmed and excited by the bumps in the road. This was his first ride in a traditional electric vehicle and he was amazed at the primitive nature of this kind of travel. The magnetic streeting in the 2060s started the downfall of many typically commuter vehicles, but the infrastructure took time to convert minor roadways. Many electric battery and solar-powered methods of transportation were still manufactured up until the late 2090s because it took so long. Of course, specialty vehicles and vehicles specifically marketed for off-road travel, such as jeeps and work trucks, which they were currently traveling in, were still actively being built. Nonetheless, Clarke had never had a reason to be in one because of his family's affluence and position in New Boston.

Clarke was amazed by how incredibly unsafe the jeep felt, and he was exhilarated at how it actually operated. He tried to conceal his enthusiasm, though, and pulled open his screen, flipped it to the highest security settings, and altered the display to only be visible at the angle his eyes were looking at the screen. This technology made it so someone literally standing over your shoulder couldn't read your screen. The protocol was developed during the aftermath of a national security incident in the previous administration, where an undersecretary caught a glimpse of nuclear launch codes and nearly launched several of them before he was shot by an old night security guard making his rounds. The interesting part, though, was how the security guard almost missed the secretary because he had to pee and backtracked to the bathroom.

Clarke's anxiety was reeling again, and he just wanted to ensure that he didn't forget anything from his set of instructions. After his retinas were scanned and the security screen locked on to his eyes, he navigated to the briefing information and reviewed it several times. He was going to check in at Les Misérables Hotel, where he would connect to the DoDLW servers via a dirty connection and await further instructions. He guessed that it was just a measure to ensure that if he was caught before he got to the hotel, nothing would have really been compromised. He closed his screen and peered out the bulletproof window.

The road seemed to trail past him so slowly because he was used to frictionless travel, which was well over 200 km/h on the highway. This jeep, on the other hand, was probably going slower than 100 km/h. It amused him to feel the bumps in the road, which were left in disrepair because the actual surfaces were largely antiquated anyway. Resulting from the unbalanced roadways, the driver would actually change lanes to avoid larger holes completely. Clarke thought it was interesting that driving an old-style car actually took skill, because the magnetic streeting made it possible to have a true autopilot—the road wouldn't let accidents happen. He could drive his family's car at the age of twelve without issue, yet he would not be allowed to drive it by himself until he had turned eighteen. The teen-car Alex had driven was lost in the accident and Claire refused to buy another one because she was convinced that the model was faulty. That didn't really bother Clarke all that much; he was comfortable sitting in the back of cars anyway, and this trip was no different.

Clarke turned his attention back to the inside of the car as they exited from the highway and pulled onto a smaller road system. The driver slowed to a stop in a small town with only several buildings over ten stories tall and pushed on her earpiece. Clarke noticed that the rest of the caravan had stopped as well. The driver listened to the instructions through her earpiece:

"All vehicles, we are at a security halt for five minutes. We are sending out the advanced team to check into the hotel and conduct a final sweep for invalids and concealed dangers. Be advised, Mr. Polo is to remain in the car until deposited on location."

Unbeknownst to the driver, Clarke heard the instructions as well and he felt that he was actually in danger just by entering Houston. His citizenship status warranted protection due to the ongoing conflict just south of the area, and so many wealthy individuals moved away, far away. Citizens first class didn't really move into war zones all that often unless they had something to bring to the fight. In this situation, Clarke was posing as a manufacturer, but he didn't know what exactly he was supposed to be manufacturing.

It began to dawn on him that he was likely doing something nefarious. He was in an armored caravan running on traditional wheels, of all things, and they were treating him like he was a high-value target for some enemy troops. This was not what he agreed to. He was supposed to go into the city as just another civilian and find the underground, where the rebels were moving equipment back and forth. Clarke thought that the underground would be fairly obvious because they were moving vehicles of war through some sort of a tunnel system. Now he realized that he would be really pressed in simply getting out of the guards' watch, let alone wanting to be out of their protection.

Clarke's heart was racing as he continued to sit as nonchalantly as he could in the back seat of the up-armored transport. He felt himself sweating through his shirt and his foot started to unconsciously tap up and down.

Then the vehicle began slowly rolling forward and Clarke felt a wave of relief, which was short-lived because just a moment later he saw an intense white light off to the right side of the vehicle in a north-northwest direction. He saw it arc higher, and as it happened, the driver floored the jeep and shouted to no one in particular, "Here we go! Let's get it!" She laughed like an excited veteran headed into combat and, a little more disturbing, she laughed like a reckless child about to do something she knows is bad.

"Buckle up, sir!" she said moments before the artillery round impacted short of its target. This type of artillery, which Clarke would later learn about in detail, was effective regardless, and the shockwave was strong enough to uproot trees and turn over transport cars from over 400 meters away. In other words, if the Fire Direction Center was off target by nearly a half kilometer, it would still prove to be an effective round and was considered a marginal hit. The shockwave hit the jeep as it was accelerating past eighty km/h and Clarke felt the weighed-down vehicle lift off the ground on the right side.

"That one wasn't even close," the driver said as Clarke reached for his seat belt and fumbled with it. His hands were shaking so severely that he couldn't get it to line up properly for a minute as the jeep climbed past 110 km/h. Another round arced high. The round illuminated several kilometers as bright as daylight as it rocketed toward the convoy. The leading vehicle slammed on its breaks and so did the other trucks and jeeps—all except the jeep Clarke was in. Instead, the headlights were turned off and something fell off the jeep, making it extremely lighter.

"I've got you, Clarke," the driver said quietly enough that it wasn't registered by her earpiece, but Clarke caught it over the whine of the electric engine as it turned sharply off road directly toward the artillery point.

Who in the world is this? Clarke thought to himself. *If they know that name, then they know my mission. Why would—How did they—Is this a good thing?* His thoughts raced as fast as the jeep was moving over the rough terrain. Clarke had never experienced anything like it. The round landed behind them and on the far side of the road, not more than a hundred meters away from the stopped caravan. He looked through the rear window of the jeep and saw several trucks in the front half of the convoy get launched into the air toward them and the trailing vehicles being pushed, flipped, and otherwise disabled as a result of shrapnel piercing them.

"They're all dead, aren't they," Clarke said as he turned around. His driver nodded and didn't say anything else. He felt a little sick again, just like with that poor soldier at the airport with his suitcase. Clarke then reached to find something to vomit in. He started muttering prayers under his breath as he looked under the seat cushions, in the seat back liners, and in the storage compartments on the door for a little bag or box, or anything. There was nothing. The driver pointed to the glove box, as she couldn't reach it.

"Get up here, and get the sick bag before you make me sick, man," she said as a third round launched into the night and the jeep began cruising at about 140 km/h on a small abandoned state road toward Lavon and Lavon Lake. The driver pointed at the third round after Clarke climbed over the center console and found his sick bag, which he promptly used.

"That one is to take them out completely," she said with a sardonic grin. "Well, that went all right, didn't it?"

Clarke tied up his bag and set it down in one of the cup holders while furrowing his brow. "Who do you think you are?" he said indignantly. "I need to get to my hotel and start up my business headquarters relocation." He said this on the fly, as the documents he had were so bare-bones that the only critical piece of information was that he get to Les Misérables Hotel at all costs.

"Clarke," the driver said, "I'm Analyn Zheng. I'm on your team."

"Oh." He was dumbfounded. He didn't know what to do.

"Things went to hell, and this plan would have ended up with you dead at that hotel tomorrow morning." Clarke looked over quizzically before Analyn continued, "They were going to poison your dinner, man. You didn't stand a chance."

"What went wrong?" Clarke said a little quickly, his voice cracking. His heart was still beating fast with adrenaline, anxiety, stress, and, oddly enough, relief. He cleared his throat and intentionally relaxed his shoulders against the seat back and lessened his grip on the armrest and center console. His sweaty hands left imprints on the soft fabric and leather.

Analyn was grinning and then explained, "The underground knew you were coming, and they wanted you on their side. From what a little birdy told me; you want to be on their side too."

Clarke looked away and hung his head in thought. He didn't know what he should do or if there would be a way for him to make it out of this situation alive if he refused. His pounding heartbeat started to subside as he realized that he was going into friendly hands, though; after all, Analyn was his teammate.

"So what side are you on, Analyn?" Clarke said, trying to both avoid an awkward silence and garner more information about his own situation.

"I'm not on anybody's side, Clarke," she said, then quickly added, "well, I guess I'm committed after this little maneuver, though." Both of them laughed a little bit more than was comfortable for either of them, but it broke the tension well enough.

"So, you're calling me Clarke, my cover name is Daniel, and my real name is—"

"Don't say it!" Analyn said, cutting him off. "Your true name is something that should never be said to anyone. Remember, you officially died. If you do anything using that name, the entire State police and federal army will come crashing down on us, not just you. This movement is far more important than getting sentimental about your name."

"Geez, okay, fine then." They sat in silence for a moment as Analyn drove the jeep around several larger impact craters and off road to avoid several disabled military vehicles. Clarke opened his mouth to try and speak but closed it when he decided to keep his question to himself. It was obvious that Analyn was not happy with him nearly saying his true name. He remembered back when he was at the park with his brother and saw that *1984* imagery for the first time and shuddered. He thought back on how the government monitored nearly all unsecure locations. It would be true for Houston not only because it was a major city, but also because it was an active war zone. Undoubtedly, the State was listening in for anything that would help push the Mexican army back and purge the resistance from their streets. So maybe saying his real name wasn't a good idea after all.

"You should use the name Clarke," Analyn said. "No one knows the name Daniel other than a few of the key leaders in the Revolutionaries. Most of the higher-ups only knew who Clarke was because the spy network is heavily classified. Only the general has all the intelligence. It'll be easier to explain when we get there."

Clarke was amazed at how complicated his situation was. He remembered receiving his enhancements from doctors and nurses who knew him, and there were several other indicators along the way, but what else happened behind the scenes? Which people were spies tracking him? Was it just some of the doctors or were people like Dan and Colonel Hudson involved? He was thinking back hard on the past couple weeks and visualizing all of the major events that took place. He had a feeling that several of his 'friends' were actually spying for the underground. One that came to him in particular was Captain Coleman. She was very forthcoming about so much information, likely because there was absolutely no monitoring up in the sky. And what on earth was the Revolutionaries?

"This is incredible," Clarke said as he began to accept his reality. "This operation was very well coordinated. Were you in on it from the beginning?"

"Nah," Analyn said coolly, "I was a part of the plan like you were, though. They put a little bird into the ear of some high-ranking military officer and let it play out. I think that the selection committee was in on it too; how else can you explain the three of us being picked?"

"I'm not sure what you mean."

"Me, you, and Lewis. All of us are from party members' families, we all were trained in code making as kids, and are all part of the underground already. We were selected for some higher reason, but I had to get you here safe before they will tell me what exactly we are doing."

Just then they started to slow down as they made a sharp curve toward the lake and came to a stop about a hundred meters away from the shoreline. Analyn pulled her earpiece out and put the car into park as she waited. Both of them surveyed their surroundings in the dark night and the soft glow from the light pollution from Houston. Clarke didn't know it, but they were only twenty kilometers from the heart of the city and only thirty kilometers or so from active combat. He took a moment to appreciate the stars he could see through the thin layer of smog drifting away from the city. Despite his own situation, he smiled at God's amazing universe.

About five minutes had come and gone when out in the middle of the lake there was a quick green flash, like from a laser pointer shining on the water. Analyn put the car back into drive and slowly proceeded toward the lake. Clarke began to recognize that there were actually two laser pointers—one green slightly off to their right and one red slightly off to their left. Analyn used the two indicators to line herself up so the lasers were reflecting just outside the wheel well. Once she was satisfied and the lasers recognized that they were aligned, Analyn accelerated into the lake.

Clarke had heard about this type of tunnel before and had gone through one when he was a young boy. Otherwise he would have been freaking out. Instead, he was thrilled. Analyn looked over at him and smiled to see her compatriot's excitement. About ten meters into the lake, they began to go down a slope that very quickly made them disappear under the water. This tunnel was a zero-density barrier between the water and was virtually invisible. Essentially, water flowed freely through it until it was engaged. Analyn explained it to Clarke like a breathable plastic bag tethered to the ground and inflated only when it was being used—a sort of on-demand bubble using a specific frequency, not unlike a garage door opener. Satellite surveillance, ground reconnaissance, and electronic equipment would never pick it up because it wasn't something that could really be viewed. Clarke saw the water flow around the jeep completely as they descended on an invisible ramp toward the bottom of the lake. When it went completely dark, Analyn turned the headlights back on and ended their blackout drive. Eventually, the invisible ramp met the solid surface of the lake bed and continued underground into an actual tunnel.

They had entered the underground in Houston.

Chapter 18—Reunion

The tunnel continued for a couple of miles, snaking deeper and deeper under the earth, and Clarke lost all sense of direction. All he knew was that Houston had done some very serious emergency preparation and knew exactly what precautions were necessary when the war got to them. Clarke was impressed with the nearly perfect archways every hundred meters, which made it easy to keep track of distance. On one pillar he actually noticed a sign with the exact depth, cardinal direction, and distance from the exit they had just come down. The financing on this network was impressive.

Analyn came to a stop at an intersection and made a turn, which led them to a large open room, where an entire fleet of vehicles were charging and ready to be dispatched. Amazingly, there were groups of people acting like this was an average day and like nothing had happened.

"How many people are down here, a couple hundred?" Clarke asked impulsively before he could bite his tongue.

"Thousands," Analyn said. "There are places here that I haven't seen yet. It's an entire city under the city, man. There are over a hundred entrances and I gave up trying to map it because it's so big. I just asked for a map after a couple weeks and they gave me one."

"Hundreds of entrances?" Clarke echoed and Analyn nodded. "How do they keep them secure?"

"You saw what we just drove through, right?" Analyn shook her head, rolled her eyes, and drew in a long breath like she was going to explain something simple to a small child. "Well, obviously there aren't a hundred lakes like that one, but there are a few. And then there are false walls in public bathrooms like *Harry Potter*, doors in trees like *The Nightmare before Christmas*, and false sewer covers like the *Teenage Mutant Ninja Turtles.*"

"I'm not sure I understand you," Clarke said with a puzzled expression. He almost laughed at the absurdity of what Analyn was saying but decided against it when she sighed again. He didn't know it, but her family collected pop culture items and prevented its destruction. Analyn motioned for him to get out of the car and walk with her toward a smaller, person-sized tunnel jutting off of the large open room. She went on to explain how each of the three references was from a major work of art during the late 20th and early 21st centuries, which made them obscure enough so most people today would never think of them independently, and since those books and movies were outlawed, only members of the underground would even know what to look for.

Just like the road they came in on, there were posts in the smaller tunnel with arrows and distances pointing to underground landmarks. For instance, after they had walked fifty meters, there was a support post with the number fifty and an arrow pointing to the direction they had just come from. Analyn and Clarke came to a larger tunnel with a handful of people milling about with carts of vegetables and other goods for sale in a small open-air style market lit by artificial windows every five meters or so. The smell of handcrafted furniture lacquer mixed with the large bowls of traditional spices, filling the area with both a sense of normal life and the stark contrast of living underground. Some shopkeepers wore soft expressions of acceptance, while others hung their heads in defeat, and still more were clearly happy to be free. Clarke began to take into consideration how much of a financial cost this network must have incurred. This must have run close to the trillion-dollar amount from what he had just seen. It was incredible; the walls were constructed out of milled stone and granite, while the floors were more of an 18th-century cobblestone. There were no wires of any kind indicating that there was at least one central power source transmitting to all devices in the area. Clarke pulled up his screen and noticed the soft blue band across the side indicating that it was actively receiving power. Usually, these types of devices would only cover a hundred square meters or so, but there wasn't a single power source in sight, which probably meant that the power unit was built into the tunnel somehow.

"They are embedded in the walls," Analyn said when she noticed her new friend looking at his screen. "The guys who are paying for this stuff are filthy rich and want to benefit everyone down here."

Clarke nodded and put his screen away as they made their way across the square into another tunnel. They continued through the network of passages, rooms, vehicle access roads, and public buildings cut out of the tunnel walls for about a half-hour until they came upon a great hall filled with beautiful stained-glass windows, paintings, and iconic imagery of Christian, Jewish, and even Islamic art. Clarke was awestruck when he saw an actual fresco of Da Vinci's *Last Supper*. The plaster image was about four meters tall and twelve meters wide. Some other artwork caught his attention too, but he didn't know the names. One was of an old man hugging what appeared to be a large scroll, which was called *Love of the Torah*, and several mosaics filled with calligraphy in Persian and Arabic. Clarke recognized the script and remembered being taught in school that it must be Islamic in nature because for a Muslim the word was never made flesh and it was therefore a sin to depict God in art. In Islam, it is blasphemous to show God in human form because, according to their faith, God never took human form—Jesus was a prophet and nothing more. Many Islamic artists focused on geometric patterns and beautiful script to honor the word of God.

Clarke didn't want to leave the room but Analyn was growing impatient, so he stole a last glance at the great hall and proceeded through another tunnel with his newfound friend and guide. Eventually, they came to a T-intersection and made a left turn, which came to a dead end about fifty meters later. Analyn winked at Clarke and pretended to count fifteen bricks up from the ground, two bricks from the left, and pushed on a particularly grimy-looking brick that countless others used and hadn't bothered to clean. Clarke guessed that the grime he had seen was not obvious to the natural eye and Analyn wanted to go through the motions of showing a new refugee how to enter the door. The door easily swung inward to the underground resistance headquarters complex, where people in gray jumpsuits were busy working at different terminals lining the perimeter of the room. There were several small doors on either side of this main room and another door on the far end that was higher than the others because it was situated behind a small three-step staircase and a small balcony overseeing the work space. Above the steps was a red and white flag with one black star and a gold fringe—it was the commander's office. Clarke caught several majors and a few colonels poking their heads out of their offices who quickly turned back around. One of the screens a lieutenant was working at showed incoming artillery on the southeast side of Houston and several buildings collapsing—it was a live feed based on what Clarke could see.

No wonder everyone is ignoring us, Clarke thought to himself. *Combat is happening right now.* Analyn motioned for Clarke to stand by as she went and knocked on the far door. A middle-aged man wearing a black jumpsuit greeted her and gave her a hug. The man had a gold star on one lapel and the half arc on the other. He looked vaguely familiar but Clarke couldn't place it. If he was supposed to know him, Clarke was sure that he would figure out where he knew the man from. During the embrace Clarke could hear the conversation and tried to give them privacy, but one of the first things that Analyn said was, "Clarke can hear us across this room over all the noise in the office." So, the general didn't even bother to try and filter out the rest of the conversation. The man was aware of the enhancements and probably played a big part in ensuring that the tracking devices were disabled.

"Good morning, young man. I am General Morgan, commander of the Revolutionaries," he said. "Come on over here into my office; I have some questions for you, as well as some answers." He then turned around and walked back through his door. Analyn gestured for Clarke to hurry up, and nobody else in the room bothered to question why Clarke was there. They either knew already or they just didn't care. Regardless, Clarke felt awkward going through the headquarters without really being screened. Then again, the general just invited him to his personal office, so clearly Clarke was a welcomed individual.

Clarke walked up the steps and entered the door cautiously. Something felt odd but he couldn't place what it was. He was uncomfortable in this situation and wasn't sure if he was considered a prisoner of war or a defector. He looked around the rather large office and saw a grand desk centered on one wall with a faux window behind it showcasing an open field and rolling hills in the distance. Knowing that they were deep underground, it was a very disturbing and unnatural sensation to see rolling green hills. Either way, the warm light radiated across the desk as if it were mid-morning. The general had several small display stands with statues of religious figures, ancient or mythical heroes, and a fine dining service for four. On the opposite wall was a small conference table for about eight officers to sit and discuss various issues and finalize plans with the general's consent. A large screen was mounted to the wall where the table terminated. In the center of the room was a small couch, several armchairs, and a solid wood coffee table with a couple books, stacks of actual printed papers, and a set of Russian dolls.

Clarke only took a moment to survey the room and instantly realized that the general was actually his uncle. The dolls were deliberately placed on the table so Clarke would see them and make the connection. He had never met Jo-Ann's father—he was always away for something—but he instinctively knew that it was him. Now Clarke understood why Jo-Ann's father was away so often. He must have been coordinating this base for two or three decades. He also thought that maybe General Morgan was responsible for starting the actual underground in New Boston. New Boston's underground only really started around the time Clarke was born, and it was just coming to fruition when he was getting ready to finish high school. The crude tunnels were being developed so slowly over time that it had taken nearly eighteen years for about five kilometers' worth of tunnels and meeting spaces to be completed. If the funding for Houston's underground was similar to New Boston, then Houston must have been started over forty years ago and was clearly the heart of the network.

"Well," the general said, "take a seat, Clarke, we've been expecting you."

"That you have been, sir," he said in response as he moved to one of the armchairs and reached for the Russian dolls. "How is your daughter? I haven't seen her for quite some time."

The general smiled in recognition and sat across from him on the couch. Clarke began taking out the dolls and setting them down on the table in a neat row. The first one had St. Stephen holding three stones and a palm frond. Analyn let out a fake sneeze from the corner of the room and used it as an excuse to get a tissue from one of the tables near Clarke so as to see what he was doing from a better angle.

"She's doing well enough. Actually, I'm pretty sure she is getting ready to start her tenth grade, the year she officially learns about this war. Tell me, what did the school teach you?"

"Not the half of it," Clarke said and set down the fourth doll very meticulously. It was a beautiful rendition of St. Sebastian with several small arrows sticking out of him. This of course was the saint his church community was named after and made him homesick. "They do a very good job explaining the events leading up to the actual invasion for the citizens first class, but several of my friends weren't told anything about that history. Instead, they were taught local history and a make-believe story about why so many people immigrated to the Southeast region."

"That's what I thought. The teachers either don't know themselves, are threatened to stay silent, or have bought into the system. It's sad, really." The general leaned forward and watched Clarke intently as he laid St. Valentine's doll down which was wearing dark red vestments.

"I was hoping that you could tell me why I'm here though, sir. I've been dragged around and have been given so many names, I'm not sure who I am anymore." Clarke was speaking truthfully and came off a little arrogant but he didn't care. He was tired of being tossed around and acting as a pawn in some grandiose game between corrupt politicians, a corrupt armed force, and whatever the Revolutionaries really were. Clarke trusted that God would deliver him to a safe end, but where was that end? He knew that he had tried to stay on the right path, but this was getting to be a very difficult thing over the past couple weeks. The simple fact that he was responsible for several people's deaths was inexcusable, and he was beginning to feel that hiding underground was wrong. He didn't want to hide anymore or pretend to be someone he wasn't. He was weary and wanted rest.

Clarke put the second to last of the nesting dolls–St. Dennis which was holding his head in his own hands—on the table, then turned his attention to the littlest one, which was still in his hand. "You know, sir, these things sometimes conceal tokens for safekeeping. Actually, I remember one time when I was shown how to open them, and I was very surprised at what I had found. Mostly because I had no idea what it was. I still don't know what it is, but I've seen it a lot recently and know that it has something to do with this place, and well, you, sir."

"Go on," the general said patiently as if he knew that Clarke needed to get some steam out. The man had seen so much, and he wanted this young man to feel comfortable and better about what was going on. Rather than interrupting him, he let Clarke continue expressing himself.

"Well, sir, I was hoping you could tell me what it is."

"What is what?"

"This." Clarke raised the small doll of St. Anthony which was decorated with white lily stalks and softly shook it. Then he began to open it the same way his dream had shown him not so long ago, saying, "It's the golden half circle on your lapel, sir. It's important and I don't know why."

The general smiled widely and stood up. He put his hand out and indicated that Clarke should remain seated on the couch, then walked over to the desk on the side of the room and opened a drawer. He rummaged around for a moment and pulled out small trinkets before lifting up a large book. He then closed the drawer and walked back to the couch, asking Clarke, "What can you tell me about fish?"

"Well, a lot, sir," Clarke intuitively replied. "I used to fish all the time as a kid." His voice trailed off as he remembered Alex.

The general let out a short chuckle. Then he opened the book to about the middle, where he read, "But they said to him, 'five loaves and two fish are all we have here.' Then he said, 'Bring them here to me,' and he ordered the crowds to sit down on the grass. Taking the five loaves and two fish, and looking up to heaven, he said the blessing, broke the loaves, and gave them to the disciple, who in turn gave them to the crowds."

"Okay, but what does that have to do with my question? What is that half circle?" Clarke was getting irritated with the older man's stalling.

"What about this one." General Morgan flipped through a couple of pages. "As he was walking by the Sea of Galilee, he saw two brothers, Simon who is called Peter, and his brother Andrew, casting a net into the sea; they were fishermen. He said to them, 'Come after me, and I will make you fishers of men.'"

Clarke recognized the passage but didn't understand what it had to do with his question still. The symbol was a golden arc with no reference or coding on it. The readings the general had just read were great and all, but it wasn't answering his question.

"Ancient Christians used the ichthys as a symbol for God himself," General Morgan said in a hushed voice, leaning over the table. This conversation was the boldest pronouncement of religion that Clarke had ever seen since he was drafted, and it felt as though it was not just taboo, but dangerous. They locked eyes and Clarke swallowed hard before breaking away.

"They would draw a half circle in markets, or on walls, or in their clothing when they needed help. Other Christians would see that symbol and draw the second half to make the ichthys." He stared at Clarke blankly, and when he saw that Clarke still hadn't understood, he took a piece of paper from the stack on the table and a pen from his pocket. "Look here. This is the half arc you are familiar with." He drew the shape. "It was a symbol of distress. Then someone who could help would come along and finish it up like this." He drew the inverse arc so two points connected on one side and the arcs intersected at the other side. "Ichthys."

A rush of memory flooded Clarke's head and he reeled backward as all his thoughts focused on the man who took Alex, the medical czar in the hospital who sent a message to his family, the Russian dolls both from his past and just now. All of these people were somehow connected to the underground and he had missed such an easy symbol. Clarke couldn't believe that he missed the symbolism, considering how often he had seen it recently, because although it was subtle, it was completely obvious if you were looking for it. He stood up and felt dizzy with anxiety. Analyn rushed over and steadied him.

"What is going on—why am I here? What do you want?" Clarke was nearly shouting. He was feeling trapped. All of his emotion and loss of control over his situation brought on a feeling of futility. He felt powerless, like a pawn in some grand scheme.

"I want you safe," the general said. "Your mother is very dear to me and I made a promise to her about ten years ago, just after your brother was taken."

"What did my mom ask you to do?"

"She made me swear that when you came of age, I would bring you here." He stood up and walked back to his desk and placed the Bible back in the drawer. Then he walked over to a small box and pulled out several handwritten letters that had yellowed with age. As he read over them himself, he shut the lid to the box and slowly walked back to the couch with a gentle smile on his face. There was silence for a little while as General Morgan read over the letter.

"I knew when that terrible accident happened she would ask for you to be protected, so I began making contacts with the military and infiltrated as far as I could to make sure you were drafted into a program that would get you out of Alabama. I don't expect you to understand it, but that place is a lot less safe than here. Here you will be able to live freely and grow up in a just society, like it was generations ago. The only downside is—"

"The only downside is that I'm going to permanently live underground, is that it?" Clarke couldn't believe the words that were coming out of his mouth. He was overcome with emotion thinking about Alex again, and how his mother had sent him away with a letter just like a draft notice. In a way, his mother's letter was more definitive, she sent him away with stinging words he was never supposed to know about.

"Yes," he paused. "You are now officially part of the underground and will have the opportunity to take on any profession you wish and associate with anyone regardless of citizenship class because it doesn't exist down here. If only you knew the extent of our network, you would feel more freedom than you have ever known."

"What if I don't want it?"

"What do you mean?"

"What if I don't want to just stop at my own freedom; what if I want to help others become free? Can I do that? Maybe join your movement and fight like they are up in the streets?" Clarke felt a firm resolve build up inside him as a rush of determination and the sensation of his calling came to fruition. He had been moved by God and knew that he would be a defender of the weak and fight for freedom above the ground too.

"That can be arranged, but I'd rather you be safe, like your mother asked of me." The general was getting sentimental as he pored over the letters again. "You know that she had more influence in New Boston than your father did, right? She actually coordinated the long-range tunnels to the suburbs and adjacent cities. Without her, New Boston would likely be completely written off our defensive posture, but we will try to pull them into our network. You see, our tunnels reach several hundred kilometers and are nearly connected to Tulsa, Memphis, and New Orleans. The Revolutionaries have been asked to try and reach New Boston, but not to engage in any combat whatsoever. That is the most critical part. If we can connect these cities together, we can create a new government and retake control of the system. We won't have to live underground anymore and people will be free. That's what we want; we want a new United States."

"Why would New Boston be written off? What's going on?" Clarke didn't understand the situation fully, but he was sure if he could see a map or sit in on an intelligence briefing, then it would make sense. He was a pretty bright individual and was clearly capable of complex thought and strategy.

"We have word from our network of infiltrators that the underground in New Boston might be compromised. If it is, then connecting to them would be a huge mistake. It's safer to let the city burn than try to pull them in at this point," Analyn said. The general looked over at her with a frown and his eyebrows pulled sharply inward. "What? That's the truth, sir. If you won't tell him, I will."

Clarke looked back at the general, silently asking for his rejection of that idea. Clarke didn't want it to be true. His whole life was in that city and he knew so many good people that didn't deserve to die in a bombing or whatever might happen. His thoughts went to his parents, and specifically his father. Clarke thought about how after Alex had died, Robert was in distress and Claire became distraught. Robert would be devastated to have lost Clarke as well, let alone knowing that the whole city was on the brink of destruction.

"Look, Clarke," General Morgan said with a sigh and put the letters into the stack of papers on the table. "So many cities have been destroyed in the past couple of years because we were unable to keep them hidden. Our system here is unique, though. We are well hidden, we are deep underground, and we have the war on top of us providing us cover. It's complicated, but if it comes to losing another city or sacrificing our movement, then I'm afraid that one city will suffer. I don't like it, but your mother knew better than anyone what was at stake. Don't waste that, please."

"What can I do to help?" Clarke said softly. "I want to be of some use. After all, I have the skills to be useful; maybe I can do something with them."

Analyn shook her head in absolute disagreement but the general grinned.

"I already have a mission for you, Captain Anicius," General Morgan said.

Part III—At War

Chapter 19—The Mission

There were two flashes down the abandoned street and then a series of loud bangs. A team of gray-suited Revolutionaries spilled out into the alley from behind a dumpster where they exited the underground. Moving in a rolling-T formation, they cleared the alley all the way to where it deposited onto the main surface street. Their powered body armor and wraparound helmets made them look like they were fighting on a space station rather than a bombed street, but that was how conventional battles had been fought for the past quarter century. The tall buildings they were between were originally over fifty stories tall but had since been blown out and partially collapsed. Rubble was strewn for hundreds of meters after the Mexican-Persian armies bombed the city making mounted movements nearly impossible. So, the Revolutionaries made use of this hidden entrance as a way to get foot soldiers onto the battlefield and confound both the foreign and domestic aggressors.

The two soldiers who operated in the front were twenty-year-old identical twins, Lewis and Shane Abubakari. Lewis was a member of the original group Clarke was supposed to be a part of in the United States Army, but his brother, Shane, was actually hidden from the world since his birth. They simply took turns going to school and taught one another when they got home. Clarke later learned that Lewis was drafted into the army in a legitimate way, but his parents had party connections and were able to get him committed to go to Houston, where he would intentionally link up with the Revolutionaries. Shane, on the other hand, could not go with his brother, and since he didn't exist according to the government, he couldn't become a member of society anyway, so his parents coordinated directly with the underground and got him to Houston for safety. If he were discovered at his home during a raid, he would have been arrested and most likely executed for desertion of some kind.

The two were apart for less than six months as one became enhanced and trained in the military while the other learned the Houston underground as best as he could. By the time Lewis had defected, Shane had already picked out their weapon systems, powered body armor, and identically numbered helmets—a result from a clerical error during manufacturing. Outside of their missions, Clarke never knew which one was which, but that didn't affect the mission; they did their job exceptionally well and had never even come close to imminent danger. They were of average build and quite sarcastic, almost to the point that they were kicked out of the underground because of their comments during a command briefing a couple weeks ago. Immaturity aside, they were the best assets that Clarke could have been paired with.

The team leader, Analyn Zheng, stood between the two and held her rifle between their heads pointed down the alley. Clarke followed behind and covered their six o'clock with a direct-energy emitter mounted to his chest plate for stability because it required both hands to operate.

It was now November 2nd and this was Clarke's twentieth mission since he entered the Revolutionaries and he was getting pretty good at his job. Since three quarters of the team was enhanced, they made for the perfect reconnaissance team. Lewis, Clarke, and Analyn were able to hear enemy conversations from half a kilometer away without the use of any equipment that would give away their own position. They could see individual soldiers moving from over four kilometers away with their naked eye if they had direct line of sight, and if they brought binoculars with them, they could read the print on a can of rations from that same distance. Clarke was the first to figure out that their dental implants were useful in tapping into radio frequencies, and given enough effort, they could listen in on tactical unit movement clear across the battlefield.

On a typical mission, the four of them would work their way to an observation post, usually an abandoned rooftop. Shane would provide security while the three others gathered all the intelligence they could for a couple hours. They were instructed to abort mission if any enemy troops were moving in their immediate area. Today they were moving to Phoenix Tower, which luckily had not collapsed despite sustaining several bombings that had cratered the streets surrounding it and knocked out nearly all of the glass windows. They reached the southern doors into the building and quickly cut the hinges with a portable plasma cutter in a matter of seconds. Then they climbed thirty-five flights of stairs to the rooftop and set up their observation post.

Shane covered the stairwell entering the area while the others sealed off the access points to that level by welding shut all the doors. Afterward, they poised themselves on the western, northern, and southern corners of the building and began recording everything they could catch. At first there was only radio traffic talking about troop resupplies and sleep rotations, which was good information but hardly useful because the Revolutionaries didn't actually attack either side. In all honesty, Clarke thought that they merely pitted the American army and the Mexican-Persian armies against one another to keep the war from spreading. The way the Revolutionaries operated like ghosts made both sides of the broader war feel like their enemy was always one step ahead. For instance, one Revolutionary attack on the Persian army was on Area Bahrandeh, the site of the next Persian forward operating power plant, a top-secret area that was never spoken about over radio or other communication devices. The Persian army did nothing wrong. They used proper protocol for radio frequencies, all their couriers knew how to transport information, and the people they trusted with their secrets were reliable. Little did they know that enhanced soldiers for an underground movement disrupted their plans by infiltrating their area of operations and listening to meetings through open windows. It felt like the Revolutionaries were intentionally creating a stalemate to spare the rest of the United States while sacrificing what was once their own city. After the first few years of the war in southern Texas, most of the wealthy fled Houston to other major U.S. cities or even Canada and Australia. Much of the underground became flooded with refugees from all citizen classes as travel restrictions prohibited free movement.

The streets were left at about a third of their regular occupancy when the bombing started; less than half of that population now remained. Analyn's team saw imagery reminiscent of wars in third world countries in downtown Houston. Nobody was out while the sun was down. Most buildings were self-sufficient at this point and used solar power or biomass to keep lights, appliances, and other utilities running properly. Unfortunately, many of the upper levels of the buildings were destroyed completely, most of the solar power strips and storage systems were rendered faulty, and biomass fuel simply stopped being supplied. This was how Clarke, Shane, Analyn, and Lewis were able to maneuver through the town without being accosted—the remaining inhabitants recognized that the Revolutionaries had never been aggressors and simply let them operate in the daytime. The several night missions Clarke had been on were even easier because no one was out; it was simply too dangerous for the average citizen. The Mexican army would shoot artillery into the city very unpredictably during the night and disrupt American military movements.

"No way, guys," Lewis said after about ten minutes of silence. "They are talking about prisoner locations."

"Which side?" asked Analyn. "Who has the prisoners, and who are the prisoners?"

"Just a second," Lewis said. "They're just going on and on about how their prisoner—it sounds like just one dude—has been difficult, like he just keeps trying to escape. ... It's definitely the Mexican army talking to the Persians about transferring him to a permanent facility. That way he can be actually chained up in a concrete box or something. ... No way." Lewis paused as he screwed up his face and focused intently. "They have one of our guys who's been in the field for months. Remember how he missed the last couple checks? Now they are saying that Phillip is very polite, he just keeps trying to escape. They think that moving him farther away will knock some sense into him."

"Try and figure out where exactly he's being held," Analyn said. "We might make a tactical decision and go get him if we have the chance."

"Boss, he's right around the corner at that old megachurch," Lewis said, referring to Joel Osteen's Lakewood Church, which had been passed down through the Osteen family for several generations. The building had several additions to increase seating and now resembled more of a stadium than a church. When religious services became outlawed, the State confiscated it and coincidentally converted it into an actual sports stadium where several professional sports teams played and practiced. It was such a massive complex that it would not only be difficult to safely enter it, but next to impossible to locate a single prisoner. Analyn took several seconds of silence to determine what she wanted to do.

"I think I got something," Clarke said, looking out of a shattered window to the south. "There is a Persian mounted patrol heading this way. Looks like three up-armored trucks with railguns and some sort of personnel carrier, hang on." He pulled up his binoculars and slid over the selector from 5x magnification to the heat settings. "Yeah, they have about fifteen soldiers in there, not counting what's inside the trucks. They just passed Brays Bayou."

"We won't make it down in time," said Analyn as she came over, looking at the dust trail. "They aren't even five klicks out." She crouched down behind a pillar and rested her chin on the butt of her rifle in thought. This was a difficult decision to make and she never had to make a choice like this before. An enemy patrol had never come this close to them, yet here they were. There was never an operational opportunity to get a prisoner of war, yet there was one now. Protocol dictated that they should avoid contact and return to base in the event that their location was compromised, as it was now. Unfortunately, there were no safe routes away from Phoenix Towers, and even if they were able to slip down the tower and out of sight, there would be no way to reach the stadium without drawing attention to themselves. In the open streets, a small team stood no chance; however, in tight quarters, numbers were irrelevant. Analyn wanted to follow protocol and return to base, but she knew that they wouldn't even make it down the stairs before the patrol would be coming up and that Phillip would likely be tortured if he wasn't rescued right now. She had already made up her mind, but wanted to have her team's support. She motioned for the team to withdraw to where Shane was posted at the stairway.

"Look, we have three options," Analyn said under her breath. "We either try to make it down these stairs right now and run like hell to get back to base, or we stand fast but hope they didn't notice we were here. I personally think that they probably tagged us already with a satellite when we crossed I-69. If I'm right, they probably have a platoon going into the building and their trucks providing cover—we'd be screwed trying to get out."

"What's the third option?" Lewis said. "You just told us that the first choice would be suicide, and the second would also be luck; what's that other choice you are keeping to yourself?"

"We head down a couple levels to where those old cubicles were. It'll create chaos for them to try and clear that level and we might be able to create a funnel for them to enter into." Analyn paused. "What do you guys think?"

"I vote not suicide," said Shane. Lewis nodded his approval while pulling out some candy from a vest pocket and taking a bite.

"Clarke?" Analyn asked. Clarke stared blankly into the middle distance and wrapped his head around what was happening. He knew that had he not said anything about the patrol, it would likely be too late already, but now that they stood a fighting chance, he felt compelled to take it. Not to mention the prisoner—he was part of the Revolutionaries. Clarke knew what was likely to happen if they couldn't get to Phillip in time. Nobody told Clarke what the Mexican-Persian armies did to prisoners of war but he had read enough history books to have a pretty good idea. Clarke couldn't leave anyone to die, not if he could help it.

"Let's do it," Clarke said and locked eyes with Analyn. "I may not want to kill anyone, but I will to save our lives, we need to make it out of this place to save our guy at the Church. You guys are my family now and I'm not going to let anything end that." Clarke felt that the missions he had gone on in the past few months made him understand and appreciate what it meant to be a soldier and relying on the man, and woman, to his left and right. It was nothing like the brief period he experienced in the United States Army; this was real to him. He knew that all three of them would look out for him, and he would do the same for them. The bonds he developed over the short period of time with the Revolutionaries and his team in particular made him feel truly alive for the first time since he was a boy playing, fishing, and hiking with his brother. These newest connections in his life showed him what it meant to be cared about in a platonic way—a real brotherhood that was worth his total devotion. In a way, this new family was even closer than his old one back in Alabama.

They rushed down to the twenty-seventh floor, where they saw an entire level of a cubicle farm. There had probably been over two hundred desks on this one open floor when it was blown apart, and now remnants of the dividers were toppled on top of desks, chairs, broken computer components, and various other office equipment. It was difficult to assess where they should go in the first place, let alone an actual defensive posture.

"All right, guys," Analyn said confidently, "I'll post myself on the opposite side with a direct line of sight to this stairwell. Lewis, I want you on my left and about fifteen meters forward. Shane, weld the other doors shut and when you're done, go to my right. Your shorter blasts will need to be closer to be really effective. Clarke, you will be right next to the kill zone behind that overturned table. If you so much as see the muzzle of a barrel come through that door, you are to shoot. Hopefully it won't come to that."

Shane had already moved over to the adjacent stairwell entrance and started welding it shut. With luck he would get all three of the other entrance doors done before the enemy came up to this level. The other three were fortifying their positions with thick pieces of the rubble and office equipment. Lewis shoved an old copy machine into his primary fighting position and created a sort of cave by covering it with several layers of cubicle dividers on top. This left him a window reminiscent of a machine gun bunker. Analyn did something fairly similar, except she was nearly on the floor and slid backward into position under a collapsed support pillar, then pulled over a chunk of concrete and a chair to act as concealment. Clarke slid several larger pieces of the dividers in front of his position and kicked a hole into the middle of one so he had his own window to shoot through. He didn't need to see much, just the doorway itself.

If anything comes through this door, pull that trigger, Clarke said to himself while he looked down at his direct-energy emitter. He still wasn't quite sure what his weapon did, but he knew that it was definitely a valuable asset on their missions if he was responsible for the entire rear security. He had seen the other weapons that his team members were using at a shooting range and was personally taken by the high-velocity rifle—the weapon Analyn used. The twins used a sort of electrical arc gun that was lethal and held enough energy for over a hundred discharges per battery. They both carried five batteries.

Shane finished up and rushed over to the spot Analyn had previously identified as a suitable fighting position. It was very well covered behind a pillar and had a vantage on both sides. He was beginning to harden his site when they started to hear boots climbing the stairs.

"These guys are loud," Clarke whispered under his breath. "I think it's a squad."

"So, let's estimate that as a third of their total strength," Analyn whispered back. "Expect the Persians to come in waves, they always fight like that. They'll just walk into the same trap over and over."

Clarke nodded before he remembered that nobody could see him. He had gotten so used to very low-decibel communication and being able to visually confirm from across rooftops that he couldn't believe he forgot that they were all literally covered in debris and garbage. He drew a sharp breath in and said, "One more floor."

The bootsteps got louder and heavy breathing became audible. All of Analyn's team knew that these soldiers were exhausted from the climb up in their heavy plated armor. They must have carried up nearly fifty kilograms in Kevlar and ballistic plating. Despite all their military's advancements in weaponry, they hadn't yet figured out powered body armor. That was one blessing Clarke thanked God for right at that very instant. His team only had to wear a vest, helmet, and bag that contained what was essentially a battery—totaling maybe a fifth of the weight compared to their aggressors.

BANG!

Analyn shot a soldier as he rounded the staircase to the next level. A series of angry shouts and confused screaming overtook the advancing squad. Several of the enemy soldiers fired wildly into the room and another lobbed in a flashbang and a fragmentation grenade to no avail. The enhancements Lewis, Analyn, and Clarke had rendered the flashbang pointless and their cover stopped all damage from the other grenade. Shane, on the other hand, was disoriented for a brief period of time, but that didn't affect the overall outcome.

BANG!

BANG!

Analyn shot the next two as they tried to pick up their dead comrade. The trailing team pushed low and approached the doorway from a crouched position. It was clear that Analyn didn't have the angle to shoot, but Lewis did. He waited for them to peer around the corner for a cursory glance, then he fired several precise arcs across the room and connected with one of them. Another member of that team used the opportunity of his point man going down to try and breach the fatal funnel. Clarke did not hesitate. He pressed his thumbs down on the triggers and, as succinctly as possible to describe, the enemy's shoulder and the greater part of his chest was vaporized. His arm fell to the ground because there was nothing there to hold it up and blood ran freely as he collapsed dead on the threshold.

Clarke vomited, but he wasn't the only one. It was clear that both Shane and Lewis couldn't keep it together either, nor could a soldier on the other side of the wall separating them.

"I think there are only four left," Analyn said from under her pile of rubble. "Lewis, give 'em a parting gift from us, will ya?" Lewis unclipped a grenade hanging from his vest, hesitated a moment, frowned, then pulled the pin and lobbed it into the stairwell. It bounced twice, rolled for a second, then detonated. The reverberation shifted the pile of cover in front of Clarke and his view of the doorway was rendered unusable. The soldiers in the hallway were not quite dead, although they were surely dying and unable to fight back. Analyn had instructed them to stay put while the second wave came up. None of the Revolutionaries understood why the Persians fought in such an archaic way. What they were doing was almost definitely committing suicide. Clarke would later find out that this was a show of their fierce nature, the fact that they stared into the face of death and did not blink. Clarke found it oddly admirable albeit futile.

"Everyone doing all right?" Analyn asked. "Adjust your cover and make sure you have something behind you too, we don't know if they are headed up any other stairs."

Clarke rushed from around his position and fixed what he could, but his window couldn't be helped—the piece was wedged too firmly between the wall and a pillar. Shane took his time and fixed himself a much better position with nearly a 360-degree view of the room. Lewis was pretty silent and Clarke knew that he was struggling with how he killed those soldiers. Clarke doubted Lewis had actually killed anyone before in combat.

It all happened so fast and none of them had really digested the first wave when the second wave started rushing up the stairs. This team was stacked just the same with antiquated body armor but advanced weaponry. They tossed in the same grenades, which again were fairly ineffective, and one by one they were picked off. This squad didn't even have the mindset to crouch when they approached, and Analyn got seven of them. Clarke got the eighth.

"You guys wait this out for a little while," said Analyn. "I think that they could have a third squad setting up a perimeter or something. I'll take a look out of a window." Then she crawled out of her little cave toward the exterior wall and started to lay down precise shots. Every third or fourth shot she would move to a different side of the building and shoot again. After five minutes she gave the all clear and everyone let out a sigh of relief—they would survive. The rest of the team visibly relaxed as they came out of their fighting positions and made for the stairs. They took the stairs slowly so they could communicate while they had guaranteed cover.

"All right, Lewis, you have the most information on where we are going. Did you pick up anything about Phillip's actual location?" Analyn asked as they rounded the twenty-fourth floor.

"Well, they kept talking about how he would keep getting down, like from the ceiling or something, and getting across the balcony," Lewis said wearily.

"That's good. We know that he will be in the upper levels," Analyn said. "Try to get a read on that while we move. Keep me informed." Lewis nodded. "Clarke, you were looking out the south side. What could you make out for a route to the stadium?"

"The interstate is raised over here; we could just go under it at ground level most likely. Maybe we could go subterranean and come out closer, though," said Clarke.

"No, we don't have time if they are moving him today. It would take us nearly an hour to get back to the tunnels and we can't even guarantee that there is anything closer anyway," Analyn said, shaking her head as the team rounded the twentieth level. "We'll use the cover from the highway. And there is likely enough of a barrier on the street anyway. It might just be a lot of crouching or crawling." She sighed.

It was silent as they continued down the stairs. Clarke felt bad for Lewis because it was obvious that he was having a hard time with tossing that grenade, but he didn't know what to say. As they came to the tenth level, Clarke put his hand on Lewis's shoulder and gave a light squeeze and said, "Let's pray for them later, right now we need to focus, okay?" Lewis paused and allowed Clarke to take another step down so they were on the same level and he looked at Clarke with watery eyes. He was unable to speak and simply nodded with a quivering lip. Clarke gave him another gentle squeeze and patted him on the back. They both smiled and returned to their assigned positions. Neither one of them recognized the importance of that moment for years to come, but in an instant, they became each other's confidants. In situations like this, it was very difficult to remember that they were still not even twenty years old and their childhoods had been sheltered from death and trauma.

They were coming down to the fifth level and Analyn called for a halt to go over the plan. Lewis had interjected several key pieces of information about the guards and where the Mexican army had left the stadium unprotected. Based on this intelligence, they decided to go in through a covered garage entrance and through a series of unlit maintenance hallways. There was only one company covering the entire stadium and they definitely didn't have enough personnel to cover all the possible routes. They left almost all routes woefully undermanned, or worse, unmanned. It was a strategic disadvantage for the Mexican army and Analyn's team was going to capitalize on their opportunity. Essentially, Analyn's plan was to go as stealthily as possible, which meant she would not be firing her rifle but everyone else could use their own weapons because they were nearly silent discharges.

The team moved in pairs to provide effective overwatch. Shane and Lewis naturally moved as a pair and then Analyn and Clarke went afterward. Clarke was right about the cover from the interstate, and aside from getting across the parking lots and small remnants of buildings dotting the area, they were concealed from satellite view. At street level they were mostly concerned with being flanked from a side street that they couldn't see from up in the Phoenix Towers. Luckily, the stadium was only about half a kilometer away, and they got into the facility no more than ten minutes from when they left the doors of their observation post.

All of them knew what they were doing at this point. Clarke, for the first time in a long time, wasn't the most nervous one there. He knew that the anxiety he felt on a usual basis wasn't even close to the adrenaline and nervousness he had coursing through his veins right now, but Lewis looked terrified, like he couldn't pull his trigger again. Analyn didn't seem to notice as they were moving through the corridors in the pitch black. Shane had his hands on Lewis's back because he couldn't see in the dark hallways. Analyn was leading the way because she had a map downloaded on the team leader's tactical screen. The tac-screen, as it was called, was tough enough to withstand an EMP, being run over by a ten-ton truck, and even a direct hit from a high-velocity round. It also had a function that rendered it completely useless to unauthorized personnel—even a fellow team member. This way the information was completely secure, and in the event that a team leader went down, the information was permanently lost. The way operational security was managed was incredibly well done by the Revolutionaries and would become a model for future warfighting functions.

Analyn took several sharp turns into an even darker hallway. The screen's display was showing a lumen rating of less than one percent so it didn't actually illuminate anything, but Analyn could still read it. When she came to a sudden stop, Clarke walked over to Lewis and gave him another reassuring look and reached for his hand. They held hands for a moment and Clarke mouthed the Lord's Prayer. Lewis figured it out after a line or two and copied Clarke. Lewis squeezed his hand when they finished and mouthed "thank you" to Clarke and then wiped away another silent tear.

Clarke was beginning to worry about Lewis on this mission but felt his prayers may have made Lewis calm down and remember what they were doing and why it mattered. Whenever he caught Lewis's attention in those tunnels, he mouthed the prayer again. Finally, after about twenty minutes of snaking through the maintenance hallways and staircases, they made their way to the highest level of the open stadium. It was pitch black except for one small area about a quarter of the way around the stadium to their left.

Chapter 20—The Escape

A nalyn put away her tac-screen and unslung her rifle from her shoulder. Everyone knew that noise discipline would be critical, but not having a weapon would be a bigger mistake. Nobody said anything to Analyn as they slowly maneuvered around a row of seats to access the most direct route to the light source. Analyn led the way, followed by Lewis, who still had his twin clutching his shoulder as they moved. The light that was illuminating the area some 200 meters away was not bright enough for Shane to operate in yet. Clarke brought up the rear as usual and simply followed about five meters behind Shane. Analyn stepped over a row of chairs and was followed by Lewis; Shane needed a little help but managed just fine. Analyn called for a halt as a flashlight shone out in the dark from the opposite side of the stadium. It was quite obvious that it was just a standard security check, but they were still caught off guard by it and everyone's pulse quickened.

They slowly continued to the light source and stopped every couple of minutes to better assess their situation. Unfortunately, with their enhanced hearing, the pulse of their blood in their eardrums made it difficult to concentrate; if anything, Shane was their most valuable asset as he didn't have this problem. Analyn pulled Shane to the front as the light began to make their area operable for him and he led the pace. This was new for him, but he intuitively knew why he was put at the front this time. Usually, Shane was second or third in the formation because he did not have enhancements, which were helpful in scouting an area, but now Analyn was willing to risk it. Not only was he expendable because he didn't have the super-soldier abilities, but his weapon made the least amount of noise if they needed to fight.

He inched closer and closer and crouched lower and lower as they approached one of the last barriers to the lit portion of the balcony. Shane climbed over the partition smoothly and headed for the shadows to his left. Just then they heard a sneeze from directly in front of them. Everyone was so focused on Shane getting over the hurdle that they hadn't been watching the far side of the lit area. A guard had apparently walked out from the entrance tunnel and started to smoke before he let out his sneeze. Clarke thought it was sheer luck that Shane wasn't spotted, but now they were separated and hadn't communicated any plan to him. They were all planning on going over the short wall, but now they couldn't without risking being seen before they found Phillip. Lewis recognized that Shane was cut off too and Clarke could hear his friend's rapid breathing begin taking over him. In his childhood Clarke remembered his anxiety causing severe mental breakdowns, which he was taught were anxiety or panic attacks. Clarke saw his friend struggling even more and wanted to help, but he was so high stress at the moment himself that he didn't know what to do—this was a bad situation all around. Analyn was at the partition when the guard sneezed again and spit off the balcony.

"How far away is he?" Analyn said under her breath. The guard didn't hear anything.

"About ten meters," Clarke responded. "I think we can avoid him, though, just wait it out, you know? How long could he smoke before someone comes looking for him anyway?" Analyn nodded and internally they hoped that Shane would stay put and out of sight while the guard finished up. Clarke turned his attention back to Lewis, who was starting to tear up and shake a bit. His nose began to drip tears and mucus as he started to silently cry. They were only about two meters apart and Clarke took the risk and crawled over to him. As he was reaching up to grab Lewis's shoulder, his weapon knocked against a metal piece of the chair and created a loud ringing echo like a hollow metal pole being rapped with a rock. The guard immediately turned to face the noise and cautiously stepped toward it.

Analyn pointed and motioned for Clarke to shoot when the guard got to the partition. Clarke nodded and swallowed hard; he wasn't ready to shoot again, not after what he now knew his weapon did. Nonetheless, he readied himself and pulled up his direct-energy emitter and aimed it at where the guard would be when he followed the open path to right above Analyn. The click of the soldier's boots echoed in the darkness and Clarke's palms began to sweat. Another few steps and Clarke would be killing another person. He didn't know if he could do it. He had to do it; their own lives were at risk. He had to do it; Lewis needed to be reassured that what he did earlier would be okay. He had to do it.

The guard was reaching for his flashlight as he took the final step to the divider where Analyn was positioned directly on the opposite side. He reached to set his hand on the concrete half-wall and peer around the corner to an area that was concealed by darkness, but he never managed to turn his flashlight on or set his hand down. Clarke pressed his thumbs to the triggers and closed his eyes for two seconds as the direct-energy beam turned the guard's entire torso into nothing. It was all over in less than five seconds. The man's head and shoulders fell but Analyn caught it before it made a noise, and Clarke noticed Shane nearly dive to stop the legs from collapsing as well. Shane quickly picked them up and flipped them over the partition so there would be no immediate visual trace that he was ever there.

WE HAVE A PLAN

Clarke felt like he was going to vomit again and Lewis was actively dry heaving while all of it took place. But none of them had any time to formulate their next move when they saw a ravaged man with a thick brown beard and wild hair tear into their field of vision. He was headed straight for them.

"It's Phillip!" Lewis said out loud. Not that noise discipline mattered really, as about ten seconds after Phillip came running barefoot out of the tunnel entrance a host of Mexican soldiers wearing their tan and brown summer fatigues came chasing him and firing non-lethal rounds in his direction. Clarke heard several direct hits and saw the muscle spasms take over the man, but he kept running. It looked like Phillip knew that this was his last chance of escaping and he wasn't going to relent. Phillip turned to the aisle where the encounter with the soldier just took place and was hobbling as fast as he could.

Meanwhile, Analyn had backed up so she could see what was happening. When Phillip was hit yet again and dropped to a knee and then collapsed, Analyn shot the leading member of the assault square in the chest. Lewis popped up and discharged his weapon at the next soldier with a brilliant flash of light. Shane must have had the same thought and took out another. Analyn took aim and hit another one. Clarke felt that he was also needed in this fight and fired another beam into the remaining mass of soldiers. Five of them dropped dead instantly as their heads and upper bodies vanished, while two started to scream and one slipped into shock when he realized his right arm was gone. The screaming quickly ended with two bright flashes of light from Shane's weapon.

"We're getting pretty good at this, boys!" Analyn said triumphantly. Lewis shot her a sideways glance and Clarke let out a deep sigh. He knew what he had just done was fundamentally wrong, but he had to do it. This was different than getting his own soldiers killed like at the airport; this was actually war. Moral ambiguity aside, they were all starting to understand what war was now.

Shane rushed over to Phillip and turned him over. There were several spots where the tranquilizers hit and more spots where non-lethal rounds slapped into his back which had already begun to create massive bruising and what looked like internal bleeding. One of the rounds got the inside of his leg and was freely bleeding. It wasn't an arterial bleed, but it was bad. Phillip was in rough shape, but started to return to consciousness as the team tended to him. Shane was already pulling out the tri-tipped tranquilizers from his skin with a sickening pop, and Lewis opened his aid bag and steadied himself before injecting Phillip with a blue-green compound. The syringe was shaking wildly as he plunged the liquid into Phillip.

"Remember that stuff they gave us back at Powell? This is it," Lewis said. "I figured it would come in handy during some sort of night watch, but I think this is a better use right now."

Phillip reeled and took a dramatic inhale as he surveyed his surroundings. His look of concern was quickly washed away as he noticed their gray jumpsuits. He let out a smile and a short laugh before reaching for his side, which Analyn noticed was red, splotchy, and very swollen.

"We need to move, now," Analyn said quietly. The team picked up Phillip and carried him over the divider, where he began to fight them so they would set him down.

"I know the way," Phillip said raggedly as his head bobbed unsteadily and blood-contaminated drool dripped from the corner of his mouth. Clarke noticed that Phillip's eyes were black and going in and out of focus, as if his body knew he should be unconscious but the drugs were preventing it. It was a sick sensation to see someone in so much pain, bleeding from so many wounds, a wrist wrapped tightly in a bandage, yet willing to carry on. Later, Clarke would be told that Phillip was hardened by the war and had a mental resolve like no other. Phillip staggered forward and fell to his knee.

"You're in no state to be walking, Phillip. Just tell us where to go," Analyn whispered into his ear. "We will do what you want if it gets us out of here."

Lewis grabbed Phillip under the arm and pulled him to his feet. Phillip nodded at Analyn and looked over to Lewis in a daze. He pulled Analyn in and rested his bristly beard on her neck and said, "Section ... 228, security locker ... Delta 24." Analyn pulled out her tac-screen and found the section labeled 228. She started to walk forward into the darkness and the team followed as quickly as they could. While they moved, Analyn had added on heat signatures of the building and was able to see where the soldiers were posted. The team leader's screen was capable of adding many different types of filters, sensors, and active monitors, which couldn't be used in covert or clandestine missions—that didn't matter now. The thermal filter that Analyn had just toggled on allowed her to see her team's heat signature with a blue outline. The benefit to this was that all non-blue heat signatures would be the enemy. Fortunately, the thermal filters indicated that the security element was spread too thinly to be effective in such a large building and no one was on their path to section 228. They continued to move across the balcony in darkness with Analyn as the point, Lewis supporting Phillip, and Clarke guiding Shane. They were not concerned with noise discipline at the moment, but they did not talk anyway.

As they went over the third partition from the lighted area, a siren wailed throughout the stadium. The enemy knew what had happened and they started to swarm the balcony.

"Quickly! We got to get out of the open area before they turn on all the lights!" Analyn nearly shouted. The five of them made for the nearest tunnel, which Clarke saw was numbered 223. They weren't too far away, maybe a hundred meters down a hallway from their destination. As they went through the tunnel Clarke looked back and saw a small trail of blood drops and smears where Phillip had walked. It was only a matter of time until they were caught. He sensed the enemy closing in as he ran up to Analyn.

"We have a problem," Clarke said, gesturing with his thumb over his shoulder to the tunnel entrance. "Our guy is leaking something fierce; they're going to catch up." The blood rushed out of Analyn's face as the situation dawned on her. Analyn was the most tactically sound member of the team, and she knew that they only survived the Phoenix Towers an hour ago because they had an excellent defensive posture. In this huge open area, they stood no chance against a company-sized element, even if they had already taken out a squad.

"We can't help it," Analyn said solemnly. "He needs to get to section 228, and I think I know why. Clean up what you can, okay?" Clarke nodded and rushed to several offices looking for a mop or hose or something to erase the tracks. While he did so, the team passed sections 224 and 225. Finally, Clarke found towels and quickly drenched one with his own water, and then he ran back to the tunnel at section 223 and began to wipe the floor as rapidly as possible.

There was a loud sound as the halogen stadium lights began to flicker on—dimly at first, then slowly brightening up. Clarke was barely out of the tunnel entrance when he started to hear footsteps on the balcony where the squad of soldiers lay dead. Clarke began to rush his cleanup and abandoned drying the floor as he got as much blood as possible and advanced toward his team. He caught up to them just a couple second later as they passed section 227. Clarke continued to mop up the blood as it was dripping from Phillip's boot onto the sealed concrete floors, and the team drifted toward the bank of security lockers on the far side of the hallway. The lights started to get brighter from the tunnels and the team collectively knew that they were running out of time until there would be a major problem.

"Clarke, Shane!" Analyn whispered loudly. "Find the Delta bank." Clarke and Shane rushed ahead of the group and entered the security doors to the storage lockers. The room was rectangular and longer than it was wide. They faced rows and rows of hundreds of identical lockers. The two stared at each other with wide eyes and a look of helplessness. Then they took off in different directions. Neither one knew exactly what they were looking for other than it would be hard to find. Clarke saw foreign characters followed by Roman numerals and recognized the numbering system almost immediately. The lockers were stacked three high and numbered top to bottom, left to right. Finding locker twenty-four would be easy, but there was no way to identify the Delta bank—there were no letters, only foreign script.

"I think it's a different language," Shane shouted from the opposite side of the room. The room wasn't all that big, but there were probably fifty different rows with over a thousand different lockers on each side of each row. Finding Delta 24 was just not going to happen before Analyn got into the room because they didn't know how it was organized.

"What language do you think it is? I can't figure it out," Clarke said. "The numbers are definitely Roman numerals, though."

"Oh, that's what Roman numerals look like," Shane said as the entrance door opened and the three others spilled into the room. Phillip wasn't walking anymore; Lewis was more or less dragging him.

"Clarke, get out there and clean up that mess," Analyn said with her voice shaking. Clarke could tell that Analyn was nervous and trying to remain composed. If Analyn lost her head, they would all surely die. Clarke came back to the entrance door and jumped around Lewis and Phillip as he pulled out the bloodied towel and left the room. "Do you have any more of that injection?" she asked.

"No, that was all I had. I was only prepared for a single day mission to the observation post, nothing like this," Lewis said and lowered Phillip to the floor. "I can't carry him much further; bro weighs at least a hundred kilos."

"Help him out when we get moving again," Analyn said to Shane. "Where is the locker?"

"That's the thing, we can't find the Delta bank. They aren't labeled alphabetically, or even using English letters at all," Shane said. "Even the numbers are out of order." Clarke came back through the door and dropped the soaking wet towel with a splat. It was so saturated that blood began to run off it toward a little drain nearby.

"I don't recognize the script before the Roman numerals," Clarke said. "It's got to be some other language or maybe even just random symbols—I can't find any two that are the same."

Just then Phillip stirred and tried to sit up. Analyn helped pull him against the nearest wall of lockers. He lifted up his hand weakly and touched his forefingers together and his thumbs to form a sloppy triangle. Clarke felt a burst of memory come to him. He remembered when he used to go out with Alex to the woods and Alex would teach him about lots of different subjects. One memory in particular came back vividly—geometry.

"WHAT IS THE STRONGEST shape?" the then sixteen-year-old Alex had asked. "Do you think it's a circle? A square? A rhombus?"

Charlie, who was only six at the time, screwed up his face and puffed out his cheeks as he thought about this question. A circle could be crushed like a marble flattened by a hammer. A square could fall to one side if the pressure was strong like standing on a cardboard box. Charlie had come to know how his brother taught different subjects and almost always left out the right answer from his questions. Alex had said that it was to make him think harder and not just be given the answer.

"Well?" Alex asked again.

"It's got to be a triangle," Charlie said. "It's the only shape you didn't say!"

"Yes, the triangle is the strongest shape, but did you know why?"

"No. You haven't told me yet."

Alex went on to teach Charlie about the pyramids and ancient Egyptians, the Nile River, and even the Greeks.

THAT WAS ALL CLARKE needed to remember—delta was a Greek letter represented by a triangle. The meaning of it was deeper than that, though; for the Revolutionaries, the delta was literally the symbol of change, just like its use in mathematic equations, where graphing the change in x over the change in y will show the slope of a line.

"We're looking for a triangle," Clarke said somberly, as if detached from his current predicament. Clarke looked down onto Phillip's face and saw a brief smile before he fell back into unconsciousness. The entire team stood up and let Phillip lean against the lockers as they took to the aisles looking for a little one-centimeter by one-centimeter picture of a triangle. Minutes went by and the first dozen rows were cleared without so much as a three-sided symbol. Lewis was the closest to the door when he heard footsteps in the hallway. He moved toward the door and listened for a few moments while the rest of the team continued searching.

"I found it!" Shane said from the middle of a row. "But this number is definitely not twenty-four, what number is this?"

"LXI is sixty-one," Clarke said. "Also, that's not a triangle, it's a nabla. The Greeks differentiated by orientation; this one is upside down—see? It's got to be a different locker." He thought for a moment and then wanted to check something. He ran to the edge of the rows and counted them; there were only forty-eight. Clarke thought that was odd as many buildings constructed in this style and era liked to use standardized numbers such as ten, twenty-five, fifty, and one hundred; forty-eight just didn't make any sense. He double checked his count again and furrowed his brow when he landed at the forty-eighth row once more.

"Clarke, what are you doing?" Lewis whispered to him. "We need to find that locker!"

"I don't think it's as simple as that," Clarke said. "None of the lockers numbered XXIV have a triangle on them, and we aren't going to find it on a locker unless-" Clarke took off for the far wall and noticed that there were lockers on it just like there were on the other side.

The number forty-eight is the Angel's number, he thought to himself and then counted backward to the row he determined would be number twenty-four. The door began to open where Lewis was standing who shot an arc at the soldier opening it up.

"We're out of time, boys!" Lewis said as the man fell limply forward into the room. "His squad will find out he's missing pretty soon if they are already conducting sweeps of this level. Dang! It's only been ten minutes since we got here." Lewis dragged the man into the room, then closed the door again. He was secretly hoping that it would be one person at a time coming through this door. Although he hated having killed several people in the past couple hours, he now felt the adrenaline in his veins and the struggle he had at first was a distant memory; he was living in a fight or flight capacity and he chose to live. Lewis thought about how Clarke literally vaporized people to save the team from capture or even death itself. It was now his turn to help them by keeping the enemy out of the room.

"Analyn, Shane, come here," Clarke called out, and they came rounding the corner only a moment later. "It's going to be here, in this row. Don't look for a locker, it'll be something else." Analyn gave a puzzled look of disapproval. "Trust me, I think it's an exit. I think Phillip was looking for an exit into the underground."

The other two lit up with surprise and their minds began to race too. The entrances they had been used to would be put to the test. If there was an entrance in this room, then it would be well hidden. The marker of a triangle would be on it, and now they had narrowed it down to this single row—a meter-wide strip in a room nearly a hundred meters wide.

Just then the door creaked open and Lewis arced another two blasts. The team only saw two quick flashes of brilliant white light and the sound of two bodies smacking hard against the tile floor.

"Keep going, guys, I got this. They don't have any clue we're here, but they will soon," Lewis called from the door.

Shane started at the far end of aisle twenty-four, looking for patterns in the ceiling tiles, while Analyn looked at the floor. Clarke went back to locker XXIV and saw that it was a symbol he didn't recognize. Then he went to the front end of the aisle and tried to take in his surroundings. Aisle twenty-four was the middle of the room. He looked to his left and saw a line in the tile cut at what appeared to be a 45-degree angle. He looked to his right and saw an identical line going the opposite way. Clarke had another theory and ran to the door just to check. As he did so, he looked down the aisles and saw that the line continued through each one. The door opened again as he was getting close. Lewis arced another flash and the body fell in.

"What are you doing, Clarke?" Lewis said angrily. "You're going to get yourself killed running around like that." Then he got up from his position and moved the body onto the pile he had already created as a short barrier between the door and himself. Clarke would have laughed if he knew that they weren't dead. The scene was ridiculous.

There were three dead Mexican soldiers stacked haphazardly about three meters from the doorway, and a skinny American was dragging a fourth to the pile. All the while a man was unconscious and sitting upright just around the corner. Clarke pushed the thought out of his mind and ran to where the line would be in the floor. Jackpot.

Clarke didn't bother checking the far side of the room to be certain that there was a giant inlaid delta on the floor of this room. He ran to the center of aisle twenty-four and saw the line cutting through the middle between lockers numbered MD and MDIII. This was the center of the entire room and Clarke knew that it was indicated for a reason. He felt the floor and the lockers and nothing was budging. He struggled for a minute or two, sensing that every second they were stuck in the room their chances of survival were dwindling. Then he felt a hand on his shoulder and looked up; it was Phillip.

Analyn and Shane were trying to find patterns in the ceiling tiles and arguing about whether they were flat or curved. None of that mattered obviously, but Clarke was busy figuring it out by himself and didn't think to tell them that he was on to something. Phillip put his finger to his lips and stumbled backward to what appeared to be no place in particular. Then he slipped a little on the drops of blood he was leaving in his trail and leaned hard on one of the lockers. He slid on his bare, beaten, and bleeding back down to the floor, where he pressed a small chip in the tile shaped like a triangle to reveal a hidden cross-shaped keyhole. He reached under the edge of the closed locker, number DCCLXXVII, and plucked a small key attached to a little braided leash of high-strength steel and diamond. The key was spectacular crystal with intricate etchings of angels and water. The leash was only about four inches long and barely had enough give to fit into the keyhole. Phillip turned the key and a dull click escaped from the lockers behind Phillip. Then he returned the key to its place under the locker and covered the keyhole back up with the little chip. The entire process took maybe thirty seconds. Analyn and Shane hadn't even noticed that Phillip was in the aisle and, in the meantime, Lewis had shot another two soldiers dead.

"Pull on this column of lockers and get out of here," Phillip slurred as he slipped back into unconsciousness. Clarke was beginning to worry about the loss of blood Phillip had been suffering from. It may have only been drops coming off him every few seconds, but internally it looked really bad. When he slumped over again, Clarke noticed that the wound on his side was bulging to a sickening size and was a deep purple. Clarke didn't know if Phillip would make it, but he knew that if they didn't get out, none of them would survive.

"Hey guys, let's go!" Clarke said. "I've got it, right through here."

Immediately, Clarke yanked on whatever he could grab from the face of the lockers and the hidden door cleanly swung open. This particular entrance was woven into the architecture of the building and they needed to follow it wherever it led. Hopefully it was a direct connection to the underground, but they had no way of knowing. A couple seconds later, Analyn took out her tac-screen again and entered the doorway. She made an immediate left and went down a narrow staircase. Lewis had run up by this time and saw Phillip lying in a slowly expanding pool of his own blood and hung his head.

"I've got him, you two go ahead," Clarke said.

"I'll get his feet," said Shane. "Lou, you go ahead." Lewis nodded sadly and disappeared into the tunnel after Analyn. Clarke reached under Phillip's arms and hauled him up while Shane grabbed him from between the knees. Moving dead weight was not easy, and going down stairs was even harder. The simple fact that Shane volunteered to do something without his brother made it obvious to Clarke that whatever was going on with Lewis was severe. Normally, the twins talked back and forth about everything whenever they had a free moment, and on missions they were serious, but they would still joke. This was different; Clarke's concern for Lewis must be nothing compared to Shane's concern.

The team proceeded down the stairs and made twists and tight turns, which were difficult to pass through with Phillip being unconscious, but they made it. Regardless of the few times that Shane or Clarke fell while carrying the man, the team made it down to below the foundation of the stadium. That's where the tunnel widened and they breathed a sigh of relief.

It wasn't over yet, though, as they had to rush to get Phillip to the hospital where he would undergo emergency surgeries and blood transfusions to save his life. Analyn had ended their radio silence the second they broke ground level by grabbing the nearest comms device and alerting the hospital that they were on their way. It wasn't far and Phillip stood a chance if they could start working on him immediately. They were moving through the hallways and pushing past people with concerned faces when Phillip came to and looked up at Clarke. He smiled.

"I always knew that I'd see you again." He reached up to touch Clarke's face and that's when Clarke noticed the man's facial features. His eyes, and the smile he would recognize even if there was a bushy beard and blood covering his cheeks. Clarke's mouth hung open in recognition as Phillip reached up and twisted Clarke's baseball cap. They reached the hospital shortly thereafter and rushed through the door to the operation room. Doctors and nurses were rushing around to have everything prepped when their newest patient arrived, but they were not ready for the severity of his blood loss. One of the tranquilizers had apparently ripped a part of an artery on his inner thigh, and although it was technically not a hemorrhage, he had been openly bleeding for around forty-five minutes, and even just a few drops at a time added up to over a liter of blood. Clarke and

Shane hobbled awkwardly to the operating table and set him down; he was unconscious again.

Clarke stood in awe, still dumbstruck, still in disbelief. Then a doctor snapped in his face to bring him back to the current situation.

"You need to get out of this room so we can save him," the doctor said. Then he noticed the glazed look on Clarke's face and the deep brown and maroon bloodstains covering the front of his jumpsuit before changing his tone. "Hey, please go to the observation room and get something to drink."

Clarke absentmindedly followed the instructions and made his way out of the operating room toward where he was directed to go. The doctor called over a nurse, who nodded and helpfully escorted Clarke in a kind and caring way. She was told to treat him for shock.

Chapter 21—Mind Games

Nobody was sure that Phillip would survive as the operations were approaching the twelfth hour. Clarke and the nurse, Miss Catherine Baker, had talked for several hours about what happened on the mission. Clarke didn't even know where the rest of his team was taken to, nor did he know how long he had been talking with Nurse Baker. Nurse Baker identified that Clarke was suffering from a traumatic incident and would likely have flashbacks for years to come. He had broken down and cried several times during their conversation as he talked about having to shoot at people and being a support for Lewis. He had confided in Ms. Baker that none of them would have made it out alive if Lewis had not kept it together and defended the room. Clarke felt the burden lessen as he spoke with her, and slowly he calmed down.

About four hours after getting back to the underground, Clarke returned to his billet, which was just a short ten-minute walk through several shoulder-width, one-way tunnels from the hospital. He grabbed his hygiene kit for a well-deserved hot shower. Nothing was working out the way he had planned when he volunteered to act as a scout for the Revolutionaries. He tried to stay calm and in control of his breathing but couldn't. He started to sob in the shower. The people in the other stalls poked their heads out in concern, but Analyn, being the good team leader that she was, had walked in and shouted at them to leave Clarke alone. She herself had been medically and psychologically evaluated like Clarke, but far more quickly and, as always, she was in excellent overall health. Clarke prayed a short prayer of thanks that Analyn had been so good to him ever since they met. The connection he felt was so strong, like a long-lost cousin who shared the same interests and skills; they defended each other and stood up for one another.

Clarke let the water rush over his shoulders and down his body, and he just stood there as steam from the other stalls poured in and fogged up the opaque glass. A few minutes later, with tears still rolling down his face, the water cut off. The underground was serious about rationing water and there were very few exceptions to this policy; Clarke held one of these exceptions today. He and the rest of the team were authorized leave, extended water use, and extra rations for the next week while they were assessed by the psychologists and debriefed by the intelligence teams. Nobody questioned it when Clarke had his retinas scanned and hit the button for more water. The shower gave him an additional five minutes, which displayed both under the showerhead and on the shower door in a countdown timer. He sighed and closed his eyes.

After his shower, Clarke returned to his billet and saw that Shane was already fast asleep and Analyn was lying down facing the wall. Based on her breathing pattern, though, Clarke could tell that she wasn't sleeping yet. Clarke went to his bed and put his hygiene kit away and looked at himself in the mirror. His eyes were puffy and swollen from tears, and he saw several bruises on his shoulders and chest from the few impacts with the ground and probably from moving the debris around in Phoenix Towers. He pulled on a shirt, and as he started to button up the side buttons, he realized how sore his arms were. Clarke hadn't realized how heavy Phillip was, nor how far he had actually carried him. He ran through the path in his head. They had gone down over a dozen staircases and he remembered passing a pillar that said 2100 meters with an arrow to the exit they had used. Then they made a turn into the primary underground tunnel network. All in all, he figured that he and Shane probably carried their comrade about three kilometers before they set him down in the operation room.

He massaged his forearms as he sat on his bed and wondered what the next few days would hold. Clarke pulled his screen out from a drawer under his bed and navigated to his schedule. He anticipated the debriefings from the intel guys to last for a couple of hours, but he still had not received a revised schedule. It still showed that they should be in debriefings right now, but that clearly wasn't happening. On his other missions, they would sit in a copper and lead-lined room with a couple of skinny guys in glasses and business suits who took notes on old-fashioned legal pads and stored all of it in a two-step authentication lock bag before it was processed on an air-gapped storage system. Clarke had never learned how the bags or the intelligence systems worked, but the bag looked like it was a biometric fingerprint scanner and an old-fashioned digital key. He had no clue where the intelligence cell actually processed their data. The only thing Clarke did know about the intelligence guys was that they took physical security incredibly seriously.

Clarke was also curious about what would happen next. Phillip had been missing for months now—long enough that Clarke hadn't even had the opportunity to meet with him since joining the Revolutionaries. Who was he? What did he do for the Revolutionaries exactly? What would he be doing when he got out of the hospital?

If he gets out of the hospital, Clarke thought to himself and shuddered. He instinctively knew that it was incredibly unlikely that Phillip would make it through the night. Clarke felt like he was robbed of time with Phillip. He put his screen away and slid himself down so he was lying with his head to the wall. For the past few hours, he struggled to come to grips with the fact that Phillip was his brother Alex. Alex was supposed to be dead, but beyond a shadow of a doubt, Clarke knew that it was him. Everything that he remembered about his brother was not just similar to Phillip, it was identical. Alex knew how to survive on his own, he knew codes and secrets. He knew patterns, riddles, lost knowledge, and above all, he was daring. Clarke felt nostalgic thinking about the times he went out camping with his brother for the weekend and started to smile. He had been through the toughest day of his life so far and finally had something personal to hope for.

Minutes turned to hours and Clarke lay awake in his bed. The light from the room shut off after ten minutes of no movement and the ambient light from the faux windows cast long shadows over the room. Clarke reached over to the screen on the wall nearest him to check the clock, which displayed 0238. He wanted to sleep but his head kept racing and going over the day's events. He couldn't believe that the entire mission from start to finish was less than six hours; it felt like weeks. He went from never firing his weapon before to killing a dozen people in the span of about two hours. Clarke tried to think about anything else but he just couldn't. He was trapped in a mental fight with himself, and no matter how hard he tried, he couldn't escape the memory of every time he pulled the triggers. Clarke felt the blood pulsing strongly in his neck. His chest tightened every once in a while as he fought off tears and additional anxiety attacks. He didn't even notice how much he was sweating under the thin sheets until he went to scratch his leg. He rolled over and saw Lewis sitting up on his bed with his arms wrapped around his knees, shaking silently.

Clarke quickly sat up and the noise he made caught Lewis's attention. He raised his head and looked over at Clarke with bloodshot eyes and tears rolling down his dark face. Even though there was no light, Clarke could see tear trails down his cheek and the tension in Lewis's jaw. The boy was trying his hardest not to cry or make any noise. Clarke threw off his blanket and swung his legs over the side of the bed.

Leaning forward, he said, "Do you need help?"

Lewis did nothing for a moment but continued to shake involuntarily as he tried to control himself, then he quickly nodded his head and bounced a little on the bed. Tears started to flow freely from his eyes, and Clarke leapt across the room to Lewis and embraced him. They both started to cry together and held each other tight. They had gone through some serious stressors together, and their bond was solidified that night as they sat silently side by side and just showed compassion for their fellow soldier—a brother.

Clarke asked for the time and Lewis looked at the screen on his wall, 0331. They had cried themselves out and their nerves were backing down to manageable levels. The entire time that Clarke sat on Lewis's bed, neither one of them spoke. Clarke reached over for one last hug before going back to his bed to get some sleep, but Lewis grabbed his elbow and stopped him.

"Thank you," was all Lewis said before letting him go. Clarke simply offered a quick grin and wiped his nose before turning back around to lie in his own bed. Both of them shifted around for a few minutes before Lewis fell asleep. Clarke heard his breathing get into a rhythm impossible to imitate and finally felt so overcome with exhaustion that he too fell into a dreamless sleep.

The next day Clarke was woken up when Analyn yawned from her bed around seven in the morning. He slowly opened his eyes to the warm replicant sunlight shining down across his chest and extending toward the foot of his bed. That feeling of warm sunlight waking him up was the reason he picked this particular bed. But even though he was greeted by the day with a familiar warmth, Clarke was brutally exhausted. He wanted to go back to sleep, but his screen pinged with a message he knew he needed to see because everyone else's screen had also pinged at the same time. Clarke pulled his blankets aside, swung his feet over the bed, and picked up his screen from the drawer. Sure enough, it was his daily schedule update that had his first meeting in fifteen minutes. He closed his eyes and sighed as he fought the urge to just lie back down again.

As Clarke wrestled with the notion of just ignoring his schedule for another ten or so minutes, he received a message from Lewis. Clarke read it quickly and looked up to see Lewis looking over at him with a soft grin.

Thank you so much. You don't know how much what you did yesterday helped me. I'm not in a good place still, but I know that if you are here with me, I'll be okay. You are so strong and I hope to stay friends with you after all of this is over.

Clarke simply gave a short smile in response to the message and thanked God that they all made it out of yesterday alive. Of course, Clarke knew that Lewis was not all right despite the note he just received. He wanted to do everything possible to help Lewis, but what was he supposed to do about it? There were still so many suicides that happened daily in the underground, even though the people there were treated equally and were able to live almost normal lives. It would be unthinkable to lose such a close friend, and Clarke thanked God that nobody he knew had killed themselves. Still, it was bound to happen one day, especially if things kept getting worse, or even just stayed the same, for that matter.

Clarke realized that he was absentmindedly staring at Lewis and then cracked a smile. He mouthed the words "any time," before he got down from his bed and started getting dressed in a gray jumpsuit. The uniform he wore yesterday was so saturated in Phillip's blood that the medical staff had actually confiscated it to prevent exposing anyone else to possible pathogens. Clarke did not put on the body armor or vest because his schedule had him in debriefings throughout the morning and it would just be uncomfortable to wear for no reason. Clarke didn't like wearing the jumpsuit either, but it was his uniform and he dealt with it. It felt to him like he was going to work in a labor camp or some sort of hard, dirty job, instead of sitting in on meetings and discussing surveillance points. Nonetheless, he zipped it up his side and flipped down the collar to show his captain bars embroidered on the lapel. The entire team had been promoted to captain when they defected and joined the Revolutionaries, but it still felt odd to Clarke. According to General Morgan, it was the most honorable thing they could have done, and he wanted to appropriately recognize them because of their experience, skill, and devotion to freedom.

The rest of the team was finishing lacing up their boots as Clarke put on his baseball cap again. He realized that there was thick dust, sweat, and some smeared blood from Phillip on it and he fought back a wave of emotion. He struggled against the tears, then smacked some of the dust off and put it on anyway. The uniform for the Revolutionaries was fairly flexible. Since they did not have issued headgear, their commanders didn't really care what they wore. Clarke had already seen several cowboy hats, a few visors, and even some rather crude homemade attempts at berets, but most soldiers wore some sort of baseball cap or nothing at all. Nobody else on his team wore a hat and nobody cared that he wore his baseball cap.

Clarke waited for Analyn to stand up and move to the door before following her. Shane and Lewis moved together just a few feet behind Clarke. Analyn made a left down the hallway to the intelligence suites with copper and lead-lined walls, but according to the schedule, Clarke was supposed to go right to the medical bays. Clarke slowly turned right and looked over his shoulder as Lewis and Shane followed after Analyn. They both looked at Clarke with identically puzzled faces and Clarke shrugged silently. They all knew that this was odd and there was no real explanation for it. They simply went their separate ways for the day.

As he rounded the corner to the hospital entrance, Clarke saw the military medical czar he had met at the hospital in Alabama wearing the exact same secret police uniform as before and standing just as rigidly and unnaturally. Clarke didn't feel like having any conversation with the man and just walked past him. Clarke felt a little guilty about not stopping to say hello, but he was in a bit of a hurry. After a couple steps, Clarke abruptly stopped walking, closed his eyes, and took a deep breath before turning around for a moment to apologize to the man. At the same time, the man turned and the light from the nearest faux window caught the golden arc on his lapel just right. Clarke smiled and the man gave a quick nod, encouraging Clarke to go see Phillip. He thought back to when this man was trying to communicate something important to him in that hospital room that was for his eyes and ears only. Clarke thought about it as he entered the hospital and scanned his screen before heading to the designated room on his schedule.

He opened the door and saw that it was a triage room of some kind with about twenty beds separated by movable walls. Unsure of where to go, he just sat on the nearest bed and waited for a few minutes. As he sat, he thought about things he used to do with Alex. Stuff like building fires or setting snares for rabbits in the woods. He remembered back to when he must have been about seven years old and caught his first rabbit. Alex was so proud of his little brother back then. Before he lost consciousness yesterday, he looked up at his little brother filled with pride.

Ms. Baker knocked on the door briefly and was going to open it regardless of any objection. She went over to Clarke and pulled out several WAB-MIVSS, placing one over his heart, his right temple, and left forearm. The screen to her left lit up and displayed every vital sign Clarke knew about and several other numbers he had no clue what they were.

"Sorry to be doing this to you," the nurse said sympathetically, "but Phillip needs more blood, and since," she broke off for a second as she caught herself and cleared her throat. "Since you have the same blood type as him, we are going to be taking 500 mL from you to give to him. We just need to make sure that you don't have any illness right now."

"Me and Al—Phillip have the same blood type?" Clarke said, excited to know something more about his brother, even if it was something impersonal like blood type.

"Yes, sir. Both of you are B positive." She looked at the screen for a moment and then peeked over at Clarke through the corner of her eyes for a fleeting second and continued with her work. "Well, it looks like your body is absolutely healthy, so we will go ahead and start the blood draw, if that's okay."

She used the screen to request a needle and bag for a blood draw and it was printed under the table Clarke was resting on. Ms. Baker used the WAB-MIVSS on his arm to locate the vein she would use and simply let the device handle the rest. A second later Clarke watched his blood flow from his arm down the narrow tube and disappear below him. He had never given blood before and it was a fascinating experience. The hospitals above ground used nanobot technology to carry oxygen and repair damaged tissues while the blood was being naturally rebuilt. Apparently, the underground either didn't have the technology available, or couldn't afford it.

"So, I said that your body was in great health, but from these readings I see that your head isn't doing so great," Ms. Baker said in a motherly tone. "I know what we talked about yesterday, but this is something different. I already have enough to diagnose you with post-traumatic stress disorder, but from what I see, you also have severe anxiety and recently onset depression." She paused and waited for a response. When none came, she continued, "Would you care to talk with me about it?"

Clarke shook his head. He knew what he wanted right now. He couldn't get it out of his mind since she said that he and Alex had the same blood type. He wanted to see his brother more than anything in the world. Now he was starting to fight back tears again and he clenched his jaw. Clarke looked away from the nurse and focused on the screen displaying his vital signs, where he saw several of the unknown readings begin to rise with his anxiety. He also saw that his pulse was getting faster and his blood pressure was going up.

He felt like he was going to explode if he kept it all in, but he tried to keep it together as he calmly asked, "Could I see Alex?"

Ms. Baker stood in shock, not knowing what to say or do. Her mouth hung open as she held her breath, looking for a response. Eventually she relented and nodded with a sincere smile. After the bag was completely filled, she took off the WAB-MIVSS and guided Clarke through the back door to the recovery rooms. This corridor was narrow and only had five beds. There was only one occupant. Clarke rushed over, giving no heed to Ms. Baker, and flung the door open, pausing only to see Phillip covered in sensors. His left ankle was in a cast and he had pins sticking out from his side where they had to drain the internal bleeding. Clarke went over to his brother and reached around his shoulders and started to cry. Phillip was sleeping and awoke both confused and alarmed. The screens on the wall started flashing, but Ms. Baker didn't stop Clarke. She was tearing up too as she hooked up the bag of blood to one of the WAB-MIVSS on Phillip's arm.

Phillip eventually realized what was happening and embraced his brother for the first time in over ten years.

Chapter 22—Battle Stations

C larke felt very relieved that Phillip was going to recover quickly. His situation was only as bad as it was because he had been tranquilized in so many different spots yesterday, and his liver hadn't yet processed out the other times he had been shot earlier that week and the week before that. From what Phillip said, it was causing his blood to thin and any small scratch would just bleed until it was treated with a coagulant. The two of them sat and talked for several hours that day, until Phillip began drifting in and out of consciousness during conversations. A doctor came in several times and injected him with a stimulant to keep him awake because, as the doctor put it, his consciousness needed to be controlled for proper monitoring until they were sure he was stable.

"Thanks, Doc," Phillip said after the third time this had happened. His eyes opened wider, and Clarke could tell that he really wanted to get up and move but knew better.

"Remember that time we went sledding down the hill by Lake Adams?" Clarke asked. "I flew so high before hitting that bush." He started to pull up his pant leg. "I still have the scar, see?"

Phillip smiled and nodded. "I remember that! You were going pretty fast; I was surprised that you didn't actually break anything. To be honest, I thought you were going to get hurt and I was scared, so I closed my eyes the second I saw you go off that ramp."

"Wait a minute, you were scared?" Clarke said in disbelief. "You were never scared!"

"Well, you weren't very good at a lot of the things I tried to show you. Mr. Valentine showed me so much out in those woods, and I wanted to pass that to you before I left." His voice began to trail off. "That's why you were so young when we started camping and everything."

There was a pause in their conversation and Clarke thought that Phillip was falling back asleep, but he was actually just trying to compose himself.

"A couple weeks after I left, Mom told me that you were there when I left and really upset that I didn't say goodbye." His face was screwed up and he held back his emotions as best as he could. "I should have gone up to you; Dad and Mr. Valentine knew that you were listening, and I still didn't go up."

Clarke took off his hat and leaned back in his chair. He was taken so off guard that Claire had known Alex was alive—the entire thing was kept from him. He started to get angry, but knew that he couldn't do anything about it. After all, that was the past—literally ten years ago. So much had changed in his own world, yet here he was, with his big brother, almost as if it were only a couple of months and they were swapping stories about their life.

"Dad was so heartbroken. Why did you leave us?" Clarke said.

"The time was right." Phillip paused for a while thinking about it all. "You know the accident I supposedly died in? Well, someone in the New Boston underground did drown and we were about the same age, so it was a perfect way to hide me. Mr. Valentine remotely piloted a car with the poor kid into Lake Adams right smack dab in the middle of town so the body would be recovered quickly. After that, me and him made it through the countryside all the way here by ourselves." He looked over at Clarke and motioned for his screen. Clarke unclipped it from his wrist and laid it out on Phillip's lap. "Here is the news story about my death—I've memorized the headline."

Local Boy Drowns in Car Accident

According to eyewitness accounts, Alexander Prescott, eighteen, of New Boston, Alabama narrowly avoided an oncoming supply truck and plunged into Lake Adams. First responders arrived at the scene in the first five minutes, but Alexander had already died. The family requested no autopsy be performed but did allow his organs to be harvested.

Clarke finished reading and looked up at Phillip.

"Depressing, isn't it?" Phillip said. "The poor guy who did die had no name, no family mentioned, and will never be known. I've tried to find the family, but they seem to have never made it out of the New Boston underground."

Clarke reminisced for a moment about people he saw only in passing while attending Mass. Human trafficking was something rarely spoken about between members of the underground in New Boston. Nearly everyone knew that people were trying to flee the more oppressive parts of the United States and the best way to passively aid them was simply pretending they didn't notice.

Clarke pulled over the screen and opened up his own obituary, which was far less dramatic:

Charlie Prescott, son of Robert and Claire Prescott. 02 September, 2095–08 February, 2113.

They both laughed at the absurdity. Clarke had legally died and simply vanished from existence. Nobody in the community cared that he died, nobody asked questions, and worst of all, they were primed to just accept the fact that a kid from their community had disappeared. It wasn't odd for newspapers not to cover the specifics when a citizen first class disappeared or died, while stories from the same day discussed at length the arrest and execution of citizens second class for crimes such as petty theft or not holding open a door for a party member. There was something inhumane about ignoring a death. The way people acted as if nothing happened when a citizen first class simply entered the ether was disturbing.

"They didn't even bother to come up with some cause of death," Clarke said. "They just publicly stated that I was dead, end of story, nothing follows."

"I've heard things about the military recruitment process, but never that before. What happened?" Phillip asked. Clarke explained his letter and the process he underwent for his enhancements, which impressed Phillip. He continued his story after a couple demonstrations of reading print from far distances and leaving the room to listen through the door. Most people never asked what he was capable of, but Phillip felt right at home—after all, he was asking his brother. Clarke talked about Fort Powell and Lieutenant Colonel Hudson in depth, to the point that he felt Phillip was actually debriefing him. But when he got to his medically induced coma, Phillip stopped him.

"What was the name of the nurse?" Phillip asked and sat upright.

"Bear, I think. Why?"

"You said you had a corrupted message from her, right?" Clarke nodded. "Show me." Clarke pulled open the message and Phillip looked at it:

Charlie,

If you are reading this, I know you don't remember me. Over the past several weeks, the medical procedures and drugs you have taken for your conscription have modified your memories. Please try to remember that you have friends and family who are trying to give people a safe life. The videos I sent have a password that is my first name. You know me. When you remember, you will understand why it was you.

Stay safe,

Your Bear

Phillip toggled the settings of the attached video files and ran them through several different types of rendering software that Clarke had no clue about. Clarke was barely following what Phillip had done when all of a sudden, he typed in 'Therese' and a video was projected on the screen of ten-year-old Alex rocking the baby Charlie in a bassinet. A girl, maybe three or four years old, reached over the side and gave a big kiss to the baby, who simply looked upward at her lips and showed a big toothless smile.

Another short video showed a slightly older Alex running around their garden with a small kite and the girl blowing bubbles with the now toddler Charlie. Another video of the girl reading a book to the toddler on the armchair in the upstairs hallway—the very same chair where Clarke had read all of his favorite books as a teenager.

There were probably a dozen videos like this, all only a couple seconds long, but the two sat there in silence and watched them repeat several times. Clarke was in awe that he had no memory of the girl, but clearly she was close to him. Phillip watched the videos and was dumbstruck. He knew who she was and could not believe that he was seeing her again.

"Who is that?" Clarke asked. "I don't remember her."

"That's our sister, Therese. She was, how can I say this, taken during a raid at a traffic stop one night when you were about four. She must have only been seven or eight. I thought that she was gone. I'm pretty sure that both Mom and Dad thought that too."

"Wait a minute. Was that when I was stuffed inside the suitcase?" Phillip nodded. "Well, I saw her and she looked after me in Fort Powell. She is alive and she gave me these videos for a reason, not just to get some tears out of me," Clarke said. "We have to do something."

Clarke thought back on that night when Claire shoved him into an old blue and gray striped suitcase they only coincidentally had with them. The chaos that he didn't understand as his arms were pushed in and the seals were fastened around him. First on his right side, then the bag was flipped on its side and the bottom was fastened. Then it was flipped again and Charlie tried to get his hands back out but Claire shot him a look of horror and he understood that this was serious. The only thing that bothered him about the memory was that there was no girl there; he didn't remember Therese at all.

Clarke hung on that for a little while before his attention was called to his screen, where he noticed that there was still another video that didn't play.

"Hang on. There is still one more video. It's a massive file; that's why it hasn't started to play yet. Let's see if there's something in this one," Phillip said.

The video finally opened and was a self-recording from Therese's screen, with her face all distorted and the background in a fishbowl lens. She leaned back and came into focus before saying:

"Charlie, if you've opened this, you should know by now that I'm your sister Therese. I don't have much time and I'm not exactly prepared to do this quite yet, but this information is for the Revolutionaries' headquarters in Houston from the operatives in the Department of Defensive Land Warfare and surrounding cities. The date is 29 July, 2113. The eastern seaboard has been connected. There are tunnels now connecting all major cities. The fastest connection from Houston to us is through New Orleans. Put all efforts into that tunnel before the government figures it out. The war in Texas will be over soon when they drop the tactical nuclear warheads. The federal government has openly expressed that they need to secure the borders and will go to extreme lengths to do so. The official plan is to drop the bombs at sunrise on 8 November, as a symbolic end of the war with Mexico."

Someone walked into the room where Therese was recording and she abruptly stood up and covered the camera. Their voices were muffled as she actually sat on her screen to cover it up. There were a couple of shouts and then a door slamming. Therese got up and crouched back down in front of the camera.

"I have to go; I don't have time for any more information." Her eyes were watery and she sniffed. "I love you."

The video recording ended and left the last image of her lips quivering for the three seconds it took the screen to close out the video. Clarke stood up and grabbed his screen.

"I need to go, now!" he said excitedly. "General Morgan needs to know this immediately—it's November 3rd today."

"Wait," Phillip said, "I have to talk with him too. Let's see if he can't come to us instead."

Phillip reached for Clarke's screen again and tapped it several times to navigate to an alert panel and indicate that there was an urgent request for the general in the hospital. Phillip slid the screen back over to Clarke with a smile and grabbed Clarke's free hand to give it a squeeze. They sat there for a few minutes in silence as they waited for General Morgan to arrive. The screen had sent a response that he was on his way, but that his location was several kilometers away and it would take some time. The most likely scenario was that he would get in a car and drive through one of the wider tunnels adjacent to the hospital and arrive momentarily.

"Could you play those other videos again for a while? I'd like to see her," Phillip said.

"Of course." Clarke pulled open the files and set the screen down on the bed. They let it loop for a couple of minutes until Lewis, Shane, and Analyn walked in through the door. They stood along the wall at attention, waiting to be told otherwise.

"Relax, guys, you saved my life," Phillip said. "You don't need the formalities right now."

"Yes sir, Colonel Sayah, sir," Analyn said and then stood at ease.

"Colonel? Nobody told me that," Clarke said and laughed. Phillip smiled and let out a short chuckle but then grabbed at his side in pain. A nurse walked in quickly and switched the now-empty bag of Clarke's blood with a small gray liquid that he recognized as nanobots. The nanobots would flush out the tranquilizer from Phillip's liver, help his wounded side and broken ankle heal faster, and also assist in building his blood back to appropriate levels. A process that would take a month just twenty years ago would now be done in a couple of days. In fact, Phillip was known to heal quickly, and he would be discharged the next morning after another couple shots of medicines and stimulants.

The three soldiers on Clarke's team were clearly uncomfortable standing in the room as Phillip lay in pain, but they were grateful that he made it back to the hospital—he was an icon in the Revolutionaries, a true leader and a hero to many. Phillip would never tell Clarke about how many people he had saved and how far his messages had reached, but others would tell him because it was so admirable. As much as General Morgan was the administrative leader and tactician, Colonel Sayah was the most caring and adept in turning the tides of the struggle.

A few awkward minutes passed until the general walked into the room. The three against the wall snapped to attention and Clarke stood up too.

"At ease, carry on," General Morgan said as he walked to the foot of the bed. "Now, what did you have that couldn't wait?"

"I have intelligence on the American, Mexican, and Persian troop movement for the next few months in the Texas theater of war. Clarke, could you bring up the tactical map?" Phillip said confidently yet respectfully. Clarke navigated to where the map was stored and had it projected on the wall behind him. The medical data moved to the outer edges of the screen, and the majority of the wall showed the traditional U.S.-Mexico border with overlays of the currently occupied territory and known unit identifications. They were being updated in real time with satellite tracking systems. Phillip focused in on Houston and drew a line from the northwest to the southeast through the city.

"The Mexican-Persian armies only have forces on this half of the city." He indicated the southern portion. "Their next move is to take their armored infantry and artillery units from here to here." He drew an arrow from the northwest to the northeast. "That would create a wedge in the southeast. The U.S. plans on pulling out of the region completely and falling back to Alexandria and Shreveport, Louisiana. Sir, they've given up and surrendered," Phillip said with a cold and stony face. "At least that's what it appears to be."

General Morgan cocked his head to the side and furrowed his brow, creating deep creases on his forehead that spoke to his true age. He pursed his lips and stood upright before speaking in a low and serious tone.

"What do you mean, 'appears to be'?" General Morgan said, doing a very poor job at concealing his concern. Phillip didn't answer at first and stared right through the general.

"If you don't mind, tell me what's going on. I sort of need to know this so I can develop a plan." General Morgan didn't flinch when he spoke and waited for a response. What he didn't know was that Phillip was struggling to decide if he should show the general the video or not, since it was so personal. Phillip relented.

"Captain Anicius, please play the video you received," he said. "Sir, when Clarke was being briefed at Fort Powell, a Nurse Bear sent him some files. They are concerning, no doubt, but, well, just watch." Clarke played the video of Therese for the group, and Analyn's team started to buzz with a short chatter about what it meant.

General Morgan looked over at Clarke and Phillip and said, "We have some work to do." Then he turned around and rushed out the door, undoubtedly back to the operations cell. He started to give orders to begin shifting all tunneling efforts to New Orleans so the Southwest Region could be connected to the Southeast Region. The existing tunnels in that direction would be widened to support increased vehicle movement as well. When the tunnels were completed, the Revolutionaries would be poised to capture the politically corrupt leaders and complete a coup d'état. Clarke realized that everything had been set in motion decades ago and the Revolutionaries had been biding their time to strategically strike at the heart of the corrupt government and bring about a new one. He saw that these last few months had been the most action that anyone in the Revolutionaries had actually seen. Now their movement was bigger than a mercy mission; it was about to break out into an actual and announced rebellion, and he was one of the final pieces in the puzzle for exploiting the government's weaknesses. Clarke gave the Revolutionaries not only an extra soldier, but an enhanced one. He was knowledgeable about one of the undergrounds the larger organization needed to connect with to unite all the pockets of resistance in the southeast United States, and his detailed knowledge from Fort Powell gave them years of data they otherwise wouldn't have had.

After General Morgan got the wheels spinning on the logistics behind shifting the resources to the New Orleans tunnels, he went to his network of reconnaissance and surveillance in Houston. There were seven teams of four soldiers each, and Analyn was one of the team leaders. They were instructed to evacuate the city no later than 1300 on 7 November so there would be enough time to seal off all the entrances preceding the nuclear detonation. The Revolutionaries recognized that the city was lost and they were responsible for saving as many innocent lives as possible. It was merely a coincidence that wiping out the foreign militaries would mutually benefit both the U.S. forces and themselves by forestalling subsequent violence. The risk of using the bombs was that it may provoke retaliatory strikes. It was out of their hands, though, and General Morgan made that perfectly clear. The Revolutionaries were to do whatever they could to protect Americans.

The tunnels would be dug as fast as possible, and the city would be evacuated. They had their orders. The reconnaissance and surveillance teams were sent out that same hour and spread as far as possible through the city. Although the city was widely abandoned, it was estimated to still shelter over a hundred thousand people, many of whom were citizens third class. The tragedy of internment during the second world war would pale in comparison if the United States government dropped tactical nuclear weapons over a major U.S. city. The number of dead would be astronomical, although the government would never have acknowledged the suffering or loss of life—especially citizens third class. The Revolutionaries would ensure that they did their part as well as they could.

Analyn's team was sent through the same exit they used the day before and found themselves in that same alley. Analyn's tac-screen guided them to population centers of vagabond encampments in abandoned warehouses and other large communities, where they immediately spread the message that they only had four and a half days to get out or go underground. Then the team left one area and relied on word of mouth to spread the message. They went from encampment to encampment the entire day and pleaded with people to seek refuge in the underground. It was close to sunset when they reentered the underground, and they already noticed the increased population. Every team in the reconnaissance and surveillance section did the same thing from the 3rd to the 5th of November.

The tunneling teams at the far ends of the tunnels were well over 200 kilometers away and diverting them would take some time; besides, there was only enough space to operate with a finite amount of people and tools. The tunneling division decided that round-the-clock manning of the tunnel to New Orleans would be the best solution, and they employed nearly a thousand of the new refugees to help. They were thankful for being saved, and many felt compelled to help in the war effort in any way they could. The necessary tools and personnel were shipped out before the next morning, and the rotation started immediately on the 5th of November. Temporary sleeping quarters were brought with them, as well as all of the different apparatuses for supporting a couple thousand workers, including sanitation, food, and medical services.

Engineers began to seal off the exits and hatches to the surface streets throughout the underground at 1300 on the 6th. The best estimates were that it would take a full twenty-four hours to have each and every one sufficiently hardened from nuclear blasts. The extra time was for the necessary inspections, to shore up the larger exits beyond a doubt, and also to brace the larger tunnels for the shockwaves. Regardless, everyone was to be moved to the deepest levels or out of the projected impact areas before midnight on the 6th.

NOBODY ASIDE FROM THE pilots of the planes dropping the bombs or the victims of the blast had any clue what the explosions looked like or saw the brilliant light sweep over the area as the sun crept over the horizon. The entire city was razed to the ground, and not a single person, American or otherwise, was left standing. The United States had just targeted Houston, Texas, with nuclear weapons.

Meanwhile, the tunnel to New Orleans was being worked round the clock and General Morgan's plan was coming to fruition. The citizens above were saved and provided much-needed manpower to support their movement. In effect, General Morgan had converted the last holdouts in the city to rebel. Reports of the destruction came back from the surface a couple of days later on the 10th of November, and all of the former Houston residents firmed up their resolve. Many of them volunteered for combat forces, while others had trade skills from various industries, including mechanics, electrical engineers, chefs, welders, farmers, and doctors. All of them freely offered their services to the Revolutionaries. The standing army had nearly doubled overnight and all operations were expanded dramatically.

Phillip was back on his feet and was ready to take charge of his command once again. The reconnaissance and surveillance platoon became a company-sized element. New recruits were trained to be interrogators, secret couriers, and analysts. Many of the new recruits with a knack for theft or secrecy swelled the formation. They now had a reason to use their skills for a purpose higher than their own self-interest. They understood that this was a mission worth fighting for and would give their life to see a freed America.

Everyone understood that the class system was unjust but had never rebelled against it. There was no hope in doing so when law after law was passed that further stripped away rights to the point of futility. Now their cause was strong enough to make a change. The Revolutionaries' network was far-reaching and had already infiltrated the corrupt government, despite how stringent the screening procedures were. If anything, the Revolutionaries' strength came from patience and deliberate action. The original organizers knew that it would be a war fought in the shadows until the time was ripe. The few who were still alive when the tunneling first started nearly fifty years ago also knew that they likely wouldn't live to see the day when open military action would take place.

General Morgan held his head high as he spoke with Colonel Sayah and Captain Anicius in his war room.

"Gentlemen, these past few months have been the most action we have seen in this struggle." He drew a long breath in. "But we still need to improve our stance before making any strike. Don't worry, though—we have a plan."

About the Author

Gregory Ulseth is a Chemical Officer in the United States Army with a Master's Degree in Public Administration from Augusta University and author of *We Have a Plan*. His military education background includes interrogation and strategic debriefing, certified Persian-Farsi linguist, reports officer, and HAZMAT response training. Raised in a religious household and fond of conjectural history, Gregory's writing revolves around religion and "what if" world building. His hobbies include playing guitar, basketball, ultimate frisbee, the boardgame of the day with his kids, and irritating his wife in a loving way. Gregory is a father of eight and uses his writing to inspire his children to reach past what they think is possible. *A jack of all trades is a master of none, but oftentimes better than a master of one.*

YOU   CAN   CONNECT   WITH   ME   ON:
https://www.instagram.com/ulsethii

CPSIA information can be obtained
at www.ICGtesting.com
Printed in the USA
BVHW071304240921
617461BV00006B/495

9 781393 840664